The Empty H

CERTAIN HOUSES, LIKE CERTAIN PE
proclaim at once their character for evil. In the ... ...
no particular feature need betray them; they may boast an open
countenance and an ingenuous smile; and yet a little of their company leaves the unalterable conviction that there is something
radically amiss with their being: that they are evil. Willy nilly, they
seem to communicate an atmosphere of secret and wicked
thoughts which makes those in their immediate neighbourhood
shrink from them as from a thing diseased.

And, perhaps, with houses the same principle is operative, and
it is the aroma of evil deeds committed under a particular roof,
long after the actual doers have passed away, that makes the
gooseflesh come and the hair rise. Something of the original passion of the evildoer, and of the horror felt by his victim, enters the
heart of the innocent watcher, and he becomes suddenly conscious
of tingling nerves, creeping skin, and a chilling of the blood. He is
terror-stricken without apparent cause.

There was manifestly nothing in the external appearance of
this particular house to bear out the tales of the horror that was
said to reign within. It was neither lonely nor unkempt. It stood,
crowded into a corner of the square, and looked exactly like the
houses on either side of it. It had the same number of windows as
its neighbours; the same balcony overlooking the gardens; the
same white steps leading up to the heavy black front door; and, in
the rear, there was the same narrow strip of green, with neat box
borders, running up to the wall that divided it from the backs of
the adjoining houses. Apparently, too, the number of chimney pots
on the roof was the same; the breadth and angle of the eaves; and
even the height of the dirty area railings.

And yet this house in the square, that seemed precisely similar
to its fifty ugly neighbours, was as a matter of fact entirely different—horribly different.

Wherein lay this marked, invisible difference is impossible to
say. It cannot be ascribed wholly to the imagination, because persons who had spent some time in the house, knowing nothing of
the facts, had declared positively that certain rooms were so disagreeable they would rather die than enter them again, and that the
atmosphere of the whole house produced in them symptoms of a

genuine terror; while the series of innocent tenants who had tried to live in it and been forced to decamp at the shortest possible notice, was indeed little less than a scandal in the town.

When Shorthouse arrived to pay a "weekend" visit to his Aunt Julia in her little house on the seafront at the other end of the town, he found her charged to the brim with mystery and excitement. He had only received her telegram that morning, and he had come anticipating boredom; but the moment he touched her hand and kissed her apple-skin wrinkled cheek, he caught the first wave of her electrical condition. The impression deepened when he learned that there were to be no other visitors, and that he had been telegraphed for with a very special object.

Something was in the wind, and the "something" would doubtless bear fruit; for this elderly spinster aunt, with a mania for psychical research,[1] had brains as well as will power, and by hook or by crook she usually managed to accomplish her ends. The revelation was made soon after tea, when she sidled close up to him as they paced slowly along the seafront in the dusk.

"I've got the keys," she announced in a delighted, yet half awesome voice. "Got them till Monday!"

"The keys of the bathing-machine, or—?" he asked innocently, looking from the sea to the town. Nothing brought her so quickly to the point as feigning stupidity.

"Neither," she whispered. "I've got the keys of the haunted house in the square—and I'm going there tonight."

Shorthouse was conscious of the slightest possible tremor down his back. He dropped his teasing tone. Something in her voice and manner thrilled him. She was in earnest.

"But you can't go alone—" he began.

"That's why I wired for you," she said with decision.

He turned to look at her. The ugly, lined, enigmatical face was alive with excitement. There was the glow of genuine enthusiasm round it like a halo. The eyes shone. He caught another wave of her excitement, and a second tremor, more marked than the first, accompanied it.

---

[1] Algernon Blackwood was a member of England's Society for Psychical Research, the earliest established academic organization dedicated to psychic studies. SPR was founded in 1882 in West Kensington, London, and is now a worldwide organization, responsible for the oversight body for the International Congresses of Physiological and Experimental Psychology. It is likely Blackwood was inspired to write *The Empty House* based on his experiences as a member of SPR.

THE ALGERNON BLACKWOOD COLLECTION

THE ALGERNON BLACKWOOD COLLECTION

ALGERNON BLACKWOOD

The Algernon Blackwood Collection by Algernon Blackwood: *The Empty House, The Damned, The Willows, The Wendigo*

Published 2019 by Aiwass Books.

First Printing: 2020.

ISBN: 9798615170171.

CONTENTS

"Thanks, Aunt Julia," he said politely; "thanks awfully."

"I should not dare to go quite alone," she went on, raising her voice; "but with you I should enjoy it immensely. You're afraid of nothing, I know."

"Thanks so much," he said again. "Er—is anything likely to happen?"

"A great deal has happened," she whispered, "though it's been most cleverly hushed up. Three tenants have come and gone in the last few months, and the house is said to be empty for good now."

In spite of himself Shorthouse became interested. His aunt was so very much in earnest.

"The house is very old indeed," she went on, "and the story—an unpleasant one—dates a long way back. It has to do with a murder committed by a jealous stableman who had some affair with a servant in the house. One night he managed to secrete himself in the cellar, and when everyone was asleep, he crept upstairs to the servants' quarters, chased the girl down to the next landing, and before anyone could come to the rescue threw her bodily over the banisters into the hall below."

"And the stableman—?"

"Was caught, I believe, and hanged for murder; but it all happened a century ago, and I've not been able to get more details of the story."

Shorthouse now felt his interest thoroughly aroused; but, though he was not particularly nervous for himself, he hesitated a little on his aunt's account.

"On one condition," he said at length.

"Nothing will prevent my going," she said firmly; "but I may as well hear your condition."

"That you guarantee your power of self-control if anything really horrible happens. I mean—that you are sure you won't get too frightened."

"Jim," she said scornfully, "I'm not young, I know, nor are my nerves; but with you I should be afraid of nothing in the world!"

This, of course, settled it, for Shorthouse had no pretensions to being other than a very ordinary young man, and an appeal to his vanity was irresistible. He agreed to go.

Instinctively, by a sort of subconscious preparation, he kept himself and his forces well in hand the whole evening, compelling an accumulative reserve of control by that nameless inward process of gradually putting all the emotions away and turning the key upon them—a process difficult to describe, but wonderfully effective, as all men who have lived through severe trials of the inner man well understand. Later, it stood him in good stead.

But it was not until half-past ten, when they stood in the hall, well in the glare of friendly lamps and still surrounded by comforting human influences, that he had to make the first call upon this store of collected strength. For, once the door was closed, and he saw the deserted silent street stretching away white in the moonlight before them, it came to him clearly that the real test that night would be in dealing with two fears instead of one. He would have to carry his aunt's fear as well as his own. And, as he glanced down at her sphinxlike countenance and realised that it might assume no pleasant aspect in a rush of real terror, he felt satisfied with only one thing in the whole adventure—that he had confidence in his own will and power to stand against any shock that might come.

Slowly they walked along the empty streets of the town; a bright autumn moon silvered the roofs, casting deep shadows; there was no breath of wind; and the trees in the formal gardens by the seafront watched them silently as they passed along. To his aunt's occasional remarks Shorthouse made no reply, realising that she was simply surrounding herself with mental buffers—saying ordinary things to prevent herself thinking of extraordinary things. Few windows showed lights, and from scarcely a single chimney came smoke or sparks. Shorthouse had already begun to notice everything, even the smallest details. Presently they stopped at the street corner and looked up at the name on the side of the house full in the moonlight, and with one accord, but without remark, turned into the square and crossed over to the side of it that lay in shadow.

"The number of the house is thirteen," whispered a voice at his side; and neither of them made the obvious reference, but passed across the broad sheet of moonlight and began to march up the pavement in silence.

It was about halfway up the square that Shorthouse felt an arm slipped quietly but significantly into his own, and knew then that their adventure had begun in earnest, and that his companion was already yielding imperceptibly to the influences against them. She needed support.

A few minutes later they stopped before a tall, narrow house that rose before them into the night, ugly in shape and painted a dingy white. Shutterless windows, without blinds, stared down upon them, shining here and there in the moonlight. There were weather streaks in the wall and cracks in the paint, and the balcony bulged out from the first floor a little unnaturally. But, beyond this generally forlorn appearance of an unoccupied house, there was nothing at first sight to single out this particular mansion for the evil character it had most certainly acquired.

Taking a look over their shoulders to make sure they had not been followed, they went boldly up the steps and stood against the huge black door that fronted them forbiddingly. But the first wave of nervousness was now upon them, and Shorthouse fumbled a long time with the key before he could fit it into the lock at all. For a moment, if truth were told, they both hoped it would not open, for they were a prey to various unpleasant emotions as they stood there on the threshold of their ghostly adventure. Shorthouse, shuffling with the key and hampered by the steady weight on his arm, certainly felt the solemnity of the moment. It was as if the whole world—for all experience seemed at that instant concentrated in his own consciousness—were listening to the grating noise of that key. A stray puff of wind wandering down the empty street woke a momentary rustling in the trees behind them, but otherwise this rattling of the key was the only sound audible; and at last it turned in the lock and the heavy door swung open and revealed a yawning gulf of darkness beyond.

With a last glance at the moonlit square, they passed quickly in, and the door slammed behind them with a roar that echoed prodigiously through empty halls and passages. But, instantly, with the echoes, another sound made itself heard, and Aunt Julia leaned suddenly so heavily upon him that he had to take a step backwards to save himself from falling.

A man had coughed close beside them—so close that it seemed they must have been actually by his side in the darkness.

With the possibility of practical jokes in his mind, Shorthouse at once swung his heavy stick in the direction of the sound; but it met nothing more solid than air. He heard his aunt give a little gasp beside him.

"There's someone here," she whispered; "I heard him."

"Be quiet!" he said sternly. "It was nothing but the noise of the front door."

"Oh! get a light—quick!" she added, as her nephew, fumbling with a box of matches, opened it upside down and let them all fall with a rattle on to the stone floor.

The sound, however, was not repeated; and there was no evidence of retreating footsteps. In another minute they had a candle burning, using an empty end of a cigar case as a holder; and when the first flare had died down he held the impromptu lamp aloft and surveyed the scene. And it was dreary enough in all conscience, for there is nothing more desolate in all the abodes of men than an unfurnished house dimly lit, silent, and forsaken, and yet tenanted by rumour with the memories of evil and violent histories.

They were standing in a wide hallway; on their left was the open door of a spacious dining room, and in front the hall ran, ever narrowing, into a long, dark passage that led apparently to the top of the kitchen stairs. The broad uncarpeted staircase rose in a sweep before them, everywhere draped in shadows, except for a single spot about halfway up where the moonlight came in through the window and fell on a bright patch on the boards. This shaft of light shed a faint radiance above and below it, lending to the objects within its reach a misty outline that was infinitely more suggestive and ghostly than complete darkness. Filtered moonlight always seems to paint faces on the surrounding gloom, and as Shorthouse peered up into the well of darkness and thought of the countless empty rooms and passages in the upper part of the old house, he caught himself longing again for the safety of the moonlit square, or the cosy, bright drawing room they had left an hour before. Then realising that these thoughts were dangerous, he thrust them away again and summoned all his energy for concentration on the present.

"Aunt Julia," he said aloud, severely, "we must now go through the house from top to bottom and make a thorough search."

The echoes of his voice died away slowly all over the building, and in the intense silence that followed he turned to look at her. In the candlelight he saw that her face was already ghastly pale; but she dropped his arm for a moment and said in a whisper, stepping close in front of him—

"I agree. We must be sure there's no one hiding. That's the first thing."

She spoke with evident effort, and he looked at her with admiration.

"You feel quite sure of yourself? It's not too late—"

"I think so," she whispered, her eyes shifting nervously toward the shadows behind. "Quite sure, only one thing—"

"What's that?"

"You must never leave me alone for an instant."

"As long as you understand that any sound or appearance must be investigated at once, for to hesitate means to admit fear. That is fatal."

"Agreed," she said, a little shakily, after a moment's hesitation. "I'll try—"

Arm in arm, Shorthouse holding the dripping candle and the stick, while his aunt carried the cloak over her shoulders, figures of utter comedy to all but themselves, they began a systematic search.

Stealthily, walking on tiptoe and shading the candle lest it should betray their presence through the shutterless windows, they went first into the big dining room. There was not a stick of furniture to be seen. Bare walls, ugly mantelpieces and empty grates stared at them. Everything, they felt, resented their intrusion, watching them, as it were, with veiled eyes; whispers followed them; shadows flitted noiselessly to right and left; something seemed ever at their back, watching, waiting an opportunity to do them injury. There was the inevitable sense that operations which went on when the room was empty had been temporarily suspended till they were well out of the way again. The whole dark interior of the old building seemed to become a malignant Presence that rose up, warning them to desist and mind their own business; every moment the strain on the nerves increased.

Out of the gloomy dining room they passed through large folding doors into a sort of library or smoking room, wrapt equally in silence, darkness, and dust; and from this they regained the hall near the top of the back stairs.

Here a pitch-black tunnel opened before them into the lower regions, and—it must be confessed—they hesitated. But only for a minute. With the worst of the night still to come it was essential to turn from nothing. Aunt Julia stumbled at the top step of the dark descent, ill lit by the flickering candle, and even Shorthouse felt at least half the decision go out of his legs.

"Come on!" he said peremptorily, and his voice ran on and lost itself in the dark, empty spaces below.

"I'm coming," she faltered, catching his arm with unnecessary violence.

They went a little unsteadily down the stone steps, a cold, damp air meeting them in the face, close and malodorous. The kitchen, into which the stairs led along a narrow passage, was large, with a lofty ceiling. Several doors opened out of it—some into cupboards with empty jars still standing on the shelves, and others into horrible little ghostly back offices, each colder and less inviting than the last. Black beetles scurried over the floor, and once, when they knocked against a deal table standing in a corner, something about the size of a cat jumped down with a rush and fled, scampering across the stone floor into the darkness. Everywhere there was a sense of recent occupation, an impression of sadness and gloom.

Leaving the main kitchen, they next went towards the scullery. The door was standing ajar, and as they pushed it open to its full extent Aunt Julia uttered a piercing scream, which she instantly tried to stifle by placing her hand over her mouth. For a second Shorthouse stood stock-still, catching his breath. He felt as if his spine had suddenly become hollow and someone had filled it with particles of ice.

Facing them, directly in their way between the doorposts, stood the figure of a woman. She had dishevelled hair and wildly staring eyes, and her face was terrified and white as death.

She stood there motionless for the space of a single second. Then the candle flickered, and she was gone—gone utterly—and the door framed nothing but empty darkness.

"Only the beastly jumping candle-light," he said quickly, in a voice that sounded like someone else's and was only half under control. "Come on, aunt. There's nothing there."

He dragged her forward. With a clattering of feet and a great appearance of boldness they went on, but over his body the skin moved as if crawling ants covered it, and he knew by the weight on his arm that he was supplying the force of locomotion for two. The scullery was cold, bare, and empty; more like a large prison cell than anything else. They went round it, tried the door into the yard, and the windows, but found them all fastened securely. His aunt moved beside him like a person in a dream. Her eyes were tightly shut, and she seemed merely to follow the pressure of his arm. Her courage filled him with amazement. At the same time he noticed that a certain odd change had come over her face, a change which somehow evaded his power of analysis.

"There's nothing here, aunty," he repeated aloud quickly. "Let's go upstairs and see the rest of the house. Then we'll choose a room to wait up in."

She followed him obediently, keeping close to his side, and they locked the kitchen door behind them. It was a relief to get up again. In the hall there was more light than before, for the moon had travelled a little further down the stairs. Cautiously they began to go up into the dark vault of the upper house, the boards creaking under their weight.

On the first floor they found the large double drawing rooms, a search of which revealed nothing. Here also was no sign of furniture or recent occupancy; nothing but dust and neglect and shadows. They opened the big folding doors between front and back drawing rooms and then came out again to the landing and went on upstairs.

They had not gone up more than a dozen steps when they both simultaneously stopped to listen, looking into each other's eyes with a new apprehension across the flickering candle flame. From the room they had left hardly ten seconds before came the sound of doors quietly closing. It was beyond all question; they heard the booming noise that accompanies the shutting of heavy doors, followed by the sharp catching of the latch.

"We must go back and see," said Shorthouse briefly, in a low tone, and turning to go downstairs again.

Somehow she managed to drag after him, her feet catching in her dress, her face livid.

When they entered the front drawing room it was plain that the folding doors had been closed—half a minute before. Without hesitation Shorthouse opened them. He almost expected to see someone facing him in the back room; but only darkness and cold air met him. They went through both rooms, finding nothing unusual. They tried in every way to make the doors close of themselves, but there was not wind enough even to set the candle flame flickering. The doors would not move without strong pressure. All was silent as the grave. Undeniably the rooms were utterly empty, and the house utterly still.

"It's beginning," whispered a voice at his elbow which he hardly recognised as his aunt's.

He nodded acquiescence, taking out his watch to note the time. It was fifteen minutes before midnight; he made the entry of exactly what had occurred in his notebook, setting the candle in its case upon the floor in order to do so. It took a moment or two to balance it safely against the wall.

Aunt Julia always declared that at this moment she was not actually watching him, but had turned her head towards the inner room, where she fancied she heard something moving; but, at any rate, both positively agreed that there came a sound of rushing feet, heavy and very swift—and the next instant the candle was out!

But to Shorthouse himself had come more than this, and he has always thanked his fortunate stars that it came to him alone and not to his aunt too. For, as he rose from the stooping position of balancing the candle, and before it was actually extinguished, a face thrust itself forward so close to his own that he could almost have touched it with his lips. It was a face working with passion; a man's face, dark, with thick features, and angry, savage eyes. It belonged to a common man, and it was evil in its ordinary normal expression, no doubt, but as he saw it, alive with intense, aggressive emotion, it was a malignant and terrible human countenance.

There was no movement of the air; nothing but the sound of rushing feet—stockinged or muffled feet; the apparition of the face; and the almost simultaneous extinguishing of the candle.

In spite of himself, Shorthouse uttered a little cry, nearly losing his balance as his aunt clung to him with her whole weight in one moment of real, uncontrollable terror. She made no sound, but simply seized him bodily. Fortunately, however, she had seen nothing, but had only heard the rushing feet, for her control returned almost at once, and he was able to disentangle himself and strike a match.

The shadows ran away on all sides before the glare, and his aunt stooped down and groped for the cigar case with the precious candle. Then they discovered that the candle had not been blown out at all; it had been crushed out. The wick was pressed down into the wax, which was flattened as if by some smooth, heavy instrument.

How his companion so quickly overcame her terror, Shorthouse never properly understood; but his admiration for her self-control increased tenfold, and at the same time served to feed his own dying flame—for which he was undeniably grateful. Equally inexplicable to him was the evidence of physical force they had just witnessed. He at once suppressed the memory of stories he had heard of "physical mediums" and their dangerous phenomena; for if these were true, and either his aunt or himself was unwittingly a physical medium, it meant that they were simply aiding to focus the forces of a haunted house already charged to the brim. It was like walking with unprotected lamps among uncovered stores of gunpowder.

So, with as little reflection as possible, he simply relit the candle and went up to the next floor. The arm in his trembled, it is true, and his own tread was often uncertain, but they went on with thoroughness, and after a search revealing nothing they climbed the last flight of stairs to the top floor of all.

Here they found a perfect nest of small servants' rooms, with broken pieces of furniture, dirty cane-bottomed chairs, chests of drawers, cracked mirrors, and decrepit bedsteads. The rooms had low sloping ceilings already hung here and there with cobwebs, small windows, and badly plastered walls—a depressing and dismal region which they were glad to leave behind.

It was on the stroke of midnight when they entered a small room on the third floor, close to the top of the stairs, and arranged to make themselves comfortable for the remainder of their adventure. It was absolutely bare, and was said to be the room—then used as a clothes closet—into which the infuriated groom had chased his victim and finally caught her. Outside, across the narrow landing, began the stairs leading up to the floor above, and the servants' quarters where they had just searched.

In spite of the chilliness of the night there was something in the air of this room that cried for an open window. But there was more than this. Shorthouse could only describe it by saying that he felt less master of himself here than in any other part of the house. There was something that acted directly on the nerves, tiring the resolution, enfeebling the will. He was conscious of this result before he had been in the room five minutes, and it was in the short time they stayed there that he suffered the wholesale depletion of his vital forces, which was, for himself, the chief horror of the whole experience.

They put the candle on the floor of the cupboard, leaving the door a few inches ajar, so that there was no glare to confuse the eyes, and no shadow to shift about on walls and ceiling. Then they spread the cloak on the floor and sat down to wait, with their backs against the wall.

Shorthouse was within two feet of the door on to the landing; his position commanded a good view of the main staircase leading down into the darkness, and also of the beginning of the servants' stairs going to the floor above; the heavy stick lay beside him within easy reach.

The moon was now high above the house. Through the open window they could see the comforting stars like friendly eyes watching in the sky. One by one the clocks of the town struck midnight, and when the sounds died away the deep silence of a windless night fell again over everything. Only the boom of the sea, far away and lugubrious, filled the air with hollow murmurs.

Inside the house the silence became awful; awful, he thought, because any minute now it might be broken by sounds portending terror. The strain of waiting told more and more severely on the nerves; they talked in whispers when they talked at all, for their voices aloud sounded queer and unnatural. A chilliness, not altogether due to the night air, invaded the room, and made them cold. The influences against them, whatever these might be, were slowly robbing them of self-confidence, and the power of decisive action; their forces were on the wane, and the possibility of real fear took on a new and terrible meaning. He began to tremble for the elderly woman by his side, whose pluck could hardly save her beyond a certain extent.

He heard the blood singing in his veins. It sometimes seemed so loud that he fancied it prevented his hearing properly certain other sounds that were beginning very faintly to make themselves audible in the depths of the house. Every time he fastened his attention on these sounds, they instantly ceased. They certainly came no nearer. Yet he could not rid himself of the idea that movement was going on somewhere in the lower regions of the house. The drawing room floor, where the doors had been so strangely closed, seemed too near; the sounds were further off than that. He thought of the great kitchen, with the scurrying black beetles, and of the dismal little scullery; but, somehow or other, they did not seem to come from there either. Surely they were not outside the house!

Then, suddenly, the truth flashed into his mind, and for the space of a minute he felt as if his blood had stopped flowing and turned to ice.

The sounds were not downstairs at all; they were upstairs— upstairs, somewhere among those horrid gloomy little servants' rooms with their bits of broken furniture, low ceilings, and cramped windows—upstairs where the victim had first been disturbed and stalked to her death.

And the moment he discovered where the sounds were, he began to hear them more clearly. It was the sound of feet, moving stealthily along the passage overhead, in and out among the rooms, and past the furniture.

He turned quickly to steal a glance at the motionless figure seated beside him, to note whether she had shared his discovery. The faint candlelight coming through the crack in the cupboard door, threw her strongly marked face into vivid relief against the white of the wall. But it was something else that made him catch his breath and stare again. An extraordinary something had come into her face and seemed to spread over her features like a mask; it smoothed out the deep lines and drew the skin everywhere a little tighter so that the wrinkles disappeared; it brought into the face—with the sole exception of the old eyes—an appearance of youth and almost of childhood.

He stared in speechless amazement—amazement that was dangerously near to horror. It was his aunt's face indeed, but it was her face of forty years ago, the vacant innocent face of a girl. He had heard stories of that strange effect of terror which could wipe a human countenance clean of other emotions, obliterating all previous expressions; but he had never realised that it could be literally true, or could mean anything so simply horrible as what he now saw. For the dreadful signature of overmastering fear was written plainly in that utter vacancy of the girlish face beside him; and when, feeling his intense gaze, she turned to look at him, he instinctively closed his eyes tightly to shut out the sight.

Yet, when he turned a minute later, his feelings well in hand, he saw to his intense relief another expression; his aunt was smiling, and though the face was deathly white, the awful veil had lifted, and the normal look was returning.

"Anything wrong?" was all he could think of to say at the moment. And the answer was eloquent, coming from such a woman.

"I feel cold—and a little frightened," she whispered.

He offered to close the window, but she seized hold of him and begged him not to leave her side even for an instant.

"It's upstairs, I know," she whispered, with an odd half laugh; "but I can't possibly go up."

But Shorthouse thought otherwise, knowing that in action lay their best hope of self-control.

He took the brandy flask and poured out a glass of neat spirit, stiff enough to help anybody over anything. She swallowed it with a little shiver. His only idea now was to get out of the house before her collapse became inevitable; but this could not safely be done by turning tail and running from the enemy. Inaction was no longer possible; every minute he was growing less master of himself, and desperate, aggressive measures were imperative without further delay. Moreover, the action must be taken towards the enemy, not away from it; the climax, if necessary and unavoidable, would have to be faced boldly. He could do it now; but in ten minutes he might not have the force left to act for himself, much less for both!

Upstairs, the sounds were meanwhile becoming louder and closer, accompanied by occasional creaking of the boards. Someone was moving stealthily about, stumbling now and then awkwardly against the furniture.

Waiting a few moments to allow the tremendous dose of spirits to produce its effect, and knowing this would last but a short time under the circumstances, Shorthouse then quietly got on his feet, saying in a determined voice—

"Now, Aunt Julia, we'll go upstairs and find out what all this noise is about. You must come too. It's what we agreed."

He picked up his stick and went to the cupboard for the candle. A limp form rose shakily beside him breathing hard, and he heard a voice say very faintly something about being "ready to come." The woman's courage amazed him; it was so much greater than his own; and, as they advanced, holding aloft the dripping candle, some subtle force exhaled from this trembling, white-faced old woman at his side that was the true source of his inspiration. It held something really great that shamed him and gave him the support without which he would have proved far less equal to the occasion.

They crossed the dark landing, avoiding with their eyes the deep black space over the banisters. Then they began to mount the narrow staircase to meet the sounds which, minute by minute, grew louder and nearer. About halfway up the stairs Aunt Julia stumbled and Shorthouse turned to catch her by the arm, and just at that moment there came a terrific crash in the servants' corridor overhead. It was instantly followed by a shrill, agonised scream that was a cry of terror and a cry for help melted into one.

Before they could move aside, or go down a single step, someone came rushing along the passage overhead, blundering horribly, racing madly, at full speed, three steps at a time, down the very staircase where they stood. The steps were light and uncertain; but close behind them sounded the heavier tread of another person, and the staircase seemed to shake.

Shorthouse and his companion just had time to flatten themselves against the wall when the jumble of flying steps was upon them, and two persons, with the slightest possible interval between them, dashed past at full speed. It was a perfect whirlwind of sound breaking in upon the midnight silence of the empty building.

The two runners, pursuer and pursued, had passed clean through them where they stood, and already with a thud the boards below had received first one, then the other. Yet they had seen absolutely nothing—not a hand, or arm, or face, or even a shred of flying clothing.

There came a second's pause. Then the first one, the lighter of the two, obviously the pursued one, ran with uncertain footsteps into the little room which Shorthouse and his aunt had just left. The heavier one followed. There was a sound of scuffling, gasping, and smothered screaming; and then out on to the landing came the step—of a single person treading weightily.

A dead silence followed for the space of half a minute, and then was heard a rushing sound through the air. It was followed by a dull, crashing thud in the depths of the house below—on the stone floor of the hall.

Utter silence reigned after. Nothing moved. The flame of the candle was steady. It had been steady the whole time, and the air had been undisturbed by any movement whatsoever. Palsied with terror, Aunt Julia, without waiting for her companion, began fumbling her way downstairs; she was crying gently to herself, and when Shorthouse put his arm round her and half carried her he felt that she was trembling like a leaf. He went into the little room and picked up the cloak from the floor, and, arm in arm, walking very slowly, without speaking a word or looking once behind them, they marched down the three flights into the hall.

In the hall they saw nothing, but the whole way down the stairs they were conscious that someone followed them; step by step; when they went faster IT was left behind, and when they went more slowly IT caught them up. But never once did they look behind to see; and at each turning of the staircase they lowered their eyes for fear of the following horror they might see upon the stairs above.

With trembling hands Shorthouse opened the front door, and they walked out into the moonlight and drew a deep breath of the cool night air blowing in from the sea.

THE END

The Damned

I

"I'M OVER FORTY, FRANCES, and rather set in my ways," I said good-naturedly, ready to yield if she insisted that our going together on the visit involved her happiness. "My work is rather heavy just now too, as you know. The question is, could I work there—with a lot of unassorted people in the house?"

"Mabel doesn't mention any other people, Bill," was my sister's rejoinder. "I gather she's alone—as well as lonely."

By the way she looked sideways out of the window at nothing, it was obvious she was disappointed, but to my surprise she did not urge the point; and as I glanced at Mrs. Franklyn's invitation lying upon her sloping lap, the neat, childish handwriting conjured up a mental picture of the banker's widow, with her timid, insignificant personality, her pale grey eyes and her expression as of a backward child.

I thought, too, of the roomy country mansion her late husband had altered to suit his particular needs, and of my visit to it a few years ago when its barren spaciousness suggested a wing of Kensington Museum fitted up temporarily as a place to eat and sleep in. Comparing it mentally with the poky Chelsea flat where I and my sister kept impecunious house, I realized other points as well. Unworthy details flashed across me to entice: the fine library, the organ, the quiet workroom I should have, perfect service, the delicious cup of early tea, and hot baths at any moment of the day—without a geyser!

"It's a longish visit, a month—isn't it?" I hedged, smiling at the details that seduced me, and ashamed of my man's selfishness, yet knowing that Frances expected it of me. "There are points about it, I admit. If you're set on my going with you, I could manage it all right."

I spoke at length in this way because my sister made no answer. I saw her tired eyes gazing into the dreariness of Oakley Street and felt a pang strike through me. After a pause, in which again she said no word, I added: "So, when you write the letter, you might hint, perhaps, that I usually work all the morning, and—er—am not a very lively visitor! Then she'll understand, you see."

And I half-rose to return to my diminutive study, where I was slaving, just then, at an absorbing article on Comparative Aesthetic Values in the Blind and Deaf.

But Frances did not move. She kept her grey eyes upon Oakley Street where the evening mist from the river drew mournful perspectives into view. It was late October. We heard the omnibuses thundering across the bridge. The monotony of that broad, characterless street seemed more than usually depressing. Even in June sunshine it was dead, but with autumn its melancholy soaked into every house between King's Road and the Embankment. It washed thought into the past, instead of inviting it hopefully towards the future. For me, its easy width was an avenue through which nameless slums across the river sent creeping messages of depression, and I always regarded it as Winter's main entrance into London—fog, slush, gloom trooped down it every November, waving their forbidding banners till March came to rout them.[2]

Its one claim upon my love was that the south wind swept sometimes unobstructed up it, soft with suggestions of the sea. These lugubrious thoughts I naturally kept to myself, though I never ceased to regret the little flat whose cheapness had seduced us. Now, as I watched my sister's impassive face, I realized that perhaps she, too, felt as I felt, yet, brave woman, without betraying it.

"And, look here, Fanny," I said, putting a hand upon her shoulder as I crossed the room, "it would be the very thing for you. You're worn out with catering and housekeeping. Mabel is your oldest friend, besides, and you've hardly seen her since he died—"

"She's been abroad for a year, Bill, and only just came back," my sister interposed. "She came back rather unexpectedly, though I never thought she would go there to live—" She stopped abruptly. Clearly, she was only speaking half her mind. "Probably," she went on, "Mabel wants to pick up old links again."

---

[2] Blackwood was born on the border of London in an area known as Shooter's Hill. This borough was later incorporated into the capital, hence the author's detailed knowledge of the city. Shooter's Hill was then situated in the picturesque county of Kent, "the Garden of England," in close proximity to Blackheath, London, the notorious site of mass graves for victims of the Great Plague of London (1665-1666). Biographers point to this juxtaposition of beauty and horror in the circumambient world of the young Blackwood as an influence on his later writing.

"Naturally," I put in, "yourself chief among them." The veiled reference to the house I let pass.

It involved discussing the dead man for one thing.

"I feel I ought to go anyhow," she resumed, "and of course it would be jollier if you came too. You'd get in such a muddle here by yourself, and eat wrong things, and forget to air the rooms, and—oh, everything!" She looked up laughing. "Only," she added, "there's the British Museum—?"

"But there's a big library there," I answered, "and all the books of reference I could possibly want. It was of you I was thinking. You could take up your painting again; you always sell half of what you paint. It would be a splendid rest too, and Sussex is a jolly country to walk in. By all means, Fanny, I advise—"

Our eyes met, as I stammered in my attempts to avoid expressing the thought that hid in both our minds. My sister had a weakness for dabbling in the various "new" theories of the day, and Mabel, who before her marriage had belonged to foolish societies for investigating the future life to the neglect of the present one, had fostered this undesirable tendency.

Her amiable, impressionable temperament was open to every psychic wind that blew. I deplored, detested the whole business. But even more than this I abhorred the later influence that Mr. Franklyn had steeped his wife in, capturing her body and soul in his somber doctrines. I had dreaded lest my sister also might be caught.

"Now that she is alone again—"

I stopped short. Our eyes now made pretence impossible, for the truth had slipped out inevitably, stupidly, although unexpressed in definite language. We laughed, turning our faces a moment to look at other things in the room. Frances picked up a book and examined its cover as though she had made an important discovery, while I took my case out and lit a cigarette I did not want to smoke.

We left the matter there. I went out of the room before further explanation could cause tension. Disagreements grow into discord from such tiny things—wrong adjectives, or a chance inflection of the voice. Frances had a right to her views of life as much as I had.

At least, I reflected comfortably, we had separated upon an agreement this time, recognized mutually, though not actually stated. And this point of meeting was, oddly enough, our way of regarding someone who was dead.

For we had both disliked the husband with a great dislike, and during his three years' married life had only been to the house once—for a weekend visit; arriving late on Saturday, we had left after an early breakfast on Monday morning. Ascribing my sister's dislike to a natural jealousy at losing her old friend, I said merely that he displeased me.

Yet we both knew that the real emotion lay much deeper. Frances, loyal, honorable creature, had kept silence; and beyond saying that house and grounds—he altered one and laid out the other—distressed her as an expression of his personality somehow ('distressed' was the word she used), no further explanation had passed her lips.

Our dislike of his personality was easily accounted for—up to a point, since both of us shared the artist's point of view that a creed, cut to measure and carefully dried, was an ugly thing, and that a dogma to which believers must subscribe or perish everlastingly was a barbarism resting upon cruelty. But while my own dislike was purely due to an abstract worship of Beauty, my sister's had another twist in it, for with her "new" tendencies, she believed that all religions were an aspect of truth and that no one, even the lowest wretch, could escape "heaven" in the long run.

Samuel Franklyn, the rich banker, was a man universally respected and admired, and the marriage, though Mabel was fifteen years his junior, won general applause; his bride was an heiress in her own right— breweries—and the story of her conversion at a revivalist meeting where Samuel Franklyn had spoken fervidly of heaven, and terrifyingly of sin, hell and damnation, even contained a touch of genuine romance. She was a brand snatched from the burning; his detailed eloquence had frightened her into heaven; salvation came in the nick of time; his words had plucked her from the edge of that lake of fire and brimstone where their worm dieth not and the fire is not quenched.[3] She regarded him as a hero, sighed her relief upon his saintly shoulder, and accepted the peace he offered her with a grateful resignation.

For her husband was a "religious man" who successfully combined great riches with the glamour of winning souls. He was a portly figure, though tall, with masterful, big hands, his fingers rather thick and red; and his dignity, that just escaped being pompous, held in it something that was implacable.

---

[3] "And the devil that deceived them was cast into the lake of fire and brimstone, where the beast and the false prophet are, and shall be tormented day and night for ever and ever." – Revelation 20:10.

A convinced assurance, almost remorseless, gleamed in his eyes when he preached especially, and his threats of hell fire must have scared souls stronger than the timid, receptive Mabel whom he married. He clad himself in long frock-coats hat buttoned unevenly, big square boots, and trousers that invariably bagged at the knee and were a little short; he wore low collars, spats occasionally, and a tall black hat that was not of silk.

His voice was alternately hard and unctuous; and he regarded theaters, ballrooms, and racecourses as the vestibule of that brimstone lake of whose geography he was as positive as of his great banking offices in the City. A philanthropist up to the hilt, however, no one ever doubted his complete sincerity; his convictions were ingrained, his faith borne out by his life—as witness his name upon so many admirable Societies, as treasurer, patron, or heading the donation list. He bulked large in the world of doing good, a broad and stately stone in the rampart against evil. And his heart was genuinely kind and soft for others—who believed as he did.

Yet, in spite of this true sympathy with suffering and his desire to help, he was narrow as a telegraph wire and unbending as a church pillar; he was intensely selfish; intolerant as an officer of the Inquisition,[4] his bourgeois soul constructed a revolting scheme of heaven that was reproduced in miniature in all he did and planned. Faith was the sine qua non of salvation, and by "faith" he meant belief in his own particular view of things—"which faith, except every one do keep whole and undefiled, without doubt he shall perish everlastingly." All the world but his own small, exclusive sect must be damned eternally—a pity, but alas, inevitable. He was right.

Yet he prayed without ceasing, and gave heavily to the poor—the only thing he could not give being big ideas to his provincial and suburban deity. Pettier than an insect, and more obstinate than a mule, he had also the superior, sleek humility of a "chosen one." He was churchwarden too. He read the lesson in a "place of worship," either chilly or overheated, where neither organ, vestments, nor lighted candles were permitted, but where the odor of hairwash on the boys' heads in the back rows pervaded the entire building.

---

4 The Spanish Inquisition (*Tribunal del Santo Oficio de la Inquisición*) began in 1478 under Ferdinand and Isabella and wasn't officially disbanded until 1834. The Holy Office of the Inquisition, as it was officially known, reported to the Catholic Spanish Crown, and was active in its pursuit of heretics across Spain and the Spanish Empire.

This portrait of the banker, who accumulated riches both on earth and in heaven, may possibly be overdrawn, however, because Frances and I were "artistic temperaments" that viewed the type with a dislike and distrust amounting to contempt. The majority considered Samuel Franklyn a worthy man and a good citizen. The majority, doubtless, held the saner view. A few years more, and he certainly would have been made a baronet. He relieved much suffering in the world, as assuredly as he caused many souls the agonies of torturing fear by his emphasis upon damnation.

Had there been one point of beauty in him, we might have been more lenient; only we found it not, and, I admit, took little pains to search. I shall never forget the look of dour forgiveness with which he heard our excuses for missing Morning Prayers that Sunday morning of our single visit to The Towers. My sister learned that a change was made soon afterwards, prayers being "conducted" after breakfast instead of before.

The Towers stood solemnly upon a Sussex hill amid park-like modern grounds, but the house cannot better be described—it would be so wearisome for one thing—than by saying that it was a cross between an overgrown, pretentious Norwood villa and one of those saturnine Institutes for cripples the train passes as it slinks ashamed through South London into Surrey. It was "wealthily" furnished and at first sight imposing, but on closer acquaintance revealed a meager personality, barren and austere. One looked for Rules and Regulations on the walls, all signed By Order. The place was a prison that shut out "the world." There was, of course, no billiard room, no smoking room, no room for play of any kind, and the great hall at the back, once a chapel, which might have been used for dancing, theatricals, or other innocent amusements, was consecrated in his day to meetings of various kinds, chiefly brigades, temperance or missionary societies. There was a harmonium at one end—on the level floor—a raised dais or platform at the other, and a gallery above for the servants, gardeners, and coachmen. It was heated with hot-water pipes, and hung with Doré's pictures,[5] though these latter were soon removed and stored out of sight in the attics as being too unspiritual. In polished, shiny wood, it was a representation in miniature of that poky exclusive Heaven he took about with him, externalizing it in all he did and planned, even in the grounds about the house.

---

[5] Gustave Doré (1832-1883).

Changes in The Towers, Frances told me, had been made during Mabel's year of widowhood abroad—an organ put into the big hall, the library made livable and re-catalogued—when it was permissible to suppose she had found her soul again and returned to her normal, healthy views of life, which included enjoyment and play, literature, music and the arts, without, however, a touch of that trivial thoughtlessness usually termed worldliness. Mrs. Franklyn, as I remembered her, was a quiet little woman, shallow, perhaps, and easily influenced, but sincere as a dog and thorough in her faithful Friendship. Her tastes at heart were catholic, and that heart was simple and unimaginative. That she took up with the various movements of the day was sign merely that she was searching in her limited way for a belief that should bring her peace.

She was, in fact, a very ordinary woman, her caliber a little less than that of Frances. I knew they used to discuss all kinds of theories together, but as these discussions never resulted in action, I had come to regard her as harmless. Still, I was not sorry when she married, and I did not welcome now a renewal of the former intimacy. The philanthropist she had given no children, or she would have made a good and sensible mother. No doubt she would marry again.

"Mabel mentions that she's been alone at The Towers since the end of August," Frances told me at teatime; "and I'm sure she feels out of it and lonely. It would be a kindness to go. Besides, I always liked her."

I agreed. I had recovered from my attack of selfishness. I expressed my pleasure.

"You've written to accept," I said, half statement and half question.

Frances nodded. "I thanked for you," she added quietly, "explaining that you were not free at the moment, but that later, if not inconvenient, you might come down for a bit and join me."

I stared. Frances sometimes had this independent way of deciding things.

I was convicted, and punished into the bargain.

Of course there followed argument and explanation, as between brother and sister who were affectionate, but the recording of our talk could be of little interest. It was arranged thus, Frances and I both satisfied. Two days later she departed for The Towers, leaving me alone in the flat with everything planned for my comfort and good behavior—she was rather a tyrant in her quiet way—and her last words as I saw her off from Charing Cross rang in my head for a long time after she was gone:

"I'll write and let you know, Bill. Eat properly, mind, and let me know if anything goes wrong."

She waved her small gloved hand, nodded her head till the feather brushed the window, and was gone.

II

AFTER THE NOTE ANNOUNCING HER safe arrival a week of silence passed, and then a letter came; there were various suggestions for my welfare, and the rest was the usual rambling information and description Frances loved, generously italicized. " ...and we are *quite* alone," she went on in her enormous handwriting that seemed such a waste of space and labor, "though some others are coming presently, I *believe*. You could work here to your heart's content. Mabel quite understands, and says she *would love to have you* when you feel free to come. She has changed a bit—back to her old natural self: she *never* mentions *him*. The place has changed too in certain ways: it has more *cheerfulness*, I think. She has put it in, this cheerfulness, *spaded* it in, if you know what I mean; but it lies about uneasily and is not natural—quite. The organ is a *beauty*. She must be very rich now, but she's as gentle and sweet as ever. Do you know, Bill, I think he must have frightened her into marrying him. I get the impression she was afraid of him."

This last sentence was inked out, I but I read it through the scratching; the letters being too big to hide.

"He had an inflexible will beneath all that oily kindness which passed for spiritual. He was a real *personality*, I mean. I'm sure he'd have sent you and me cheerfully to the stake in another century—for our own good. Isn't it odd she never speaks of him, even to me?" This, again, was stroked through, though without the intention to obliterate—merely because it was repetition, probably. "The only reminder of him in the house now is a big copy of the presentation portrait that stands on the stairs of the Multitechnic Institute at Peckham—you know—that life-size one with his fat hand sprinkled with rings resting on a thick Bible and the other slipped between the buttons of a tight frock-coat. It hangs in the dining room and rather dominates our meals. I *wish* Mabel would take it down. I think she'd like to if she dared. There's not a *single* photograph of him *anywhere*, even in her own room. Mrs. Marsh[6] is here—you remember her, his housekeeper, the wife of the man who got penal servitude for killing a baby or something—you said she robbed him and justified her stealing because the story of the unjust steward was in the Bible! How we laughed over that! She's

---

[6] Mrs. Marsh is a typical Blackwood name imbued with atmospheric overtones.

just the same too, gliding about all over the house and turning up when least expected."

Other reminiscences filled the next two sides of the letter, and ran, without a trace of punctuation, into instructions about a Salamander stove for heating my workroom in the flat; these were followed by things I was to tell the cook, and by requests for several articles she had forgotten and would like sent after her, two of them blouses, with descriptions so lengthy and contradictory that I sighed as I read them—

"...unless you come down *soon*, in which case perhaps you wouldn't mind bringing them; *not* the mauve one I wear in the evening sometimes, but *the pale blue one* with lace round the collar and the crinkly front. They're in the cupboard—or the drawer, I'm not sure which—of my bedroom. Ask Annie if you're in doubt. Thanks *most* awfully. Send a telegram, remember, and we'll meet you in the motor *any* time. I don't quite know if I shall stay the *whole* month—alone. It all depends...."

And she closed the letter, the italicized words increasing recklessly towards the end, with a repetition that Mabel would love to have me, "for myself," as also to have a, "*man* in the *house*," and that I only had to telegraph the day and the train....

This letter, coming by the second post, interrupted me in a moment of absorbing work, and, having read it through to make sure there was nothing requiring instant attention, I threw it aside and went on with my notes and reading. Within five minutes, however, it was back at me again. That restless thing called "between the lines" fluttered about my mind. My interest in the Balkan States—political article that had been "ordered"—faded. Somewhere, somehow I felt disquieted, disturbed.

At first, I persisted in my work, forcing myself to concentrate, but soon found that a layer of new impressions floated between the article and my attention. It was like a shadow, though a shadow that dissolved upon inspection. Once or twice I glanced up, expecting to find someone in the room, that the door had opened unobserved and Annie was waiting for instructions. I heard the buses thundering across the bridge. I was aware of Oakley Street.

Montenegro and the blue Adriatic melted into the October haze along that depressing Embankment that aped a riverbank, and sentences from the letter flashed before my eyes and stung me. Picking it up and reading it through more carefully, I rang the bell and told Annie to find the blouses and pack them for the post, showing her finally the written description, and resenting the superior smile with which she at once interrupted. "I know them, sir," and disappeared.

But it was not the blouses: it was that exasperating thing "between the lines" that put an end to my work with its elusive teasing nuisance. The first sharp impression is alone of value in such a case, for once analysis begins the imagination constructs all kinds of false interpretation. The more I thought, the more I grew fuddled. The letter, it seemed to me, wanted to say another thing; instead the eight sheets conveyed it merely. It came to the edge of disclosure, then halted.

There was something on the writer's mind, and I felt uneasy. Studying the sentences brought, however, no revelation, but increased confusion only; for while the uneasiness remained, the first clear hint had vanished. In the end I closed my books and went out to look up another matter at the British Museum library. Perhaps I should discover it that way—by turning the mind in a totally new direction. I lunched at the Express Dairy in Oxford Street close by, and telephoned to Annie that I would be home to tea at five.

And at tea, tired physically and mentally after breathing the exhausted air of the Rotunda for five hours, my mind suddenly delivered up its original impression, vivid and clear-cut; no proof accompanied the revelation; it was mere presentiment, but convincing. Frances was disturbed in her mind, her orderly, sensible, housekeeping mind; she was uneasy, even perhaps afraid; something in the house distressed her, and she had need of me. Unless I went down, her time of rest and change, her quite necessary holiday, in fact, would be spoilt. She was too unselfish to say this, but it ran everywhere between the lines. I saw it clearly now. Mrs. Franklyn, moreover—and that meant Frances too—would like a "man in the house." It was a disagreeable phrase, a suggestive way of hinting something she dared not state definitely. The two women in that great, lonely barrack of a house were afraid.

My sense of duty, affection, unselfishness, whatever the composite emotion may be termed, was stirred; also my vanity. I acted quickly, lest reflection should warp clear, decent judgment.

"Annie," I said, when she answered the bell, "you need not send those blouses by the post. I'll take them down tomorrow when I go. I shall be away a week or two, possibly longer." And, having looked up a train, I hastened out to telegraph before I could change my fickle mind.

But no desire came that night to change my mind. I was doing the right, the necessary thing. I was even in something of a hurry to get down to The Towers as soon as possible. I chose an early afternoon train.

III

A TELEGRAM HAD TOLD ME TO COME to a town ten miles from the house, so I was saved the crawling train to the local station, and traveled down by an express. As soon as we left London the fog cleared off, and an autumn sun, though without heat in it, painted the landscape with golden browns and yellows. My spirits rose as I lay back in the luxurious motor and sped between the woods and hedges. Oddly enough, my anxiety of overnight had disappeared. It was due, no doubt, to that exaggeration of detail which reflection in loneliness brings. Frances and I had not been separated for over a year, and her letters from The Towers told so little. It had seemed unnatural to be deprived of those intimate particulars of mood and feeling I was accustomed to. We had such confidence in one another, and our affection was so deep. Though she was but five years younger than myself, I regarded her as a child. My attitude was fatherly.

In return, she certainly mothered me with a solicitude that never cloyed. I felt no desire to marry while she was still alive. She painted in watercolors with a reasonable success, and kept house for me; I wrote, reviewed books and lectured on aesthetics; we were a humdrum couple of quasi-artists, well satisfied with life, and all I feared for her was that she might become a suffragette or be taken captive by one of these wild theories that caught her imagination sometimes, and that Mabel, for one, had fostered. As for myself, no doubt she deemed me a trifle solid or stolid—I forget which word she preferred—but on the whole there was just sufficient difference of opinion to make intercourse suggestive without monotony, and certainly without quarrelling.

Drawing in deep draughts of the stinging autumn air, I felt happy and exhilarated. It was like going for a holiday, with comfort at the end of the journey instead of bargaining for centimes.

But my heart sank noticeably the moment the house came into view. The long drive, lined with hostile monkey trees and formal wellingtonias that were solemn and sedate, was mere extension of the miniature approach to a thousand semidetached suburban "residences"; and the appearance of The Towers, as we turned the corner with a rush, suggested a commonplace climax to a story that had begun interestingly, almost thrillingly. A villa had escaped from the shadow of the Crystal Palace, thumped its way down by night, grown suddenly monstrous in a shower of rich rain, and settled itself insolently to stay. Ivy climbed about the opulent redbrick walls, but climbed neatly and with disfiguring effect, sham as on a prison or—the simile made me smile—an orphan asylum. There was no hint of the comely roughness of untidy ivy on a ruin. Clipped, trained, and precise it was, as on a brand-new protestant church. I swear there was not a bird's nest nor a single earwig in it anywhere. About the porch it was particularly thick, smothering a seventeenth-century lamp with a contrast that was quite horrible. Extensive glasshouses spread away on the farther side of the house; the numerous towers to which the building owed its name secmed made to hold school bells; and the windowsills, thick with potted flowers, made me think of the desolate suburbs of Brighton or Bexhill. In a commanding position upon the crest of a hill, it overlooked miles of undulating, wooded country southwards to the Downs, but behind it, to the north, thick banks of ilex,[7] holly, and privet protected it from the cleaner and more stimulating winds. Hence, though highly placed, it was shut in. Three years had passed since I last set eyes upon, it, but the unsightly memory I had retained was justified by the reality. The place was deplorable.

It is my habit to express my opinions audibly sometimes, when impressions are strong enough to warrant it; but now I only sighed "Oh, dear," as I extricated my legs from many rugs and went into the house. A tall parlor-maid, with the bearing of a grenadier, received me, and standing behind her was Mrs. Marsh, the housekeeper, whom I remembered because her untidy back hair had suggested to me that it had been burnt. I went at once to my room, my hostess already dressing for dinner, but Frances came in to see me just as I was struggling with my black tie that had got tangled like a bootlace. She fastened it for me in a neat, effective bow, and while I held my chin up for the operation, staring blankly at the ceiling, the impression came—I wondered, was it her touch that caused it?—that something in her trembled. Shrinking perhaps is the truer word. Nothing in her face or manner betrayed it, nor in her pleasant, easy talk while she tidied my things and scolded my slovenly packing, as her habit was, questioning me about the servants at the flat. The blouses, though right, were crumpled, and my scolding was deserved. There was no impatience even. Yet somehow or other the suggestion of a shrinking reserve and holding back reached my mind.

She had been lonely, of course, but it was more than that; she was glad that I had come, yet for some reason unstated she could

---

[7] *Ilex aquifolium* is a species of holly native to western Europe.

have wished that I had stayed away. We discussed the news that had accumulated during our brief separation, and in doing so the impression, at best exceedingly slight, was forgotten. My chamber was large and beautifully furnished; the hall and dining room of our flat would have gone into it with a good remainder; yet it was not a place I could settle down in for work. It conveyed the idea of impermanence, making me feel transient as in a hotel bedroom.

This, of course, was the fact. But some rooms convey a settled, lasting hospitality even in a hotel; this one did not; and as I was accustomed to work in the room I slept in, at least when visiting, a slight frown must have crept between my eyes.

"Mabel has fitted a workroom for you just out of the library," said the clairvoyant Frances.

"No one will disturb you there, and you'll have fifteen thousand books all catalogued within easy reach. There's a private staircase too. You can breakfast in your room and slip down in your dressing gown if you want to." She laughed. My spirits took a turn upwards as absurdly as they had gone down.

"And how are you?" I asked, giving her a belated kiss. "It's jolly to be together again. I did feel rather lost without you, I'll admit."

"That's natural," she laughed. "I'm so glad."

She looked well and had country color in her cheeks. She informed me that she was eating and sleeping well, going out for little walks with Mabel, painting bits of scenery again, and enjoying a complete change and rest; and yet, for all her brave description, the word somehow did not quite ring true. Those last words in particular did not ring true. There lay in her manner, just out of sight, I felt, this suggestion of the exact reverse—of unrest, shrinking, almost of anxiety. Certain small strings in her seemed over-tight. "Keyed-up" was the slang expression that crossed my mind. I looked rather searchingly into her face as she was telling me this.

"Only—the evenings," she added, noticing my query, yet rather avoiding my eyes, "the evenings are—well, rather heavy sometimes, and I find it difficult to keep awake."

"The strong air after London makes you drowsy," I suggested, "and you like to get early to bed."

Frances turned and looked at me for a moment steadily. "On the contrary, Bill, I dislike going to bed—here. And Mabel goes so early." She said it lightly enough, fingering the disorder upon my dressing table in such a stupid way that I saw her mind was working in another direction altogether. She looked up suddenly with a kind of nervousness from the brush and scissors.

"Billy," she said abruptly, lowering her voice, "isn't it odd, but I hate sleeping alone here? I can't make it out quite; I've never felt such a thing before in my life. Do you—think it's all nonsense?"

And she laughed, with her lips but not with her eyes; there was a note of defiance in her I failed to understand.

"Nothing a nature like yours feels strongly is nonsense, Frances," I replied soothingly.

But I, too, answered with my lips only, for another part of my mind was working elsewhere, and among uncomfortable things. A touch of bewilderment passed over me. I was not certain how best to continue. If I laughed she would tell me no more, yet if I took her too seriously the strings would tighten further. Instinctively, then, this flashed rapidly across me: that something of what she felt, I had also felt, though interpreting it differently. Vague it was, as the coming of rain or storm that announce themselves hours in advance with their hint of faint, unsettling excitement in the air. I had been but a short hour in the house—big, comfortable, luxurious house—but had experienced this sense of being unsettled, unfixed, fluctuating—a kind of impermanence that transient lodgers in hotels must feel, but that a guest in a friend's home ought not to feel, be the visit short or long. To Frances, an impressionable woman, the feeling had come in the terms of alarm. She disliked sleeping alone, while yet she longed to sleep. The precise idea in my mind evaded capture, merely brushing through me, three-quarters out of sight; I realized only that we both felt the same thing, and that neither of us could get at it clearly.

Degrees of unrest we felt, but the actual thing did not disclose itself. It did not happen. I felt strangely at sea for a moment. Frances would interpret hesitation as endorsement, and encouragement might be the last thing that could help her.

"Sleeping in a strange house," I answered at length, "is often difficult at first, and one feels lonely. After fifteen months in our tiny flat one feels lost and uncared for in a big house. It's an uncomfortable feeling—I know it well. And this is a barrack, isn't it? The masses of furniture only make it worse. One feels in storage somewhere underground—the furniture doesn't furnish. One must never yield to fancies, though—" Frances looked away towards the windows; she seemed disappointed a little.

"After our thickly-populated Chelsea," I went on quickly, "it seems isolated here."

But she did not turn back, and clearly I was saying the wrong thing. A wave of pity rushed suddenly over me. Was she really frightened, perhaps? She was imaginative, I knew, but never moody; common sense was strong in her, though she had her times of hypersensitiveness. I caught the echo of some unreasoning, big alarm in her. She stood there, gazing across my balcony towards the sea of wooded country that spread dim and vague in the obscurity of the dusk. The deepening shadows entered the room, I fancied, from the grounds below. Following her abstracted gaze a moment, I experienced a curious sharp desire to leave, to escape. Out yonder was wind and space and freedom. This enormous building was oppressive, silent, still.

Great catacombs occurred to me, things beneath the ground, imprisonment and capture. I believe I even shuddered a little.

I touched her shoulder. She turned round slowly, and we looked with a certain deliberation into each other's eyes.

"Fanny," I asked, more gravely than I intended, "you are not frightened, are you? Nothing has happened, has it?"

She replied with emphasis, "Of course not! How could it—I mean, why should I?" She stammered, as though the wrong sentence flustered her a second. "It's simply—that I have this—er—this dislike of sleeping alone."

Naturally, my first thought was how easy it would be to cut our visit short. But I did not say this. Had it been a true solution, Frances would have said it for me long ago.

"Wouldn't Mabel double-up with you?" I said instead, "or give you an adjoining room, so that you could leave the door between you open? There's space enough, heaven knows."

And then, as the gong sounded in the hall below for dinner, she said, as with an effort, this thing, "Mabel did ask me—on the third night—after I had told her. But I declined."

"You'd rather be alone than with her?" I asked, with a certain relief.

Her reply was so gravely given, a child would have known there was more behind it: "Not that; but that she did not really want it."

I had a moment's intuition and acted on it impulsively. "She feels it too, perhaps, but wishes to face it by herself—and get over it?"

My sister bowed her head, and the gesture made me realize of a sudden how grave and solemn our talk had grown, as though some portentous thing were under discussion. It had come of itself—indefinite as a gradual change of temperature. Yet neither of us knew its nature, for apparently neither of us could state it plainly. Nothing happened, even in our words.

"That was my impression," she said, "—that if she yields to it she encourages it. And a habit forms so easily. Just think," she added with a faint smile that was the first sign of lightness she had yet betrayed, "what a nuisance it would be—everywhere—if everybody was afraid of being alone—like that."

I snatched readily at the chance. We laughed a little, though it was a quiet kind of laughter that seemed wrong. I took her arm and led her towards the door.

"Disastrous, in fact," I agreed.

She raised her voice to its normal pitch again, as I had done. "No doubt it will pass," she said, "now that you have come. Of course, it's chiefly my imagination." Her tone was lighter, though nothing could convince me that the matter itself was light—just then. "And in any case," tightening her grip on my arm as we passed into the bright enormous corridor and caught sight of Mrs. Franklyn waiting in the cheerless hall below, "I'm very glad you're here, Bill, and Mabel, I know, is too."

"If it doesn't pass," I just had time to whisper with a feeble attempt at jollity, "I'll come at night and snore outside your door. After that you'll be so glad to get rid of me that you won't mind being alone."

"That's a bargain," said Frances.

I shook my hostess by the hand, made a banal remark about the long interval since last we met, and walked behind them into the great dining room, dimly lit by candles, wondering in my heart how long my sister and I should stay, and why in the world we had ever left our cozy little flat to enter this desolation of riches and false luxury at all. The unsightly picture of the late Samuel Franklyn, Esq., stared down upon me from the farther end of the room above the mighty mantelpiece.

He looked, I thought, like some pompous Heavenly Butler who denied to all the world, and to us in particular, the right of entry without presentation cards signed by his hand as proof that we belonged to his own exclusive set. The majority, to his deep grief, and in spite of all his prayers on their behalf, must burn and "perish everlastingly."[8]

---

[8] "That everyone who believes in Him may have eternal life. For God so loved the world that He gave His one and only Son, that everyone who believes in Him shall not perish but have eternal life." - Gospel of John 3: 15-16.

IV

WITH THE INSTINCT OF THE healthy bachelor I always try to make myself a nest in the place I live in, be it for long or short. Whether visiting, in lodging house, or in hotel, the first essential is this nest—one's own things built into the walls as a bird builds in its feathers. It may look desolate and uncomfortable enough to others, because the central detail is neither bed nor wardrobe, sofa nor armchair, but a good solid writing table that does not wriggle, and that has wide elbow room.

And The Towers is vividly described for me by the single fact that I could not "nest" there.

I took several days to discover this, but the first impression of impermanence was truer than I knew. The feathers of the mind refused here to lie one way. They ruffled, pointed, and grew wild.

Luxurious furniture does not mean comfort; I might as well have tried to settle down in the sofa and armchair department of a big shop. My bedroom was easily managed; it was the private work-room, prepared especially for my reception, that made me feel alien and outcast.

Externally, it was all one could desire: an antechamber to the great library, with not one, but two generous oak tables, to say nothing of smaller ones against the walls with capacious drawers.

There were reading desks, mechanical devices for holding books, perfect light, quiet as in a church, and no approach but across the huge adjoining room. Yet it did not invite.

"I hope you'll be able to work here," said my little hostess the next morning, as she took me in—her only visit to it while I stayed in the house—and showed me the ten-volume Catalogue.

"It's absolutely quiet and no one will disturb you."

"If you can't, Bill, you're not much good," laughed Frances, who was on her arm. "Even I could write in a study like this!"

I glanced with pleasure at the ample tables, the sheets of thick blotting paper, the rulers, sealing wax, paper knives, and all the other immaculate paraphernalia. "It's perfect," I answered with a secret thrill, yet feeling a little foolish. This was for Gibbon[9] or Carlyle,[10] rather than for my potboiling insignificancies. "If I can't write

---

[9] Historian Edward Gibbon (1737-1794), author of the epic six volume *History of the Decline and Fall of the Roman Empire*.

[10] Thomas Carlyle (1795-1881), author of many important works of history, and an influence on Charles Dickens during his research for *A Tale of*

masterpieces here, it's certainly not your fault," and I turned with gratitude to Mrs. Franklyn. She was looking straight at me, and there was a question in her small pale eyes I did not understand. Was she noting the effect upon me, I wondered?

"You'll write here—perhaps a story about the house," she said, "Thompson will bring you anything you want; you only have to ring." She pointed to the electric bell on the central table, the wire running neatly down the leg. "No one has ever worked here before, and the library has been hardly used since it was put in. So there's no previous atmosphere to affect your imagination—er—adversely."

We laughed. "Bill isn't that sort," said my sister; while I wished they would go out and leave me to arrange my little nest and set to work.

I thought, of course, it was the huge listening library that made me feel so inconsiderable—the fifteen thousand silent, staring books, the solemn aisles, the deep, eloquent shelves. But when the women had gone and I was alone, the beginning of the truth crept over me, and I felt that first hint of disconsolateness which later became an imperative No. The mind shut down, images ceased to rise and flow. I read, made copious notes, but I wrote no single line at The Towers.

Nothing completed itself there. Nothing happened.

The morning sunshine poured into the library through ten long narrow windows; birds were singing; the autumn air, rich with a faint aroma of November melancholy that stung the imagination pleasantly, filled my antechamber. I looked out upon the undulating wooded landscape, hemmed in by the sweep of distant Downs, and I tasted a whiff of the sea. Rooks cawed as they floated above the elms, and there were lazy cows in the nearer meadows. A dozen times I tried to make my nest and settle down to work, and a dozen times, like a turning fastidious dog upon a hearth rug, I rearranged my chair and books and papers.

The temptation of the Catalogue and shelves, of course, was accountable for much, yet not, I felt, for all. That was a manageable seduction.

My work, moreover, was not of the creative kind that requires absolute absorption; it was the mere readable presentation of data I had accumulated. My notebooks were charged with facts ready

---

Two Cities. His famous dictum that "the history of the world is but the biography of great men," continues to be a topic of debate in history classes.

to tabulate—facts, too, that interested me keenly. A mere effort of the will was necessary, and concentration of no difficult kind. Yet, somehow, it seemed beyond me: something forever pushed the facts into disorder ... and in the end I sat in the sunshine, dipping into a dozen books selected from the shelves outside, vexed with myself and only half-enjoying it. I felt restless. I wanted to be elsewhere.

And even while I read, attention wandered. Frances, Mabel, her late husband, the house and grounds, each in turn and sometimes all together, rose uninvited into the stream of thought, hindering any consecutive flow of work. In disconnected fashion came these pictures that interrupted concentration, yet presenting themselves as broken fragments of a bigger thing my mind already groped for unconsciously. They fluttered round this hidden thing of which they were aspects, fugitive interpretations, no one of them bringing complete revelation. There was no adjective, such as pleasant or unpleasant, that I could attach to what I felt, beyond that the result was unsettling. Vague as the atmosphere of a dream, it yet persisted, and I could not dissipate it.

Isolated words or phrases in the lines I read sent questions scouring across my mind, sure sign that the deeper part of me was restless and ill at ease.

Rather trivial questions too—half-foolish interrogations, as of a puzzled or curious child: Why was my sister afraid to sleep alone, and why did her friend feel a similar repugnance, yet seek to conquer it? Why was the solid luxury of the house without comfort, its shelter without the sense of permanence? Why had Mrs. Franklyn asked us to come, artists, unbelieving vagabonds, types at the farthest possible remove from the saved sheep of her husband's household? Had a reaction set in against the hysteria of her conversion? I had seen no signs of religious fervor in her; her atmosphere was that of an ordinary, high-minded woman, yet a woman of the world. Lifeless, though, a little, perhaps, now that I came to think about it: she had made no definite impression upon me of any kind. And my thoughts ran vaguely after this fragile clue.

Closing my book, I let them run. For, with this chance reflection came the discovery that I could not see her clearly—could not feel her soul, her personality. Her face, her small pale eyes, her dress and body and walk, all these stood before me like a photograph; but her Self evaded me. She seemed not there, lifeless, empty, a shadow—nothing.

The picture was disagreeable, and I put it by. Instantly she melted out, as though light thought had conjured up a phantom that had no real existence. And at that very moment, singularly enough, my eye caught sight of her moving past the window, going silently along the gravel path. I watched her, a sudden new sensation gripping me. "There goes a prisoner," my thought instantly ran, "one who wishes to escape, but cannot."

What brought the outlandish notion, heaven only knows. The house was of her own choice, she was twice an heiress, and the world lay open at her feet. Yet she stayed—unhappy, frightened, caught. All this flashed over me, and made a sharp impression even before I had time to dismiss it as absurd. But a moment later explanation offered itself, though it seemed as far-fetched as the original impression. My mind, being logical, was obliged to provide something, apparently. For Mrs. Franklyn, while dressed to go out, with thick walking boots, a pointed stick, and a motor-cap tied on with a veil as for the windy lanes, was obviously content to go no farther than the little garden paths. The costume was a sham and a pretence. It was this, and her lithe, quick movements that suggested a caged creature—a creature tamed by fear and cruelty that cloaked themselves in kindness—pacing up and down, unable to realize why it got no farther, but always met the same bars in exactly the same place. The mind in her was barred.

I watched her go along the paths and down the steps from one terrace to another, until the laurels hid her altogether; and into this mere imagining of a moment came a hint of something slightly disagreeable, for which my mind, search as it would, found no explanation at all. I remembered then certain other little things. They dropped into the picture of their own accord. In a mind not deliberately hunting for clues, pieces of a puzzle sometimes come together in this way, bringing revelation, so that for a second there flashed across me, vanishing instantly again before I could consider it, a large, distressing thought. I can only describe vaguely as a Shadow.

Dark and ugly, oppressive certainly it might be described, with something torn and dreadful about the edges that suggested pain and strife and terror. The interior of a prison with two rows of occupied condemned cells, seen years ago in New York, sprang to memory after it—the connection between the two impossible to surmise even. But the "certain other little things" mentioned above were these: that Mrs. Franklyn, in last night's dinner talk, had always referred to "this house," but never called it "home"; and had emphasized unnecessarily, for a well-bred woman, our "great kindness" in coming down to stay so long with her. Another time, in answer to my futile compliment about the "stately rooms," she said quietly, "It is an enormous house for so small a party; but I stay here very little, and only till I get it straight again." The three of us were going up the great staircase to bed as this was said, and, not knowing quite her meaning, I dropped the subject. It edged delicate ground, I felt. Frances added no word of her own. It now occurred to me abruptly that "stay" was the word made use of, when "live" would have been more natural. How insignificant to recall! Yet why did they suggest themselves just at this moment …?

And, on going to Frances's room to make sure she was not nervous or lonely, I realized abruptly, that Mrs. Franklyn, of course, had talked with her in a confidential sense that I, as a mere visiting brother, could not share. Frances had told me nothing. I might easily have wormed it out of her, had I not felt that for us to discuss further our hostess and her house merely because we were under the roof together, was not quite nice or loyal.

"I'll call you, Bill, if I'm scared," she had laughed as we parted, my room being just across the big corridor from her own. I had fallen asleep, thinking what in the world was meant by "getting it straight again."

And now in my antechamber to the library, on the second morning, sitting among piles of foolscap and sheets of spotless blotting paper, all useless to me, these slight hints came back and helped to frame the big, vague Shadow I have mentioned. Up to the neck in this Shadow, almost drowned, yet just treading water, stood the figure of my hostess in her walking costume. Frances and I seemed swimming to her aid. The Shadow was large enough to include both house and grounds, but farther than that I could not see…. Dismissing it, I fell to reading my purloined book again. Before I turned another page, however, another startling detail leaped out at me: the figure of Mrs. Franklyn in the Shadow was not living. It floated helplessly, like a doll or puppet that has no life in it. It was both pathetic and dreadful.

Anyone who sits in reverie thus, of course, may see similar ridiculous pictures when the will no longer guides construction. The incongruities of dreams are thus explained. I merely record the picture as it came. That it remained by me for several days, just as vivid dreams do, is neither here nor there. I did not allow myself to dwell upon it. The curious thing, perhaps, is that from this moment I date my inclination, though not yet my desire, to leave. I purposely say, "to leave."

I cannot quite remember when the word changed to that aggressive, frantic thing which is escape.

V

WE WERE LEFT DELIGHTFULLY TO OURSELVES in this pretentious country mansion with the soul of a villa. Frances took up her painting again, and, the weather being propitious, spent hours out of doors, sketching flowers, trees and nooks of woodland, garden, even the house itself where bits of it peered suggestively across the orchards. Mrs. Franklyn seemed always busy about something or other, and never interfered with us except to propose motoring, tea in another part of the lawn, and so forth. She flitted everywhere, preoccupied, yet apparently doing nothing. The house engulfed her rather. No visitor called. For one thing, she was not supposed to be back from abroad yet; and for another, I think, the neighbor-hood—her husband's neighborhood—was puzzled by her sudden cessation from good works. Brigades and temperance societies did not ask to hold their meetings in the big hall, and the vicar ar-ranged the school-treats in another's field without explanation.

The full-length portrait in the dining room, and the presence of the housekeeper with the "burnt" back hair, indeed, were the only reminders of the man who once had lived here. Mrs. Marsh retained her place in silence, well-paid sinecure as it doubtless was, yet with no hint of that suppressed disapproval one might have expected from her. Indeed there was nothing positive to dis-approve, since nothing "worldly" entered grounds or building. In her master's lifetime she had been another "brand snatched from the burning," and it had then been her custom to give vociferous "testimony" at the revival meetings where he adorned the platform and led in streams of prayer. I saw her sometimes on the stairs, hovering, wandering, half-watching and half-listening, and the idea came to me once that this woman somehow formed a link with the departed influence of her bigoted employer. She, alone among us, belonged to the house, and looked at home there. When I saw her talking—oh, with such correct and respectful mien—to Mrs. Franklyn, I had the feeling that for all her unaggressive attitude, she yet exerted some influence that sought to make her mistress stay in the building forever—live there. She would prevent her es-cape, prevent "getting it straight again," thwart somehow her will to freedom, if she could. The idea in me was of the most fleeting kind.

But another time, when I came down late at night to get a book from the library antechamber, and found her sitting in the hall—alone—the impression left upon me was the reverse of fleeting. I can never forget the vivid, disagreeable effect it produced upon me. What was she doing there at half-past eleven at night, all alone in the darkness? She was sitting upright, stiff, in a big chair below the clock. It gave me a turn. It was so incongruous and odd. She rose quietly as I turned the corner of the stairs, and asked me respectfully, her eyes cast down as usual, whether I had finished with the library, so that she might lock up. There was no more to it than that; but the picture stayed with me—unpleasantly.

These various impressions came to me at odd moments, of course, and not in a single sequence as I now relate them. I was hard at work before three days were past, not writing, as explained, but reading, making notes, and gathering material from the library for future use. It was in chance moments that these curious flashes came, catching me unawares with a touch of surprise that sometimes made me start. For they proved that my under-mind was still conscious of the Shadow, and that far away out of sight lay the cause of it that left me with a vague unrest, unsettled, seeking to "nest" in a place that did not want me. Only when this deeper part knows harmony, perhaps, can good brainwork result, and my inability to write was thus explained.

Certainly, I was always seeking for something here I could not find—an explanation that continually evaded me. Nothing but these trivial hints offered themselves. Lumped together, however, they had the effect of defining the Shadow a little. I became more and more aware of its very real existence. And, if I have made little mention of Frances and my hostess in this connection, it is because they contributed at first little or nothing towards the discovery of what this story tries to tell. Our life was wholly external, normal, quiet, and uneventful; conversation banal—Mrs. Franklyn's conversation in particular. They said nothing that suggested revelation.

Both were in this Shadow, and both knew that they were in it, but neither betrayed by word nor act a hint of interpretation. They talked privately, no doubt, but of that I can report no details.

And so it was that, after ten days of a very commonplace visit, I found myself looking straight into the face of a Strangeness that defied capture at close quarters. "There's something here that never happens," were the words that rose in my mind, "and that's why none of us can speak of it."

And as I looked out of the window and watched the vulgar blackbirds, with toes turned in, boring out their worms, I realized sharply that even they, as indeed everything large and small in the house and grounds, shared this strangeness, and were twisted out of normal appearance because of it. Life, as expressed in the entire place, was crumpled, dwarfed, emasculated. God's meanings here were crippled, His love of joy was stunted. Nothing in the garden danced or sang.

There was hate in it. "The Shadow," my thought hurried on to completion, "is a manifestation of hate; and hate is the Devil." And then I sat back frightened in my chair, for I knew that I had partly found the truth.

Leaving my books I went out into the open. The sky was overcast, yet the day by no means gloomy, for a soft, diffused light oozed through the clouds and turned all things warm and almost summery. But I saw the grounds now in their nakedness because I understood. Hate means strife, and the two together weave the robe that terror wears. Having no so-called religious beliefs myself, nor belonging to any set of dogmas called a creed, I could stand outside these feelings and observe. Yet they soaked into me sufficiently for me to grasp sympathetically what others, with more cabined souls (I flattered myself), might feel. That picture in the dining room stalked everywhere, hid behind every tree, peered down upon me from the peaked ugliness of the bourgeois towers, and left the impress of its powerful hand upon every bed of flowers. "You must not do this, you must not do that," went past me through the air. "You must not leave these narrow paths," said the rigid iron railings of black. "You shall not walk here," was written on the lawns. "Keep to the steps," "Don't pick the flowers; make no noise of laughter, singing, dancing," was placarded all over the rose-garden, and "Trespassers will be—not prosecuted but—destroyed" hung from the crest of monkey tree and holly. Guarding the ends of each artificial terrace stood gaunt, implacable policemen, warders, jailers. "Come with us," they chanted, "or be damned eternally."

I remember feeling quite pleased with myself that I had discovered this obvious explanation of the prison feeling the place breathed out. That the posthumous influence of heavy old Samuel Franklyn might be an inadequate solution did not occur to me. By "getting the place straight again," his widow, of course, meant forgetting the glamour of fear and foreboding his depressing creed had temporarily forced upon her; and Frances, delicately minded being, did not speak of it because it was the influence of the man her friend had loved. I felt lighter; a load was lifted from me. "To trace the unfamiliar to the familiar," came back a sentence I had read somewhere, "is to understand." It was a real relief. I could talk with Frances now, even with my hostess, no danger of treading clumsily. For the key was in my hands. I might even help to dissipate the Shadow, "to get it straight again." It seemed, perhaps, our long invitation was explained!

I went into the house laughing—at myself a little. "Perhaps after all the artist's outlook, with no hard and fast dogmas, is as narrow as the others! How small humanity is! And why is there no possible and true combination of all outlooks?"

The feeling of "unsettling" was very strong in me just then, in spite of my big discovery which was to clear everything up. And at the moment I ran into Frances on the stairs, with a portfolio of sketches under her arm.

It came across me then abruptly that, although she had worked a great deal since we came, she had shown me nothing. It struck me suddenly as odd, unnatural. The way she tried to pass me now confirmed my newborn suspicion that—well, that her results were hardly what they ought to be.

"Stand and deliver!" I laughed, stepping in front of her. "I've seen nothing you've done since you've been here, and as a rule you show me all your things. I believe they are atrocious and degrading!" Then my laughter froze.

She made a sly gesture to slip past me, and I almost decided to let her go, for the expression that flashed across her face shocked me. She looked uncomfortable and ashamed; the color came and went a moment in her cheeks, making me think of a child detected in some secret naughtiness. It was almost fear.

"It's because they're not finished then?" I said, dropping the tone of banter, "or because they're too good for me to understand?" For my criticism of painting, she told me, was crude and ignorant sometimes. "But you'll let me see them later, won't you?"

Frances, however, did not take the way of escape I offered. She changed her mind. She drew the portfolio from beneath her arm instead. "You can see them if you really want to, Bill," she said quietly, and her tone reminded me of a nurse who says to a boy just grown out of childhood, "you are old enough now to look upon horror and ugliness—only I don't advise it."

"I do want to," I said, and made to go downstairs with her. But, instead, she said in the same low voice as before, "Come up to my room, we shall be undisturbed there." So I guessed that she had been on her way to show the paintings to our hostess, but did not care for us all three to see them together. My mind worked furiously.

"Mabel asked me to do them," she explained in a tone of submissive horror, once the door was shut, "in fact, she begged it of me. You know how persistent she is in her quiet way. I—er—had to."

She flushed and opened the portfolio on the little table by the window, standing behind me as I turned the sketches over—sketches of the grounds and trees and garden. In the first moment of inspection, however, I did not take in clearly why my sister's sense of modesty had been offended. For my attention flashed a second elsewhere. Another bit of the puzzle had dropped into place, defining still further the nature of what I called "the Shadow." Mrs. Franklyn, I now remembered, had suggested to me in the library that I might perhaps write something about the place, and I had taken it for one of her banal sentences and paid no further attention. I realized now that it was said in earnest. She wanted our interpretations, as expressed in our respective "talents," painting and writing. Her invitation was explained. She left us to ourselves on purpose.

"I should like to tear them up," Frances was whispering behind me with a shudder, "only I promised—" She hesitated a moment.

"Promised not to?" I asked with a queer feeling of distress, my eyes glued to the papers.

"Promised always to show them to her first," she finished so low I barely caught it.

I have no intuitive, immediate grasp of the value of paintings; results come to me slowly, and though everyone believes his own judgment to be good, I dare not claim that mine is worth more than that of any other layman, Frances had too often convicted me of gross ignorance and error. I can only say that I examined these sketches with a feeling of amazement that contained revulsion, if not actually horror and disgust. They were outrageous. I felt hot for my sister, and it was a relief to know she had moved across the room on some pretence or other, and did not examine them with me. Her talent, of course, is mediocre, yet she has her moments of inspiration—moments, that is to say, when a view of Beauty not normally her own flames divinely through her. And these interpretations struck me forcibly as being thus "inspired"—not her own. They were uncommonly well done; they were also atrocious. The meaning in them, however, was never more than hinted. There the unholy skill and power came in: they suggested so abominably, leaving most to the imagination. To find such significance in a bourgeois villa garden, and to interpret it with such delicate yet legible certainty, was a kind of symbolism that was sinister, even diabolical. The delicacy was her own, but the point of view was another's.

And the word that rose in my mind was not the gross description of "impure," but the more fundamental qualification—"unpure."

In silence I turned the sketches over one by one, as a boy hurries through the pages of an evil book lest he be caught.[11]

"What does Mabel do with them?" I asked presently in a low tone, as I neared the end. "Does she keep them?"

"She makes notes about them in a book and then destroys them," was the reply from the end of the room. I heard a sigh of relief. "I'm glad you've seen them, Bill. I wanted you to—but was afraid to show them. You understand?"

"I understand," was my reply, though it was not a question intended to be answered. All I understood really was that Mabel's mind was as sweet and pure as my sister's, and that she had some good reason for what she did. She destroyed the sketches, but first made notes! It was an interpretation of the place she sought. Brother-like, I felt resentment, though, that Frances should waste her time and talent, when she might be doing work that she could sell. Naturally, I felt other things as well....

"Mabel pays me five guineas for each one," I heard. "Absolutely insists."

I stared at her stupidly a moment, bereft of speech or wit. "I must either accept, or go away," she went on calmly, but a little white.

"I've tried everything. There was a scene the third day I was here—when I showed her my first result. I wanted to write to you, but hesitated—"

"It's unintentional, then, on your part—forgive my asking it, Frances, dear?" I blundered, hardly knowing what to think or say. "Between the lines" of her letter came back to me. "I mean, you make the sketches in your ordinary way and—the result comes out of itself, so to speak?"

She nodded, throwing her hands out like a Frenchman. "We needn't keep the money for ourselves, Bill. We can give it away,

---

11 'Evil book' sounds like the hyperbolic description of something Blackwood might have been caught reading (by his Christian parents) as a child.

but—I must either accept or leave," and she repeated the shrugging gesture. She sat down on the chair facing me, staring helplessly at the carpet.

"You say there was a scene?" I went on presently, "She insisted?"

"She begged me to continue," my sister replied very quietly. "She thinks—that is, she has an idea or theory that there's something about the place—something she can't get at quite." Frances stammered badly. She knew I did not encourage her wild theories.

"Something she feels—yes," I helped her, more than curious.

"Oh, you know what I mean, Bill," she said desperately. "That the place is saturated with some influence that she is herself too positive or too stupid to interpret. She's trying to make herself negative and receptive, as she calls it, but can't, of course, succeed. Haven't you noticed how dull and impersonal and insipid she seems, as though she had no personality? She thinks impressions will come to her that way. But they don't—"

"Naturally."

"So she's trying me—us—what she calls the sensitive and impressionable artistic temperament. She says that until she is sure exactly what this influence is, she can't fight it, turn it out, 'get the house straight', as she phrases it."

Remembering my own singular impressions, I felt more lenient than I might otherwise have done. I tried to keep impatience out of my voice.

"And this influence, what—whose is it?"

We used the pronoun that followed in the same breath, for I answered my own question at the same moment as she did:

"His." Our heads nodded involuntarily towards the floor, the dining room being directly underneath.

And my heart sank, my curiosity died away on the instant; I felt bored. A commonplace haunted house was the last thing in the world to amuse or interest me. The mere thought exasperated, with its suggestions of imagination, overwrought nerves, hysteria, and the rest.

Mingled with my other feelings was certainly disappointment. To see a figure or feel a "presence," and report from day to day strange incidents to each other would be a form of weariness I could never tolerate.

"But really, Frances," I said firmly, after a moment's pause, "it's too far-fetched, this explanation. A curse, you know, belongs to the ghost stories of early Victorian days." And only my positive conviction that there was something after all worth discovering, and that it most certainly was not this, prevented my suggesting that we terminate our visit forthwith, or as soon as we decently could. "This is not a haunted house, whatever it is," I concluded somewhat vehemently, bringing my hand down upon her odious portfolio.

My sister's reply revived my curiosity sharply.

"I was waiting for you to say that. Mabel says exactly the same. He is in it—but it's something more than that alone, something far bigger and more complicated." Her sentence seemed to indicate the sketches, and though I caught the inference I did not take it up, having no desire to discuss them with her just them indeed, if ever.

I merely stared at her and listened. Questions, I felt sure, would be of little use. It was better she should say her thought in her own way.

"He is one influence, the most recent," she went on slowly, and always very calmly, "but there are others—deeper layers, as it were—underneath. If his were the only one, something would happen. But nothing ever does happen. The others hinder and prevent—as though each were struggling to predominate."

I had felt it already myself. The idea was rather horrible. I shivered.

"That's what is so ugly about it—that nothing ever happens," she said. "There is this endless anticipation—always on the dry edge of a result that never materializes. It is torture. Mabel is at her wits' end, you see. And when she begged me—what I felt about my sketches—I mean—"

She stammered badly as before.

I stopped her. I had judged too hastily. That queer symbolism in her paintings, pagan and yet not innocent, was, I understood, the result of mixture. I did not pretend to understand, but at least I could be patient. I consequently held my peace. We did talk on a little longer, but it was more general talk that avoided successfully our hostess, the paintings, wild theories, and him—until at length the emotion Frances had hitherto so successfully kept under burst vehemently forth again.

It had hidden between her calm sentences, as it had hidden between the lines of her letter. It swept her now from head to foot, packed tight in the thing she then said.

"Then, Bill, if it is not an ordinary haunted house," she asked, "what is it?"

The words were commonplace enough. The emotion was in the tone of her voice that trembled; in the gesture she made, leaning forward and clasping both hands upon her knees, and in the slight blanching of her cheeks as her brave eyes asked the question and searched my own with anxiety that bordered upon panic. In that moment she put herself under my protection. I winced.

"And why," she added, lowering her voice to a still and furtive whisper, "does nothing ever happen? If only,"—this with great emphasis—"something would happen—break this awful tension— bring relief. It's the waiting I cannot stand." And she shivered all over as she said it, a touch of wildness in her eyes.

I would have given much to have made a true and satisfactory answer. My mind searched frantically for a moment, but in vain. There lay no sufficient answer in me. I felt what she felt, though with differences. No conclusive explanation lay within reach. Nothing happened. Eager as I was to shoot the entire business into the rubbish heap where ignorance and superstition discharge their poisonous weeds, I could not honestly accomplish this. To treat Frances as a child, and merely "explain away" would be to strain her confidence in my protection, so affectionately claimed. It would further be dishonest to myself—weak, besides—to deny that I had also felt the strain and tension even as she did. While my mind continued searching, I returned her stare in silence; and Frances then, with more honesty and insight than my own, gave suddenly the answer herself—an answer whose truth and adequacy, so far as they went, I could not readily gainsay:

"I think, Bill, because it is too big to happen here—to happen anywhere, indeed, all at once—and too awful!"

To have tossed the sentence aside as nonsense, argued it away, proved that it was really meaningless, would have been easy—at any other time or in any other place; and, had the past week brought me none of the vivid impressions it had brought me, this is doubtless what I should have done. My narrowness again was proved. We understand in others only what we have in ourselves. But her explanation, in a measure, I knew was true. It hinted at the strife and struggle that my notion of a Shadow had seemed to cover thinly.

"Perhaps," I murmured lamely, waiting in vain for her to say more. "But you said just now that you felt the thing was 'in layers', as it were. Do you mean each one—each influence—fighting for the upper hand?"

I used her phraseology to conceal my own poverty. Terminology, after all, was nothing, provided we could reach the idea itself.

Her eyes said yes. She had her clear conception, arrived at independently, as was her way.

And, unlike her sex, she kept it clear, unsmothered by too many words.

"One set of influences gets at me; another gets at you. It's according to our temperaments, I think." She glanced significantly at the vile portfolio. "Sometimes they are mixed—and therefore false. There has always been in me, more than in you, the pagan thing, perhaps, though never, thank God, like that."

The frank confession of course invited my own, as it was meant to do.

Yet it was difficult to find the words.

"What I have felt in this place, Frances, I honestly can hardly tell you, because—er—my impressions have not arranged themselves in any definite form I can describe. The strife, the agony of vainly-sought escape, and the unrest—a sort of prison atmosphere—this I have felt at different times and with varying degrees of strength. But I find, as yet, no final label to attach. I couldn't say pagan, Christian, or anything like that, I mean, as you do. As with the blind and deaf, you may have an intensification of certain senses denied to me, or even another sense altogether in embryo..."

"Perhaps," she stopped me, anxious to keep to the point, "you feel it as

Mabel does. She feels the whole thing complete."

"That also is possible," I said very slowly. I was thinking behind my words. Her odd remark that it was "big and awful" came back upon me as true. A vast sensation of distress and discomfort swept me suddenly. Pity was in it, and a fierce contempt, a savage, bitter anger as well. Fury against some sham authority was part of it.

"Frances," I said, caught unawares, and dropping all pretence, "what in the world can it be?" I looked hard at her. For some minutes neither of us spoke.

"Have you felt no desire to interpret it?" she asked presently, "Mabel did suggest my writing something about the house," was my reply, "but I've felt nothing imperative. That sort of writing is not my line, you know. My only feeling," I added, noticing that she waited for more, "is the impulse to explain, discover, get it out of me somehow, and so get rid of it. Not by writing, though—as yet." And again I repeated my former question:

"What in the world do you think it is?" My voice had become involuntarily hushed. There was awe in it. Her answer, given with slow emphasis, brought back all my reserve: the phraseology provoked me rather:—"Whatever it is, Bill, it is not of God."

I got up to go downstairs. I believe I shrugged my shoulders. "Would you like to leave, Frances? Shall we go back to town?" I suggested this at the door, and hearing no immediate reply, I turned back to look. Frances was sitting with her head bowed over and buried in her hands. The attitude horribly suggested tears. No woman, I realized, can keep back the pressure of strong emotion as long as Frances had done, without ending in a fluid collapse. I waited a moment uneasily, longing to comfort, yet afraid to act— and in this way discovered the existence of the appalling emotion in myself, hitherto but half guessed.

At all costs, a scene must be prevented: it would involve such exaggeration and overstatement. Brutally, such is the weakness of the ordinary man, I turned the handle to go out, but my sister then raised her head. The sunlight caught her face, framed untidily in its auburn hair, and I saw her wonderful expression with a start. Pity, tenderness, and sympathy shone in it like a flame. It was undeniable. There shone through all her features the imperishable love and yearning to sacrifice self for others which I have seen in only one type of human being. It was the great mother look.

"We must stay by Mabel and help her get it straight," she whispered, making the decision for us both.

I murmured agreement. Abashed and half ashamed, I stole softly from the room and went out into the grounds. And the first thing clearly realized when alone was this: that the long scene between us was without definite result. The exchange of confidence was really nothing but hints and vague suggestion. We had decided to stay, but it was a negative decision not to leave rather than a positive action. All our words and questions, our guesses, inferences, explanations, our most subtle allusions and insinuations, even the odious paintings themselves, were without definite result. Nothing had happened.

VI

AND INSTINCTIVELY, ONCE ALONE, I made for the places where she had painted her extraordinary pictures; I tried to see what she had seen. Perhaps, now that she had opened my mind to another view, I should be sensitive to some similar interpretation—and possibly by way of literary expression. If I were to write about the place, I asked myself, how should I treat it? I deliberately invited an interpretation in the way that came easiest to me—writing.

But in this case there came no such revelation. Looking closely at the trees and flowers, the bits of lawn and terrace, the rose garden and corner of the house where the flaming creeper hung so thickly, I discovered nothing of the odious, unpure thing her color and grouping had unconsciously revealed.

At first, that is, I discovered nothing. The reality stood there, commonplace and ugly, side by side with her distorted version of it that lay in my mind. It seemed incredible. I tried to force it, but in vain. My imagination ploughed less deeply than hers, or to another pattern, grew different seed. Where I saw the gross soul of an overgrown suburban garden, inspired by the spirit of a vulgar, rich revivalist who loved to preach damnation, she saw this rush of pagan liberty and joy, this strange license of primitive flesh which, tainted by the other, produced the adulterated, vile result.

Certain things, however, gradually then became apparent, forcing themselves upon me, willy-nilly. They came slowly, but overwhelmingly. Not that facts had changed, or natural details altered in the grounds—this was impossible—but that I noticed for the first time various aspects I had not noticed before—trivial enough, yet for me, just then, significant. Some I remembered from previous days; others I saw now as I wandered to and fro, uneasy, uncomfortable, almost, it seemed, watched by someone who took note of my impressions. The details were so foolish, the total result so formidable. I was half aware that others tried hard to make me see. It was deliberate.

My sister's phrase, "one layer got at me, another gets at you," flashed, undesired, upon me.

For I saw, as with the eyes of a child, what I can only call a goblin garden—house, grounds, trees, and flowers belonged to a goblin world that children enter through the pages of their fairy tales. And what made me first aware of it was the whisper of the wind behind me, so that I turned with a sudden start, feeling that something had moved closer. An old ash tree, ugly and ungainly, had been artificially trained to form an arbor at one end of the terrace that was a tennis lawn, and the leaves of it now went rustling together, swishing as they rose and fell. I looked at the ash tree, and felt as though I had passed that moment between doors into this goblin garden that crouched behind the real one. Below, at a deeper layer perhaps, lay hidden the one my sister had entered.

To deal with my own, however, I call it goblin, because an odd aspect of the quaint in it yet never quite achieved the picturesque. Grotesque, probably, is the truer word, for everywhere I noticed, and for the first time, this slight alteration of the natural due either to the exaggeration of some detail, or to its suppression, generally, I think, to the latter. Life everywhere appeared to me as blocked from the full delivery of its sweet and lovely message. Some counter influence stopped it—suppression; or sent it awry—exaggeration. The house itself, mere expression, of course, of a narrow, limited mind, was sheer ugliness; it required no further explanation. With the grounds and garden, so far as shape and general plan were concerned, this was also true; but that trees and flowers and other natural details should share the same deficiency perplexed my logical soul, and even dismayed it. I stood and stared, then moved about, and stood and stared again. Everywhere was this mockery of a sinister, unfinished aspect. I sought in vain to recover my normal point of view. My mind had found this goblin garden and wandered to and fro in it, unable to escape.

The change was in myself, of course, and so trivial were the details which illustrated it, that they sound absurd, thus mentioned one by one. For me, they proved it, is all I can affirm. The goblin touch lay plainly everywhere: in the forms of the trees, planted at neat intervals along the lawns; in this twisted ash that rustled just behind me; in the shadow of the gloomy wellingtonias, whose sweeping skirts obscured the grass; but especially, I noticed, in the tops and crests of them. For here, the delicate, graceful curves of last year's growth seemed to shrink back into themselves. None of them pointed upwards. Their life had failed and turned aside just when it should have become triumphant. The character of a tree reveals itself chiefly at the extremities, and it was precisely here that they all drooped and achieved this hint of goblin distortion—in the growth, that is, of the last few years. What ought to have been fairy, joyful, natural, was instead uncomely to the verge of the grotesque. Spontaneous expression was arrested. My mind perceived a goblin garden, and was caught in it. The place grimaced at me.

With the flowers it was similar, though far more difficult to detect in detail for description. I saw the smaller vegetable growth as impish, half-malicious. Even the terraces sloped ill, as though their ends had sagged since they had been so lavishly constructed; their varying angles gave a queerly bewildering aspect to their sequence that was unpleasant to the eye. One might wander among their deceptive lengths and get lost—lost among open terraces!— with the house quite close at hand. Unhomely seemed the entire garden, unable to give repose, restlessness in it everywhere, almost strife, and discord certainly.

Moreover, the garden grew into the house, the house into the garden, and in both was this idea of resistance to the natural—the spirit that says No to joy. All over it I was aware of the effort to achieve another end, the struggle to burst forth and escape into free, spontaneous expression that should be happy and natural, yet the effort forever frustrated by the weight of this dark shadow that rendered it abortive. Life crawled aside into a channel that was a cul-de-sac, then turned horribly upon itself. Instead of blossom and fruit, there were weeds. This approach of life I was conscious of—then dismal failure. There was no fulfillment. Nothing happened.

And so, through this singular mood, I came a little nearer to understand the unpure thing that had stammered out into expression through my sister's talent. For the unpure is merely negative; it has no existence; it is but the cramped expression of what is true, stammering its way brokenly over false boundaries that seek to limit and confine. Great, full expression of anything is pure, whereas here was only the incomplete, unfinished, and therefore ugly. There was a strife and pain and desire to escape. I found myself shrinking from house and grounds as one shrinks from the touch of the mentally arrested, those in whom life has turned awry. There was almost mutilation in it.

Past items, too, now flocked to confirm this feeling that I walked, liberty captured and half-maimed, in a monstrous garden. I remembered days of rain that refreshed the countryside, but left these grounds, cracked with the summer heat, unsatisfied and thirsty; and how the big winds, that cleaned the woods and fields elsewhere, crawled here with difficulty through the dense foliage that protected The Towers from the North and West and East. They were ineffective, sluggish currents. There was no real wind.

Nothing happened. I began to realize—far more clearly than in my sister's fanciful explanation about "layers"—that here were many contrary influences at work, mutually destructive of one another. House and grounds were not haunted merely; they were the arena of past thinking and feeling, perhaps of terrible, impure beliefs, each striving to suppress the others, yet no one of them achieving supremacy because no one of them was strong enough, no one of them was true. Each, moreover, tried to win me over, though only one was able to reach my mind at all. For some obscure reason—possibly because my temperament had a natural bias towards the grotesque—it was the goblin layer. With me, it was the line of least resistance....

In my own thoughts this "goblin garden" revealed, of course, merely my personal interpretation. I felt now objectively what long ago my mind had felt subjectively. My work, essential sign of spontaneous life with me, had stopped dead; production had become impossible.

I stood now considerably closer to the cause of this sterility. The Cause, rather, turned bolder, had stepped insolently nearer. Nothing happened anywhere; house, garden, mind alike were barren, abortive, torn by the strife of frustrate impulse, ugly, hateful, sinful. Yet behind it all was still the desire of life—desire to escape—accomplish. Hope—an intolerable hope—I became startlingly aware—crowned torture.

And, realizing this, though in some part of me where Reason lost her hold, there rose upon me then another and a darker thing that caught me by the throat and made me shrink with a sense of revulsion that touched actual loathing. I knew instantly whence it came, this wave of abhorrence and disgust, for even while I saw red and felt revolt rise in me, it seemed that I grew partially aware of the layer next below the goblin. I perceived the existence of this deeper stratum. One opened the way for the other, as it were. There were so many, yet all interrelated; to admit one was to clear the way for all. If I lingered I should be caught—horribly. They struggled with such violence for supremacy among themselves, however, that this latest uprising was instantly smothered and crushed back, though not before a glimpse had been revealed to me, and the redness in my thoughts transferred itself to color my surroundings thickly and appallingly—with blood. This lurid aspect drenched the garden, smeared the terraces, lent to the very soil a tinge as of sacrificial rites, that choked the breath in me, while it seemed to fix me to the earth my feet so longed to leave. It was so revolting that at the same time I felt a dreadful curiosity as of fascination—I wished to stay. Between these contrary impulses I think I actually reeled a moment, transfixed by a fascination of the Awful. Through the lighter goblin veil I felt myself sinking down, down, down into this turgid layer that was so much more violent and so much more ancient. The upper layer, indeed, seemed fairy by comparison with this terror born of the lust for blood, thick with the anguish of human sacrificial victims.

Upper! Then I was already sinking; my feet were caught; I was actually in it! What atavistic strain, hidden deep within me, had been touched into vile response, giving this flash of intuitive comprehension, I cannot say. The coatings laid on by civilization are probably thin enough in all of us. I made a supreme effort. The sun and wind came back. I could almost swear I opened my eyes. Something very atrocious surged back into the depths, carrying with it a thought of tangled woods, of big stones standing in a circle, motionless, white figures, the one form bound with ropes, and the ghastly gleam of the knife. Like smoke upon a battlefield, it rolled away....

I was standing on the gravel path below the second terrace when the familiar goblin garden danced back again, doubly grotesque now, doubly mocking, yet, by way of contrast, almost welcome. My glimpse into the depths was momentary, it seems, and had passed utterly away.

The common world rushed back with a sense of glad relief, yet ominous now forever, I felt, for the knowledge of what its past had built upon. In street, in theater, in the festivities of friends, in music room or playing field, even indeed in church—how could the memory of what I had seen and felt leave its hideous trace? The very structure of my Thought, it seemed to me, was stained.

What has been thought by others can never be obliterated until....

With a start my reverie broke and fled, scattered by a violent sound that I recognized for the first time in my life as wholly desirable. The returning motor meant that my hostess was back.

Yet, so urgent had been my temporary obsession, that my first presentation of her was—well, not as I knew her now. Floating along with a face of anguished torture I saw Mabel, a mere effigy captured by others' thinking, pass down into those depths of fire and blood that only just had closed beneath my feet. She dipped away. She vanished; her fading eyes turned to the last towards some savior who had failed her. And that strange intolerable hope was in her face.

The mystery of the place was pretty thick about me just then. It was the fall of dusk, and the ghost of slanting sunshine was as unreal as though badly painted. The garden stood at attention all about me. I cannot explain it, but I can tell it, I think, exactly as it happened, for it remains vivid in me forever—that, for the first time, something almost happened, myself apparently the combining link through which it pressed towards delivery:

I had already turned towards the house. In my mind were pictures—not actual thoughts—of the motor, tea on the verandah, my sister, Mabel— when there came behind me this tumultuous, awful rush—as I left the garden. The ugliness, the pain, the striving to escape, the whole negative and suppressed agony that was the Place, focused that second into a concentrated effort to produce a result. It was a blinding tempest of long-frustrate desire that heaved at me, surging appallingly behind me like an anguished mob. I was in the act of crossing the frontier into my normal self again, when it came, catching fearfully at my skirts. I might use an entire dictionary of descriptive adjectives yet come no nearer to it than this—the conception of a huge assemblage determined to escape with me, or to snatch me back among themselves. My legs trembled for an instant, and I caught my breath—then turned and ran as fast as possible up the ugly terraces.

At the same instant, as though the clanging of an iron gate cut short the unfinished phrase, I thought the beginning of an awful thing:

"The Damned ..."

Like this it rushed after me from that goblin garden that had sought to keep me:

"The Damned!"

For there was sound in it. I know full well it was subjective, not actually heard at all; yet somehow sound was in it—a great volume, roaring and booming thunderously, far away, and below me. The sentence dipped back into the depths that gave it birth, unfinished. Its completion was prevented. As usual, nothing happened. But it drove behind me like a hurricane as I ran towards the house, and the sound of it I can only liken to those terrible undertones you may hear standing beside Niagara. They lie behind the mere crash of the falling flood, within it somehow, not audible to all—felt rather than definitely heard.

It seemed to echo back from the surface of those sagging terraces as I flew across their sloping ends, for it was somehow underneath them. It was in the rustle of the wind that stirred the skirts of the drooping wellingtonias. The beds of formal flowers passed it on to the creepers, red as blood, that crept over the unsightly building. Into the structure of the vulgar and forbidding house it sank away; The Towers took it home. The uncomely doors and windows seemed almost like mouths that had uttered the words themselves, and on the upper floors at that very moment I saw two maids in the act of closing them again.

And on the verandah, as I arrived breathless, and shaken in my soul, Frances and Mabel, standing by the tea table, looked up to greet me. In the faces of both were clearly legible the signs of shock. They watched me coming, yet so full of their own distress that they hardly noticed the state in which I came. In the face of my hostess, however, I read another and a bigger thing than in the face of Frances. Mabel knew. She had experienced what I had experienced. She had heard that awful sentence I had heard but heard it not for the first time; heard it, moreover, I verily believe, complete and to its dreadful end.

"Bill, did you hear that curious noise just now?" Frances asked it sharply before I could say a word. Her manner was confused; she looked straight at me; and there was a tremor in her voice she could not hide.

"There's wind about," I said, "wind in the trees and sweeping round the walls. It's risen rather suddenly." My voice faltered rather.

"No. It wasn't wind," she insisted, with a significance meant for me alone, but badly hidden. "It was more like distant thunder, we thought. How you ran too!" she added. "What a pace you came across the terraces!"

I knew instantly from the way she said it that they both had already heard the sound before and were anxious to know if I had heard it, and how. My interpretation was what they sought.

"It was a curiously deep sound, I admit. It may have been big guns at sea," I suggested, "forts or cruisers practicing. The coast isn't so very far, and with the wind in the right direction—"

The expression on Mabel's face stopped me dead.

"Like huge doors closing," she said softly in her colorless voice, "enormous metal doors shutting against a mass of people clamoring to get out." The gravity, the note of hopelessness in her tones, was shocking.

Frances had gone into the house the instant Mabel began to speak. "I'm cold," she had said; "I think I'll get a shawl." Mabel and I were alone. I believe it was the first time we had been really alone since I arrived. She looked up from the teacups, fixing her pallid eyes on mine. She had made a question of the sentence.

"You hear it like that?" I asked innocently. I purposely used the present tense.

She changed her stare from one eye to the other; it was absolutely expressionless. My sister's step sounded on the floor of the room behind us.

"If only—" Mabel began, then stopped, and my own feelings leaping out instinctively completed the sentence I felt was in her mind:

"—something would happen."

She instantly corrected me. I had caught her thought, yet somehow phrased it wrongly.

"We could escape!" She lowered her tone a little, saying it hurriedly. The "we" amazed and horrified me; but something in her voice and manner struck me utterly dumb. There was ice and terror in it. It was a dying woman speaking; a lost and hopeless soul.

In that atrocious moment I hardly noticed what was said exactly, but I remember that my sister returned with a grey shawl about her shoulders, and that Mabel said, in her ordinary voice again, "It is chilly, yes; let's have tea inside," and that two maids, one of them the grenadier, speedily carried the loaded trays into the morning-room and put a match to the logs in the great open fireplace. It was, after all, foolish to risk the sharp evening air, for dusk was falling steadily, and even the sunshine of the day just fading could not turn autumn into summer. I was the last to come in. Just as I left the verandah a large black bird swooped down in front of me past the pillars; it dropped from overhead, swerved abruptly to one side as it caught sight of me, and flapped heavily towards the shrubberies on the left of the terraces, where it disappeared into the gloom. It flew very low, very close. And it startled me, I think because in some way it seemed like my Shadow materialized—as though the dark horror that was rising everywhere from house and garden, then settling back so thickly yet so imperceptibly upon us all, were incarnated in that whirring creature that passed between the daylight and the coming night.

I stood a moment, wondering if it would appear again, before I followed the others indoors, and as I was in the act of closing the windows after me, I caught a glimpse of a figure on the lawn. It was some distance away, on the other side of the shrubberies, in fact where the bird had vanished. But in spite of the twilight that half magnified, half obscured it, the identity was unmistakable. I knew the housekeeper's stiff walk too well to be deceived. "Mrs. Marsh taking the air," I said to myself. I felt the necessity of saying it, and I wondered why she was doing so at this particular hour. If I had other thoughts they were so vague, and so quickly and utterly suppressed, that I cannot recall them sufficiently to relate them here.

And, once indoors, it was to be expected that there would come explanation, discussion, conversation, at any rate, regarding the singular noise and its cause, some uttered evidence of the mood that had been strong enough to drive us all inside. Yet there was none. Each of us purposely, and with various skill, ignored it. We talked little, and when we did it was of anything in the world but that. Personally, I experienced a touch of that same bewilderment which had come over me during my first talk with Frances on the evening of my arrival, for I recall now the acute tension, and the hope, yet dread, that one or other of us must sooner or later introduce the subject. It did not happen, however; no reference was made to it even remotely. It was the presence of Mabel, I felt positive, that prohibited. As soon might we have discussed Death in the bedroom of a dying woman.

The only scrap of conversation I remember, where all was ordinary and commonplace, was when Mabel spoke casually to the grenadier asking why Mrs. Marsh had omitted to do something or other—what it was I forget—and that the maid replied respectfully that "Mrs. Marsh was very sorry, but her 'and still pained her." I enquired, though so casually that I scarcely know what prompted the words, whether she had injured herself severely, and the reply, "She upset a lamp and burnt herself," was said in a tone that made me feel my curiosity was indiscreet, "but she always has an excuse for not doing things she ought to do." The little bit of conversation remained with me, and I remember particularly the quick way Frances interrupted and turned the talk upon the delinquencies of servants in general, telling incidents of her own at our flat with a volubility that perhaps seemed forced, and that certainly did not encourage general talk as it may have been intended to do. We lapsed into silence immediately she finished.

But for all our care and all our calculated silence, each knew that something had, in these last moments, come very close; it had brushed us in passing; it had retired; and I am inclined to think now that the large dark thing I saw, riding the dusk, probably bird of prey, was in some sense a symbol of it in my mind—that actually there had been no bird at all, I mean, but that my mood of apprehension and dismay had formed the vivid picture in my thoughts. It had swept past us, it had retreated, but it was now, at this moment, in hiding very close. And it was watching us.

Perhaps, too, it was mere coincidence that I encountered Mrs. Marsh, his housekeeper, several times that evening in the short interval between tea and dinner, and that on each occasion the sight of this gaunt, half-saturnine woman fed my prejudice against her. Once, on my way to the telephone, I ran into her just where the passage is somewhat jammed by a square table carrying the Chinese gong, a grandfather's clock and a box of croquet mallets. We both gave way, then both advanced, then again gave way—simultaneously. It seemed, impossible to pass. We stepped with decision to the same side, finally colliding in the middle, while saying those futile little things, half apology, half excuse, that are inevitable at such times. In the end she stood upright against the wall for me to pass, taking her place against the very door I wished to open. It was ludicrous.

"Excuse me—I was just going in—to telephone," I explained. And she sidled off, murmuring apologies, but opening the door for me while she did so. Our hands met a moment on the handle.

There was a second's awkwardness—it was too stupid. I remembered her injury, and by way of something to say, I enquired after it. She thanked me; it was entirely healed now, but it might have been much worse; and there was something about the "mercy of the Lord" that I didn't quite catch. While telephoning, however—London call, and my attention focused on it—realized sharply that this was the first time I had spoken with her; also, that I had—touched her.

It happened to be a Sunday, and the lines were clear. I got my connection quickly, and the incident was forgotten while my thoughts went up to London. On my way upstairs, then, the woman came back into my mind, so that I recalled other things about her—how she seemed all over the house, in unlikely places often; how I had caught her sitting in the hall alone that night; how she was forever coming and going with her lugubrious visage and that untidy hair at the back that had made me laugh three years ago with the idea that it looked singed or burnt; and how the impression on my first arrival at The Towers was that this woman somehow kept alive, though its evidence was outwardly suppressed, the influence of her late employer and of his somber teachings. Somewhere with her was associated the idea of punishment, vindictiveness, revenge. I remembered again suddenly my odd notion that she sought to keep her present mistress here, a prisoner in this bleak and comfortless house, and that really, in spite of her obsequious silence, she was intensely opposed to the change of thought that had reclaimed Mabel to a happier view of life.

All this in a passing second flashed in review before me, and I discovered, or at any rate reconstructed, the real Mrs. Marsh. She was decidedly in the Shadow. More, she stood in the forefront of it, stealthily leading an assault, as it were, against The Towers and its occupants, as though, consciously or unconsciously, she labored incessantly to this hateful end.

I can only judge that some state of nervousness in me permitted the series of insignificant thoughts to assume this dramatic shape, and that what had gone before prepared the way and led her up at the head of so formidable a procession. I relate it exactly as it came to me. My nerves were doubtless somewhat on edge by now. Otherwise I should hardly have been a prey to the exaggeration at all. I seemed open to so many strange, impressions.

Nothing else, perhaps, can explain my ridiculous conversation with her, when, for the third time that evening, I came suddenly upon the woman halfway down the stairs, standing by an open window as if in the act of listening. She was dressed in black, a black shawl over her square shoulders and black gloves on her big, broad hands. Two black objects, prayer books apparently, she clasped, and on her head she wore a bonnet with shaking beads of jet. At first I did not know her, as I came running down upon her from the landing; it was only when she stood aside to let me pass that I saw her profile against the tapestry and recognized Mrs. Marsh. And to catch her on the front stairs, dressed like this, struck me as incongruous—impertinent. I paused in my dangerous descent. Through the opened window came the sound of bells—church bells—a sound more depressing to me than superstition, and as nauseating. Though the action was ill judged, I obeyed the sudden prompting—was it a secret desire to attack, perhaps?—and spoke to her.

"Been to church, I suppose, Mrs. Marsh?" I said. "Or just going, perhaps?"

Her face, as she looked up a second to reply, was like an iron doll that moved its lips and turned its eyes, but made no other imitation of life at all.

"Some of us still goes, sir," she said unctuously.

It was respectful enough, yet the implied judgment of the rest of the world made me almost angry. A deferential insolence lay behind the affected meekness.

"For those who believe no doubt it is helpful," I smiled. "True religion brings peace and happiness, I'm sure—joy, Mrs. Marsh, joy!" I found keen satisfaction in the emphasis.

She looked at me like a knife. I cannot describe the implacable thing that shone in her fixed, stern eyes, nor the shadow of felt darkness that stole across her face. She glittered. I felt hate in her. I knew— she knew too—who was in the thoughts of us both at that moment.

She replied softly, never forgetting her place for an instant:

"There is joy, sir—in 'eaven—over one sinner that repenteth, and in church there goes up prayer to Gawd for those 'oo—well, for the others, sir, 'oo—"

She cut short her sentence thus. The gloom about her as she said it was like the gloom about a hearse, a tomb, a darkness of great hopeless dungeons. My tongue ran on of itself with a kind of bitter satisfaction:

"We must believe there are no others, Mrs. Marsh. Salvation, you know, would be such a failure if there were. No merciful, all-foreseeing God could ever have devised such a fearful plan—"

Her voice, interrupting me, seemed to rise out of the bowels of the earth:

"They rejected the salvation when it was offered to them, sir, on earth."

"But you wouldn't have them tortured forever because of one mistake in ignorance," I said, fixing her with my eye. "Come now, would you, Mrs. Marsh? No God worth worshipping could permit such cruelty. Think a moment what it means."

She stared at me, a curious expression in her stupid eyes. It seemed to me as though the "woman" in her revolted, while yet she dared not suffer her grim belief to trip. That is, she would willingly have had it otherwise but for a terror that prevented.

"We may pray for them, sir, and we do—we may 'ope." She dropped her eyes to the carpet.

"Good, good!" I put in cheerfully, sorry now that I had spoken at all.

"That's more hopeful, at any rate isn't it?"

She murmured something about Abraham's bosom,[12] and the "time of salvation not being forever,"[13] as I tried to pass her. Then a half gesture that she made stopped me. There was something more she wished to say—to ask. She looked up furtively. In her eyes I saw the "woman" peering out through fear.

"Per'aps, sir." she faltered, as though lightning must strike her dead, "per'aps, would you think, a drop of cold water, given in His name, might moisten—?"

But I stopped her, for the foolish talk had lasted long enough. "Of course," I exclaimed, "of course. For God is love, remember, and love means charity, tolerance, sympathy, and sparing others pain," and I hurried past her, determined to end the outrageous conversation for which yet I knew myself entirely to blame. Behind me, she stood stock-still for several minutes, half bewildered, half alarmed, as I suspected. I caught the fragment of another sentence, one word of it, rather—"punishment"—but the rest escaped me. Her arrogance and condescending tolerance exasperated me, while I was at the same time secretly pleased that I might have touched some string of remorse or sympathy in her after all. Her belief was iron; she dared not let it go; yet somewhere underneath there lurked the germ of a wholesome revulsion. She would help "them"—if she dared. Her question proved it.

Half ashamed of myself, I turned and crossed the hall quickly lest I should be tempted to say more, and in me was a disagreeable sensation as though I had just left the Incurable Ward of some great hospital. A reaction caught me as of nausea. Ugh! I wanted such people cleansed by fire. They seemed to me as centers of contamination whose vicious thoughts flowed out to stain God's glorious world. I saw myself, Frances, Mabel too especially, on the rack, while that odious figure of cruelty and darkness stood over us and ordered the awful handles turned in order that we might be "saved"—forced, that is, to think and believe exactly as she thought and believed.

I found relief for my somewhat childish indignation by letting myself loose upon the organ then. The flood of Bach and Beethoven brought back the sense of proportion. It proved, however, at the same time that there had been this growth of distortion in me, and

---

[12] A biblical neverland where the dead await judgment day.

[13] Referring to "The time of salvation is now," a paraphrase of, "In the time of my favor I heard you, and in the day of salvation I helped you. I tell you, now is the time of God's favor, now."

that it had been provided apparently by my closer contact—for the first time—with that funereal personality, the woman who, like her master, believed that all holding views of God that differed from her own, must be damned eternally. It gave me, moreover, some faint clue perhaps, though a clue I was unequal of following up, to the nature of the strife and terror and frustrate influence in the house. That housekeeper had to do with it. She kept it alive. Her thought was like a spell she waved above her mistress's head.

VII

THAT NIGHT I WAS WAKENED by a hurried tapping at my door, and before I could answer, Frances stood beside my bed. She had switched on the light as she came in. Her hair fell straggling over her dressing gown. Her face was deathly pale, its expression so distraught it was almost haggard.

The eyes were very wide. She looked almost like another woman.

She was whispering at a great pace: "Bill, Bill, wake up, quick!"

"I am awake. What is it?" I whispered too. I was startled.

"Listen!" was all she said. Her eyes stared into vacancy.

There was not a sound in the great house. The wind had dropped, and all was still. Only the tapping seemed to continue endlessly in my brain. The clock on the mantelpiece pointed to half-past two.

"I heard nothing, Frances. What is it?" I rubbed my eyes; I had been very deeply asleep.

"Listen!" she repeated very softly, holding up one finger and turning her eyes towards the door she had left ajar. Her usual calmness had deserted her. She was in the grip of some distressing terror.

For a full minute we held our breath and listened. Then her eyes rolled round again and met my own, and her skin went even whiter than before.

"It woke me," she said beneath her breath, and moving a step nearer to my bed. "It was the Noise." Even her whisper trembled.

"The Noise!" The word repeated itself dully of its own accord. I would rather it had been anything in the world but that—earthquake, foreign cannon, collapse of the house above our heads! "The Noise, Frances! Are you sure?" I was playing really for a little time.

"It was like thunder. At first I thought it was thunder. But a minute later it came again—from underground. It's appalling." She muttered the words, her voice not properly under control.

There was a pause of perhaps a minute, and then we both spoke at once. We said foolish, obvious things that neither of us believed in for a second. The roof had fallen in, there were burglars downstairs, the safes had been blown open. It was to comfort each other as children do that we said these things; also it was to gain further time.

"There's someone in the house, of course," I heard my voice say finally, as I sprang out of bed and hurried into dressing gown and slippers. "Don't be alarmed. I'll go down and see," and from the drawer I took a pistol it was my habit to carry everywhere with me. I loaded it carefully while Frances stood stock-still beside the bed and watched. I moved towards the open door.

"You stay here, Frances," I whispered, the beating of my heart making the words uneven, "while I go down and make a search. Lock yourself in, girl. Nothing can happen to you. It was downstairs, you said?"

"Underneath," she answered faintly, pointing through the floor.

She moved suddenly between me and the door.

"Listen! Hark!" she said, the eyes in her face quite fixed; "it's coming again," and she turned her head to catch the slightest sound. I stood there watching her, and while I watched her, shook.

But nothing stirred. From the halls below rose only the whirr and quiet ticking of the numerous clocks. The blind by the open window behind us flapped out a little into the room as the draught caught it.

"I'll come with you, Bill—to the next floor," she broke the silence. "Then I'll stay with Mabel—till you come up again." The blind sank down with a long sigh as she said it.

The question jumped to my lips before I could repress it:

"Mabel is awake. She heard it too?"

I hardly know why horror caught me at her answer. All was so vague and terrible as we stood there playing the great game of this sinister house where nothing ever happened.

"We met in the passage. She was on her way to me."

What shook in me, shook inwardly. Frances, I mean, did not see it. I had the feeling just that the Noise was upon us, that any second it would boom and roar about our ears. But the deep silence held. I only heard my sister's little whisper coming across the room in answer to my question:

"Then what is Mabel doing now?"

And her reply proved that she was yielding at last beneath the dreadful tension, for she spoke at once, unable longer to keep up the pretence. With a kind of relief, as it were, she said it out, looking helplessly at me like a child:

"She is weeping and gna—"

My expression must have stopped her. I believe I clapped both hands upon her mouth, though when I realized things clearly again, I found they were covering my own ears instead. It was a moment of unutterable horror. The revulsion I felt was actually physical. It would have given me pleasure to fire off all the five chambers of my pistol into the air above my head; the sound—a definite, wholesome sound that explained itself—would have been a positive relief. Other feelings, though, were in me too, all over me, rushing to and fro. It was vain to seek their disentanglement; it was impossible. I confess that I experienced, among them, a touch of paralyzing fear—though for a moment only; it passed as sharply as it came, leaving me with a violent flush of blood to the face such as bursts of anger bring, followed abruptly by an icy perspiration over the entire body. Yet I may honestly avow that it was not ordinary personal fear I felt, nor any common dread of physical injury. It was, rather, a vast, impersonal shrinking—a sympathetic shrinking—from the agony and terror that countless others, somewhere, somehow, felt for themselves. The first sensation of a prison overwhelmed me in that instant, of bitter strife and frenzied suffering, and the fiery torture of the yearning to escape that was yet hopelessly uttered.... It was of incredible power. It was real. The vain, intolerable hope swept over me.

I mastered myself, though hardly knowing how, and took my sister's hand. It was as cold as ice, as I led her firmly to the door and out into the passage. Apparently she noticed nothing of my so near collapse, for I caught her whisper as we went. "You are brave, Bill; splendidly brave."

The upper corridors of the great sleeping house were brightly lit; on her way to me she had turned on every electric switch her hand could reach; and as we passed the final flight of stairs to the floor below, I heard a door shut softly and knew that Mabel had been listening—waiting for us. I led my sister up to it. She knocked, and the door was opened cautiously an inch or so. The room was pitch black. I caught no glimpse of Mabel standing there. Frances turned to me with a hurried whisper, "Billy, you will be careful, won't you?" and went in. I just had time to answer that I would not be long, and Frances to reply, "You'll find us here" when the door closed and cut her sentence short before its end.

But it was not alone the closing door that took the final words. Frances—by the way she disappeared I knew it—had made a swift and violent movement into the darkness that was as though she sprang. She leaped upon that other woman who stood back among the shadows, for, simultaneously with the clipping of the sentence, another sound was also stopped—stifled, smothered, choked back lest I should also hear it. Yet not in time. I heard it—a hard and horrible sound that explained both the leap and the abrupt cessation of the whispered words.

I stood irresolute a moment. It was as though all the bones had been withdrawn from my body, so that I must sink and fall. That sound plucked them out, and plucked out my self-possession with them. I am not sure that it was a sound I had ever heard before, though children, I half remembered, made it sometimes in blind rages when they knew not what they did. In a grown-up person certainly I had never known it. I associated it with animals rather—horribly. In the history of the world, no doubt, it has been common enough, alas, but fortunately today there can be but few who know it, or would recognize it even when heard. The bones shot back into my body the same instant, but red-hot and burning; the brief instant of irresolution passed; I was torn between the desire to break down the door and enter, and to run—run for my life from a thing I dared not face.

Out of the horrid tumult, then, I adopted neither course. Without reflection, certainly without analysis of what was best to do for my sister, myself or Mabel, I took up my action where it had been interrupted. I turned from the awful door and moved slowly towards the head of the stairs.

But that dreadful little sound came with me. I believe my own teeth chattered. It seemed all over the house—in the empty halls that opened into the long passages towards the music-room, and even in the grounds outside the building. From the lawns and barren garden, from the ugly terraces themselves, it rose into the night, and behind it came a curious driving sound, incomplete, unfinished, as of wailing for deliverance, the wailing of desperate souls in anguish, the dull and dry beseeching of hopeless spirits in prison.

That I could have taken the little sound from the bedroom where I actually heard it, and spread it thus over the entire house and grounds, is evidence, perhaps, of the state my nerves were in.

The wailing assuredly was in my mind alone. But the longer I hesitated, the more difficult became my task, and, gathering up my dressing gown, lest I should trip in the darkness, I passed slowly down the staircase into the hail below. I carried neither candle nor matches; every switch in room and corridor was known to me. The covering of darkness was indeed rather comforting than otherwise, for if it prevented seeing, it also prevented being seen. The heavy pistol, knocking against my thigh as I moved, made me feel I was carrying a child's toy, foolishly. I experienced in every nerve that primitive vast dread which is the Thrill of darkness. Merely the child in me was comforted by that pistol.

The night was not entirely black; the iron bars across the glass front door were visible, and, equally, I discerned the big, stiff wooden chairs in the hall, the gaping fireplace, the upright pillars supporting the staircase, the round table in the center with its books and flower-vases, and the basket that held visitors' cards. There, too, was the stick and umbrella stand and the shelf with railway guides, directory, and telegraph forms. Clocks ticked everywhere with sounds like quiet footfalls. Light fell here and there in patches from the floor above. I stood a moment in the hall, letting my eyes grow more accustomed to the gloom, while deciding on a plan of search. I made out the ivy trailing outside over one of the big windows ... and then the tall clock by the front door made a grating noise deep down inside its body—it was the Presentation clock, large and hideous, given by the congregation of his church— and, dreading the booming strike it seemed to threaten, I made a quick decision. If others beside myself were about in the night, the sound of that striking might cover their approach.

So I tiptoed to the right, where the passage led towards the dining room. In the other direction were the morning- and drawing rooms, both little used, and various other rooms beyond that had been his, generally now kept locked. I thought of my sister, waiting upstairs with that frightened woman for my return. I went quickly, yet stealthily.

And, to my surprise, the door of the dining room was open. It had been opened. I paused on the threshold, staring about me. I think I fully expected to see a figure blocked in the shadows against the heavy sideboard, or looming on the other side beneath his portrait. But the room was empty; I felt it empty. Through the wide bow-windows that gave on to the verandah came an uncertain glimmer that even shone reflected in the polished surface of the dinner table, and again I perceived the stiff outline of chairs, waiting tenantless all round it, two larger ones with high carved backs at either end. The monkey trees on the upper terrace, too, were visible outside against the sky, and the solemn crests of the wellingtonias[14] on the terraces below. The enormous clock on the mantelpiece ticked very slowly, as though its machinery were running down, and I made out the pale round patch that was its face.

[14] Wellingtonia is an old-fashioned English name for the giant sequoia tree (*Sequoiadendron giganteum*).

Resisting my first inclination to turn the lights up—my hand had gone so far as to finger the friendly knob—I crossed the room so carefully that no single board creaked, nor a single chair, as I rested a hand upon its back, moved on the parquet flooring. I turned neither to the right nor left, nor did I once look back.

I went towards the long corridor filled with priceless objets d'art, that led through various antechambers into the spacious music-room, and only at the mouth of this corridor did I next halt a moment in uncertainty. For this long corridor, lit faintly by high windows on the left from the verandah, was very narrow, owing to the mass of shelves and fancy tables it contained. It was not that I feared to knock over precious things as I went, but, that, because of its ungenerous width, there would be no room to pass another person—if I met one. And the certainty had suddenly come upon me that somewhere in this corridor another person at this actual moment stood. Here, somehow, amid all this dead atmosphere of furniture and impersonal emptiness, lay the hint of a living human presence; and with such conviction did it come upon me, that my hand instinctively gripped the pistol in my pocket before I could even think. Either someone had passed along this corridor just before me, or someone lay waiting at its farther end—withdrawn or flattened into one of the little recesses, to let me pass. It was the person who had opened the door. And the blood ran from my heart as I realized it.

It was not courage that sent me on, but rather a strong impulsion from behind that made it impossible to retreat: the feeling that a throng pressed at my back, drawing nearer and nearer; that I was already half surrounded, swept, dragged, coaxed into a vast prison-house where there was wailing and gnashing of teeth, where their worm dieth not and their fire is not quenched. I can neither explain nor justify the storm of irrational emotion that swept me as I stood in that moment, staring down the length of the silent corridor towards the music-room at the far end, I can only repeat that no personal bravery sent me down it, but that the negative emotion of fear was swamped in this vast sea of pity and commiseration for others that surged upon me.

My senses, at least, were no whit confused; if anything, my brain registered impressions with keener accuracy than usual. I noticed, for instance, that the two swinging doors of baize that cut the corridor into definite lengths, making little rooms of the spaces between them, were both wide-open—in the dim light no mean achievement. Also that the fronds of a palm plant, some ten feet in front of me, still stirred gently from the air of someone who had recently gone past them. The long green leaves waved to and fro like hands. Then I went stealthily forward down the narrow space, proud even that I had this command of myself, and so carefully that my feet made no sound upon the Japanese matting on the floor.

It was a journey that seemed timeless. I have no idea how fast or slow I went, but I remember that I deliberately examined articles on each side of me, peering with particular closeness into the recesses of wall and window. I passed the first baize doors, and the passage beyond them widened out to hold shelves of books; there were sofas and small reading-tables against the wall.

It narrowed again presently, as I entered the second stretch. The windows here were higher and smaller, and marble statuettes of classical subject lined the walls, watching me like figures of the dead. Their white and shining faces saw me, yet made no sign. I passed next between the second baize doors. They, too, had been fastened back with hooks against the wall. Thus all doors were open—had been recently opened.

And so, at length, I found myself in the final widening of the corridor which formed an antechamber to the music-room itself. It had been used formerly to hold the overflow of meetings. No door separated it from the great hall beyond, but heavy curtains hung usually to close it off, and these curtains were invariably drawn. They now stood wide. And here—I can merely state the impression that came upon me—I knew myself at last surrounded. The throng that pressed behind me, also surged in front: facing me in the big room, and waiting for my entry, stood a multitude; on either side of me, in the very air above my head, the vast assemblage paused upon my coming. The pause, however, was momentary, for instantly the deep, tumultuous movement was resumed that yet was silent as a cavern underground. I felt the agony that was in it, the passionate striving, the awful struggle to escape. The semi-darkness held beseeching faces that fought to press themselves upon my vision, yearning yet hopeless eyes, lips scorched and dry, mouths that opened to implore but found no craved delivery in actual words, and a fury of misery and hate that made the life in me stop dead, frozen by the horror of vain pity. That intolerable, vain Hope was everywhere.

And the multitude, it came to me, was not a single multitude, but many; for, as soon as one huge division pressed too close upon the edge of escape, it was dragged back by another and prevented.

The wild host was divided against itself. Here dwelt the Shadow I had "imagined" weeks ago, and in it struggled armies of lost souls as in the depths of some bottomless pit whence there is no escape. The layers mingled, fighting against themselves in endless torture. It was in this great Shadow I had clairvoyantly seen Mabel, but about its fearful mouth, I now was certain, hovered another figure of darkness, a figure who sought to keep it in existence, since to her thought were due those lampless depths of woe without escape.... Towards me the multitudes now surged.

It was a sound and a movement that brought me back into myself. The great dock at the farther end of the room just then struck the hour of three. That was the sound. And the movement— ? I was aware that a figure was passing across the distant center of the floor. Instantly I dropped back into the arena of my little human terror. My hand again clutched stupidly at the pistol butt. I drew back into the folds of the heavy curtain. And the figure advanced.

I remember every detail. At first it seemed to me enormous— this advancing shadow—far beyond human scale; but as it came nearer, I measured it, though not consciously, by the organ pipes that gleamed in faint colors, just above its gradual soft approach. It passed them, already halfway across the great room. I saw then that its stature was that of ordinary men. The prolonged booming of the clock died away. I heard the footfall, shuffling upon the polished boards. I heard another sound—a voice, low and monotonous, droning as in prayer. The figure was speaking. It was a woman. And she carried in both hands before her a small object that faintly shimmered—a glass of water. And then I recognized her.

There was still an instant's time before she reached me, and I made use of it. I shrank back, flattening myself against the wall. Her voice ceased a moment, as she turned and carefully drew the curtains together behind her, dosing them with one hand. Oblivious of my presence, though she actually touched my dressing gown with the hand that pulled the cords, she resumed her dreadful, solemn march, disappearing at length down the long vista of the corridor like a shadow.

But as she passed me, her voice began again, so that I heard each word distinctly as she uttered it, her head aloft, her figure upright, as though she moved at the head of a procession:

"A drop of cold water, given in His name, shall moisten their burning tongues."

It was repeated monotonously over and over again, droning down into the distance as she went, until at length both voice and figure faded into the shadows at the farther end.

For a time, I have no means of measuring precisely, I stood in that dark corner, pressing my back against the wall, and would have drawn the curtains down to hide me had I dared to stretch an arm out. The dread that presently the woman would return passed gradually away. I realized that the air had emptied, the crowd her presence had stirred into activity had retreated; I was alone in the gloomy under-space of the odious building.... Then I remembered suddenly again the terrified women waiting for me on that upper landing; and realized that my skin was wet and freezing cold after a profuse perspiration. I prepared to retrace my steps. I remember the effort it cost me to leave the support of the wall and covering darkness of my corner, and step out into the grey light of the corridor. At first I sidled, then, finding this mode of walking impossible, turned my face boldly and walked quickly, regardless that my dressing gown set the precious objects shaking as I passed. A wind that sighed mournfully against the high, small windows seemed to have got inside the corridor as well; it felt so cold; and every moment I dreaded to see the outline of the woman's figure as she waited in recess or angle against the wall for me to pass.

Was there another thing I dreaded even more? I cannot say. I only know that the first baize doors had swung to behind me, and the second ones were close at hand, when the great dim thunder caught me, pouring up with prodigious volume so that it, seemed to roll out from another world. It shook the very bowels of the building. I was closer to it than that other time, when it had followed me from the goblin garden. There was strength and hardness in it, as of metal reverberation. Some touch of numbness, almost of paralysis, must surely have been upon me that I felt no actual terror, for I remember even turning and standing still to hear it better. "That is the Noise," my thought ran stupidly, and I think I whispered it aloud; "the Doors are closing." The wind outside against the windows was audible, so it cannot have been really loud, yet to me it was the biggest, deepest sound I have ever heard, but so far away, with such awful remoteness in it, that I had to doubt my own ears at the same time. It seemed underground—the rumbling of earthquake gates that shut remorselessly within the rocky Earth—stupendous ultimate thunder. They were shut off from help again. The doors had closed.

I felt a storm of pity, an agony of bitter, futile hate sweep through me. My memory of the figure changed then. The Woman with the glass of cooling water had stepped down from Heaven; but the Man—or was it Men?—who smeared this terrible layer of belief and Thought upon the world!...

I crossed the dining room—it was fancy, of course, that held my eyes from glancing at the portrait for fear I should see it smiling approval—and so finally reached the hall, where the light from the floor above seemed now quite bright in comparison. All the doors I closed carefully behind me; but first I had to open them. The woman had closed every one. Up the stairs, then, I actually ran, two steps at a time. My sister was standing outside Mabel's door. By her face I knew that she had also heard. There was no need to ask. I quickly made my mind up.

"There's nothing," I said, and detailed briefly my tour of search. "All is quiet and undisturbed downstairs." May God forgive me!

She beckoned to me, closing the door softly behind her. My heart beat violently a moment, then stood still.

"Mabel," she said aloud.

It was like the sentence of a judge, that one short word.

I tried to push past her and go in, but she stopped me with her arm. She was wholly mistress of herself, I saw.

"Hush!" she said in a lower voice. "I've got her round again with brandy. She's sleeping quietly now. We won't disturb her."

She drew me farther out into the landing, and as she did so, the clock in the hall below struck half-past three. I had stood, then, thirty minutes in the corridor below. "You've been such a long time." she said simply. "I feared for you," and she took my hand in her own that was cold and clammy.

VIII

AND THEN, WHILE THAT DREADFUL HOUSE stood listening about us in the early hours of this chill morning upon the edge of winter, she told me, with laconic brevity, things about Mabel that I heard as from a distance. There was nothing so unusual or tremendous in the short recital, nothing indeed I might not have already guessed for myself. It was the time and scene, the inference, too, that made it so afflicting: the idea that Mabel believed herself so utterly and hopelessly lost—beyond recovery damned.

That she had loved him with so passionate a devotion that she had given her soul into his keeping, this certainly I had not divined—probably because I had never thought about it one way or the other. He had "converted" her, I knew, but that she had subscribed wholeheartedly to that most cruel and ugly of his dogmas— this was new to me, and came with a certain shock as I heard it. In love, of course, the weaker nature is receptive to all manner of suggestion. This man had "suggested" his pet brimstone lake so vividly that she had listened and believed. He had frightened her into heaven; and his heaven, a definite locality in the skies, had its foretaste here on earth in miniature—The Towers, house, and garden. Into his dolorous scheme of a handful saved and millions damned, his enclosure, as it were, of sheep and goats, he had swept her before she was aware of it. Her mind no longer was her own. And it was Mrs. Marsh who kept the thought-stream open, though tempered, as she deemed, with that touch of craven, superstitious mercy.

But what I found it difficult to understand, and still more difficult to accept, was that, during her year abroad, she had been so haunted with a secret dread of that hideous after-death that she had finally revolted and tried to recover that clearer state of mind she had enjoyed before the religious bully had stunned her—yet had tried in vain. She had returned to The Towers to find her soul again, only to realize that it was lost eternally. The cleaner state of mind lay then beyond recovery. In the reaction that followed the removal of his terrible "suggestion," she felt the crumbling of all that he had taught her, but searched in vain for the peace and beauty his teachings had destroyed. Nothing came to replace these. She was empty, desolate, hopeless; craving her former joy and carelessness, she found only hate and diabolical calculation. This man, whom she had loved to the point of losing her soul for him, had bequeathed to her one black and fiery thing—the terror of the damned. His thinking wrapped her in this iron garment that held her fast.

All this Frances told me, far more briefly than I have here repeated it. In her eyes and gestures and laconic sentences lay the conviction of great beating issues and of menacing drama my own description fails to recapture. It was all so incongruous and remote from the world I lived in that more than once a smile, though a smile of pity, fluttered to my lips; but a glimpse of my face in the mirror showed rather the leer of a grimace. There was no real laughter anywhere that night.

The entire adventure seemed so incredible, here, in this twentieth century—but yet delusion, that feeble word, did not occur once in the comments my mind suggested though did not utter. I remembered that forbidding Shadow too; my sister's watercolors; the vanished personality of our hostess; the inexplicable, thundering Noise, and the figure of Mrs. Marsh in her midnight ritual that was so childish yet so horrible. I shivered in spite of my own "emancipated" cast of mind.

"There is no Mabel," were the words with which my sister sent another shower of ice down my spine. "He has killed her in his lake of fire and brimstone."

I stared at her blankly, as in a nightmare where nothing true or possible ever happened.

"He killed her in his lake of fire and brimstone," she repeated more faintly.

A desperate effort was in me to say the strong, sensible thing which should destroy the oppressive horror that grew so stiflingly about us both, but again the mirror drew the attempted smile into the merest grin, betraying the distortion that was everywhere in the place.

"You mean," I stammered beneath my breath, "that her faith has gone, but that the terror has remained?" I asked it, dully groping. I moved out of the line of the reflection in the glass.

She bowed her head as though beneath a weight; her skin was the pallor of grey ashes.

"You mean," I said louder, "that she has lost her—mind?"

"She is terror incarnate," was the whispered answer. "Mabel has lost her soul. Her soul is—there!" She pointed horribly below. "She is seeking it …?"

The word "soul" stung me into something of my normal self again.

"But her terror, poor thing, is not—cannot be—transferable to us!" I exclaimed more vehemently. "It certainly is not convertible into feelings, sights and—even sounds!"

She interrupted me quickly, almost impatiently, speaking with that conviction by which she conquered me so easily that night.

"It is her terror that revived 'the Others.' It has brought her into touch with them. They are loose and driving after her. Her efforts at resistance have given them also hope—that escape, after all, is possible. Day and night they strive.

"Escape! Others!" The anger fast rising in me dropped of its own accord at the moment of birth. It shrank into a shuddering beyond my control. In that moment, I think, I would have believed in the possibility of anything and everything she might tell me. To argue or contradict seemed equally futile.

"His strong belief, as also the beliefs of others who have pre-ceded him," she replied, so sure of herself that I actually turned to look over my shoulder, "have left their shadow like a thick deposit over the house and grounds. To them, poor souls imprisoned by thought, it was hopeless as granite walls—until her resistance, her effort to dissipate it—let in light. Now, in their thousands, they are flocking to this little light, seeking escape. Her own escape, don't you see, may release them all!"

It took my breath away. Had his predecessors, former occu-pants of this house, also preached damnation of all the world but their own exclusive sect? Was this the explanation of her obscure talk of "layers," each striving against the other for domination? And if men are spirits, and these spirits survive, could strong Thought thus determine their condition even afterwards?

So many questions flooded into me that I selected no one of them, but stared in uncomfortable silence, bewildered, out of my depth, and acutely, painfully distressed. There was so odd a mix-ture of possible truth and incredible, unacceptable explanation in it all; so much confirmed, yet so much left darker than before. What she said did, indeed, offer a quasi-interpretation of my own series of abominable sensations—strife, agony, pity, hate, escape—but so far-fetched that only the deep conviction in her voice and attitude made it tolerable for a second even. I found myself in a curious state of mind. I could neither think clearly nor say a word to refute her amazing statements, whispered there beside me in the shivering hours of the early morning with only a wall between ourselves and—Mabel. Close behind her words I remember this singular thing, however—that an atmosphere as of the Inquisition seemed to rise and stir about the room, beating awful wings of black above my head.

Abruptly, then, a moment's common sense returned to me. I faced her.

"And the Noise?" I said aloud, more firmly, "the roar of the closing doors? We have all heard that! Is that subjective too?"

Frances looked sideways about her in a queer fashion that made my flesh creep again. I spoke brusquely, almost angrily. I repeated the question, and waited with anxiety for her reply.

"What noise?" she asked, with the frank expression of an innocent child.

"What closing doors?"

But her face turned from grey to white, and I saw that drops of perspiration glistened on her forehead. She caught at the back of a chair to steady herself, then glanced about her again with that sidelong look that made my blood run cold. I understood suddenly then. She did not take in what I said. I knew now. She was listening—for something else.

And the discovery revived in me a far stronger emotion than any mere desire for immediate explanation. Not only did I not insist upon an answer, but I was actually terrified lest she would answer. More, I felt in me a terror lest I should be moved to describe my own experiences below-stairs, thus increasing their reality and so the reality of all. She might even explain them too!

Still listening intently, she raised her head and looked me in the eyes. Her lips opened to speak. The words came to me from a great distance, it seemed, and her voice had a sound like a stone that drops into a deep well, its fate though hidden, known.

"We are in it with her, too, Bill. We are in it with her. Our interpretations vary—because we are—in parts of it only. Mabel is in it—all."

The desire for violence came over me. If only she would say a definite thing in plain King's English! If only I could find it in me to give utterance to what shouted so loud within me! If only—the same old cry— something would happen! For all this elliptic talk that dazed my mind left obscurity everywhere. Her atrocious meaning, nonetheless, flashed through me, though vanishing before it wholly divulged itself.

It brought a certain reaction with it. I found my tongue. Whether I actually believed what I said is more than I can swear to; that it seemed to me wise at the moment is all I remember. My mind was in a state of obscure perception less than that of normal consciousness.

"Yes, Frances, I believe that what you say is the truth, and that we are in it with her"—I meant to say I with loud, hostile emphasis, but instead I whispered it lest she should hear the trembling of my voice—"and for that reason, my dear sister, we leave tomorrow, you and I—today, rather, since it is long past midnight—we leave this house of the damned. We go back to London."

Frances looked up; her face distraught almost beyond recognition. But it was not my words that caused the tumult in her heart. It was a sound— the sound she had been listening for—so faint I barely caught it myself, and had she not pointed I could never have known the direction whence it came. Small and terrible it rose again in the stillness of the night, the sound of gnashing teeth. And behind it came another—the tread of stealthy footsteps. Both were just outside the door.

The room swung round me for a second. My first instinct to prevent my sister going out—she had dashed past me frantically to the door—gave place to another when I saw the expression in her eyes. I followed her lead instead; it was surer than my own. The pistol in my pocket swung uselessly against my thigh. I was flustered beyond belief and ashamed that I was so.

"Keep close to me, Frances," I said huskily, as the door swung wide and a shaft of light fell upon a figure moving rapidly. Mabel was going down the corridor. Beyond her, in the shadows on the staircase, a second figure stood beckoning, scarcely visible.

"Before they get her! Quick!" was screamed into my ears, and our arms were about her in the same moment. It was a horrible scene. Not that Mabel struggled in the least, but that she collapsed as we caught her and fell with her dead weight, as of a corpse, limp, against us. And her teeth began again. They continued, even beneath the hand that Frances clapped upon her lips....

We carried her back into her own bedroom, where she lay down peacefully enough. It was so soon over.... The rapidity of the whole thing robbed it of reality almost. It had the swiftness of something remembered rather than of something witnessed. She slept again so quickly that it was almost as if we had caught her sleepwalking. I cannot say. I asked no questions at the time; I have asked none since; and my help was needed as little as the protection of my pistol. Frances was strangely competent and collected.... I lingered for some time uselessly by the door, till at length, looking up with a sigh, she made a sign for me to go.

"I shall wait in your room next door," I whispered, "till you come." But, though going out, I waited in the corridor instead, so as to hear the faintest call for help. In that dark corridor upstairs I waited, but not long. It may have been fifteen minutes when Frances reappeared, locking the door softly behind her. Leaning over the banisters, I saw her.

"I'll go in again about six o'clock," she whispered, "as soon as it gets light. She is sound asleep now. Please don't wait. If anything happens I'll call—you might leave your door ajar, perhaps."

And she came up, looking like a ghost.

But I saw her first safely into bed, and the rest of the night I spent in an armchair close to my opened door, listening for the slightest sound. Soon after five o'clock I heard Frances fumbling with the key, and, peering over the railing again, I waited till she reappeared and went back into her own room. She closed her door. Evidently she was satisfied that all was well.

Then, and then only, did I go to bed myself, but not to sleep. I could not get the scene out of my mind, especially that odious detail of it which I hoped and believed my sister had not seen—the still, dark figure of the housekeeper waiting on the stairs below— waiting, of course, for Mabel.

IX

IT SEEMS I BECAME A MERE spectator after that; my sister's lead was so assured for one thing, and, for another, the responsibility of leaving Mabel alone—Frances laid it bodily upon my shoulders—was a little more than I cared about. Moreover, when we all three met later in the day, things went on so exactly as before, so absolutely without friction or distress, that to present a sudden, obvious excuse for cutting our visit short seemed ill-judged. And on the lowest grounds it would have been desertion. At any rate, it was beyond my powers, and Frances was quite firm that she must stay. We therefore did stay. Things that happen in the night always seem exaggerated and distorted when the sun shines brightly next morning; no one can reconstruct the terror of a nightmare afterwards, nor comprehend why it seemed so overwhelming at the time.

I slept till ten o'clock, and when I rang for breakfast, a note from my sister lay upon the tray, its message of counsel couched in a calm and comforting strain. Mabel, she assured me, was herself again and remembered nothing of what had happened; there was no need of any violent measures; I was to treat her exactly as if I knew nothing. "And, if you don't mind, Bill, let us leave the matter unmentioned between ourselves as well. Discussion exaggerates; such things are best not talked about. I'm sorry I disturbed you so unnecessarily; I was stupidly excited. Please forget all the things I said at the moment." She had written "nonsense" first instead of "things," then scratched it out. She wished to convey that hysteria had been abroad in the night, and I readily gulped the explanation down, though it could not satisfy me in the smallest degree.

There was another week of our visit still, and we stayed it out to the end without disaster. My desire to leave at times became that frantic thing, desire to escape; but I controlled it, kept silent, watched and wondered. Nothing happened. As before, and everywhere, there was no sequence of development, no connection between cause and effect; and climax, none whatever. The thing swayed up and down, backwards and forwards like a great loose curtain in the wind, and I could only vaguely surmise what caused the draught or why there was a curtain at all. A novelist might mold the queer material into coherent sequence that would be interesting but could not be true.

It remains, therefore, not a story but a history. Nothing happened.

Perhaps my intense dislike of the fall of darkness was due wholly to my stirred imagination, and perhaps my anger when I learned that Frances now occupied a bed in our hostess's room was unreasonable. Nerves were unquestionably on edge. I was forever on the lookout for some event that should make escape imperative, but yet that never presented itself. I slept lightly, left my door ajar to catch the slightest sound, even made stealthy tours of the house below-stairs while everybody dreamed in their beds. But I discovered nothing; the doors were always locked; I neither saw the housekeeper again in unreasonable times and places, nor heard a footstep in the passages and halls. The Noise was never once repeated. That horrible, ultimate thunder, my intensest dread of all, lay withdrawn into the abyss whence it had twice arisen. And though in my thoughts it was sternly denied existence, the great black reason for the fact afflicted me unbelievably. Since Mabel's fruitless effort to escape, the Doors kept closed remorselessly. She had failed; they gave up hope. For this was the explanation that haunted the region of my mind where feelings stir and hint before they clothe themselves in actual language. Only I firmly kept it there; it never knew expression.

But, if my ears were open, my eyes were opened too, and it were idle to pretend that I did not notice a hundred details that were capable of sinister interpretation had I been weak enough to yield. Some protective barrier had fallen into ruins round me, so that Terror stalked behind the general collapse, feeling for me through all the gaping fissures. Much of this, I admit, must have been merely the elaboration of those sensations I had first vaguely felt, before subsequent events and my talks with Frances had dramatized them into living thoughts. I therefore leave them unmentioned in this history, just as my mind left them unmentioned in that interminable final week. Our life went on precisely as before—Mabel unreal and outwardly so still; Frances, secretive, anxious, tactful to the point of slyness, and keen to save to the point of self-forgetfulness.

There were the same stupid meals, the same wearisome long evenings, the stifling ugliness of house and grounds, the Shadow settling in so thickly that it seemed almost a visible, tangible thing. I came to feel the only friendly things in all this hostile, cruel place were the robins that hopped boldly over the monstrous terraces and even up to the windows of the unsightly house itself. The robins alone knew joy; they danced, believing no evil thing was possible in all God's radiant world. They believed in everybody; their god's plan of life had no room in it for hell, damnation, and lakes of brimstone. I came to love the little birds. Had Samuel Franklyn known them, he might have preached a different sermon, bequeathing love in place of terror!

Most of my time I spent writing; but it was a pretence at best, and rather a dangerous one besides. For it stirred the mind to production, with the result that other things came pouring in as well. With reading it was the same. In the end I found an aggressive, deliberate resistance to be the only way of feasible defense. To walk far afield was out of the question, for it meant leaving my sister too long alone, so that my exercise was confined to nearer home. My saunters in the grounds, however, never surprised the goblin garden again. It was close at hand, but I seemed unable to get wholly into it. Too many things assailed my mind for anyone to hold exclusive possession, perhaps.

Indeed, all the interpretations, all the "layers," to use my sister's phrase, slipped in by turns and lodged there for a time. They came day and night, and though my reason denied them entrance they held their own as by a kind of squatter's right. They stirred moods already in me, that is, and did not introduce entirely new ones; for every mind conceals ancestral deposits that have been cultivated in turn along the whole line of its descent. Any day a chance shower may cause this one or that to blossom. Thus it came to me, at any rate. After darkness the Inquisition paced the empty corridors and set up ghastly apparatus in the dismal halls; and once, in the library, there swept over me that easy and delicious conviction that by confessing my wickedness I could resume it later, since Confession is expression, and expression brings relief and leaves one ready to accumulate again. And in such mood I felt bitter and unforgiving towards all others who thought differently. Another time it was a Pagan thing that assaulted me—so trivial yet oh, so significant at the time—when I dreamed that a herd of centaurs rolled up with a great stamping of hoofs round the house to destroy it, and then woke to hear the horses tramping across the field below the lawns; they neighed ominously and their noisy panting was audible as if it were just outside my windows.

But the tree episode, I think, was the most curious of all— except, perhaps, the incident with the children which I shall mention in a moment—for its closeness to reality was so unforgettable.

Outside the east window of my room stood a giant wellingtonia on the lawn, its head rising level with the upper sash. It grew some twenty feet away, planted on the highest terrace, and I often saw it when closing my curtains for the night, noticing how it drew its heavy skirts about it, and how the light from other windows threw glimmering streaks and patches that turned it into the semblance of a towering, solemn image. It stood there then so strikingly, somehow like a great old-world idol, that it claimed attention. Its appearance was curiously formidable. Its branches rustled without visibly moving and it had a certain portentous, forbidding air, so grand and dark and monstrous in the night that I was always glad when my curtains shut it out. Yet, once in bed, I had never thought about it one way or the other, and by day had certainly never sought it out.

One night, then, as I went to bed and closed this window against a cutting easterly wind, I saw—that there were two of these trees. A brother wellingtonia rose mysteriously beside it, equally huge, equally towering, equally monstrous. The menacing pair of them faced me there upon the lawn. But in this new arrival lay a strange suggestion that frightened me before I could argue it away. Exact counterpart of its giant companion, it revealed also that gross, odious quality that all my sister's paintings held. I got the odd impression that the rest of these trees, stretching away dimly in a troop over the farther lawns, were similar, and that, led by this enormous pair, they had all moved boldly closer to my windows. At the same moment a blind was drawn down over an upper room; the second tree disappeared into the surrounding darkness.

It was, of course, this chance light that had brought it into the field of vision, but when the black shutter dropped over it, hiding it from view, the manner of its vanishing produced the queer effect that it had slipped into its companion—almost that it had been an emanation of the one I so disliked, and not really a tree at all! In this way the garden turned vehicle for expressing what lay behind it all …!

The behavior of the doors, the little, ordinary doors, seems scarcely worth mention at all, their queer way of opening and shutting of their own accord; for this was accountable in a hundred natural ways, and to tell the truth, I never caught one in the act of moving. Indeed, only after frequent repetitions did the detail force itself upon me, when, having noticed one, I noticed all. It produced, however, the unpleasant impression of a continual coming and going in the house, as though, screened cleverly and purposely from actual sight, someone in the building held constant invisible intercourse with—others.

Upon detailed descriptions of these uncertain incidents I do not venture, individually so trivial, but taken all together so impressive and so insolent. But the episode of the children, mentioned above, was different. And I give it because it showed how vividly the intuitive child-mind received the impression—one impression, at any rate—of what was in the air. It may be told in a very few words. I believe they were the coachman's children, and that the man had been in Mr. Franklyn's service; but of neither point am I quite positive.

I heard screaming in the rose-garden that runs along the stable walls— it was one afternoon not far from the tea-hour—and on hurrying up I found a little girl of nine or ten fastened with ropes to a rustic seat, and two other children—boys, one about twelve and one much younger— gathering sticks beneath the climbing rose trees. The girl was white and frightened, but the others were laughing and talking among themselves so busily while they picked that they did not notice my abrupt arrival. Some game, I understood, was in progress, but a game that had become too serious for the happiness of the prisoner, for there was a fear in the girl's eyes that was a very genuine fear indeed. I unfastened her at once; the ropes were so loosely and clumsily knotted that they had not hurt her skin; it was not that which made her pale. She collapsed a moment upon the bench, then picked up her tiny skirts and dived away at full speed into the safety of the stable yard.

There was no response to my brief comforting, but she ran as though for her life, and I divined that some horrid boys' cruelty had been afoot. It was probably mere thoughtlessness, as cruelty with children usually is, but something in me decided to discover exactly what it was.

And the boys, not one whit alarmed at my intervention, merely laughed shyly when I explained that their prisoner had escaped, and told me frankly what their "gime" had been. There was no vestige of shame in them, nor any idea, of course, that they aped a monstrous reality.

That it was mere pretence was neither here nor there. To them, though make-believe, it was a make-believe of something that was right and natural and in no sense cruel. Grown-ups did it too. It was necessary for her good.

"We was going to burn her up, sir," the older one informed me, answering my "Why?" with the explanation, "Because she wouldn't believe what we wanted 'er to believe."

And, game though it was, the feeling of reality about the little episode was so arresting, so terrific in some way, that only with difficulty did I confine my admonitions on this occasion to mere words. The boys slunk off, frightened in their turn, yet not, I felt, convinced that they had erred in principle. It was their inheritance. They had breathed it in with the atmosphere of their bringing-up. They would renew the salutary torture when they could—till she "believed" as they did.

I went back into the house, afflicted with a passion of mingled pity and distress impossible to describe, yet on my short way across the garden was attacked by other moods in turn, each more real and bitter than its predecessor. I received the whole series, as it were, at once. I felt like a diver rising to the surface through layers of water at different temperatures, though here the natural order was reversed, and the cooler strata were uppermost, the heated ones below. Thus, I was caught by the goblin touch of the willows that fringed the field; by the sensuous curving of the twisted ash that formed a gateway to the little grove of sapling oaks where fauns and satyrs lurked to play in the moonlight before Pagan altars; and by the cloaking darkness, next, of the copse of stunted pines, close gathered each to each, where hooded figures stalked behind an awful cross. The episode with the children seemed to have opened me like a knife. The whole Place rushed at me.

I suspect this synthesis of many moods produced in me that climax of loathing and disgust which made me feel the limit of bearable emotion had been reached, so that I made straight to find Frances in order to convince her that at any rate I must leave. For, although this was our last day in the house, and we had arranged to go next day, the dread was in me that she would still find some persuasive reason for staying on. And an unexpected incident then made my dread unnecessary. The front door was open, and a cab stood in the drive; a tall, elderly man was gravely talking in the hall with the parlor maid we called the Grenadier. He held a piece of paper in his hand. "I have called to see the house," I heard him say, as I ran up the stairs to Frances, who was peering like an inquisitive child over the banisters....

"Yes," she told me with a sigh, I know not whether of resignation or relief, "the house is to be let or sold. Mabel has decided. Some Society or other, I believe—"

I was overjoyed: this made our leaving right and possible. "You never told me, Frances!"

"Mabel only heard of it a few days ago. She told me herself this morning. It is a chance, she says. Alone she cannot get it 'straight'.

"Defeat?" I asked, watching her closely.

"She thinks she has found a way out. It's not a family, you see, it's a Society, a sort of Community—they go in for thought—"

"A Community!" I gasped. "You mean religious?"

She shook her head. "Not exactly," she said smiling, "but some kind of association of men and women who want a headquarters in the country—a place where they can write and meditate—think—mature their plans and all the rest—I don't know exactly what."

"Utopian dreamers?" I asked, yet feeling an immense relief come over me as I heard. But I asked in ignorance, not cynically. Frances would know. She knew all this kind of thing.

"No, not that exactly," she smiled. "Their teachings are grand and simple—old as the world too, really—the basis of every religion before men's minds perverted them with their manufactured creeds—"

Footsteps on the stairs, and the sound of voices, interrupted our odd impromptu conversation, as the Grenadier came up, followed by the tall, grave gentleman who was being shown over the house. My sister drew me along the corridor towards her room, where she went in and closed the door behind me, yet not before I had stolen a good look at the caller—long enough, at least, for his face and general appearance to have made a definite impression on me. For something strong and peaceful emanated from his presence; he moved with such quiet dignity; the glance of his eyes was so steady and reassuring, that my mind labeled him instantly as a type of man one would turn to in an emergency and not be disappointed. I had seen him but for a passing moment, but I had seen him twice, and the way he walked down the passage, looking competently about him, conveyed the same impression as when I saw him standing at the door— fearless, tolerant, wise. "A sincere and kindly character," I judged instantly, "a man whom some big kind of love has trained in sweetness towards the world; no hate in him anywhere." A great deal, no doubt, to read in so brief a glance! Yet his voice confirmed my intuition, a deep and very gentle voice, great firmness in it too.

"Have I become suddenly sensitive to people's atmospheres in this extraordinary fashion?" I asked myself, smiling, as I stood in the room and heard the door close behind me. "Have I developed some clairvoyant faculty here?" At any other time I should have mocked.

And I sat down and faced my sister, feeling strangely comforted and at peace for the first time since I had stepped beneath The Towers' roof a month ago. Frances, I then saw, was smiling a little as she watched me.

"You know him?" I asked.

"You felt it too?" was her question in reply. "No," she added, "I don't know him—beyond the fact that he is a leader in the Movement and has devoted years and money to its objects. Mabel felt the same thing in him that you have felt—and jumped at it."

"But you've seen him before?" I urged, for the certainty was in me that he was no stranger to her.

She shook her head. "He called one day early this week, when you were out. Mabel saw him. I believe—" she hesitated a moment, as though expecting me to stop her with my usual impatience of such subjects—"I believe he has explained everything to her—the beliefs he embodies, she declares, are her salvation—might be, rather, if she could adopt them."

"Conversion again!" For I remembered her riches, and how gladly a Society would gobble them.

"The layers I told you about," she continued calmly, shrugging her shoulders slightly—"the deposits that are left behind by strong thinking and real belief—but especially by ugly, hateful belief, because, you see—unfortunately there's more vital passion in that sort—"

"Frances, I don't understand a bit," I said out loud, but said it a little humbly, for the impression the man had left was still strong upon me and I was grateful for the steady sense of peace and comfort he had somehow introduced. The horrors had been so dreadful. My nerves, doubtless, were more than a little overstrained. Absurd as it must sound, I classed him in my mind with the robins, the happy, confiding robins who believed in everybody and thought no evil! I laughed a moment at my ridiculous idea, and my sister, encouraged by this sign of patience in me, continued more fluently.

"Of course you don't understand, Bill? Why should you? You've never thought about such things. Needing no creed yourself, you think all creeds are rubbish."

"I'm open to conviction—I'm tolerant," I interrupted.

"You're as narrow as Sam Franklyn, and as crammed with prejudice," she answered, knowing that she had me at her mercy.

"Then, pray, what may be his, or his Society's beliefs?" I asked, feeling no desire to argue, "and how are they going to prove your Mabel's salvation? Can they bring beauty into all this aggressive hate and ugliness?"

"Certain hope and peace," she said, "that peace which is understanding, and that understanding which explains all creeds and therefore tolerates them."

"Toleration! The one word a religious man loathes above all others! His pet word is damnation—"

"Tolerates them," she repeated patiently, unperturbed by my explosion, "because it includes them all."

"Fine, if true," I admitted, "very fine. But how, pray, does it include them all?"

"Because the key-word, the motto, of their Society is, 'There is no religion higher than Truth,' and it has no single dogma of any kind. Above all," she went on, "because it claims that no individual can be 'lost.' It teaches universal salvation. To damn outsiders is uncivilized, childish, impure. Some take longer than others—it's according to the way they think and live—but all find peace, through development, in the end. What the creeds call a hopeless soul, it regards as a soul having further to go. There is no damnation—"

"Well, well," I exclaimed, feeling that she rode her hobby horse too wildly, too roughly over me, "but what is the bearing of all this upon this dreadful place, and upon Mabel? I'll admit that there is this atmosphere—this—er—inexplicable horror in the house and grounds, and that if not of damnation exactly, it is certainly damnable. I'm not too prejudiced to deny that, for I've felt it myself."

To my relief she was brief. She made her statement, leaving me to take it or reject it as I would.

"The thought and belief its former occupants—have left behind. For there has been coincidence here, a coincidence that must be rare. The site on which this modern house now stands was Roman, before that Early Britain, with burial mounds, before that again, Druid—the Druid stones still lie in that copse below the field, the Tumuli among the ilexes behind the drive. The older building Sam Franklyn altered and practically pulled down was a monastery; he changed the chapel into a meeting hall, which is now the music room; but, before he came here, the house was occupied by Manetti, a violent Catholic without tolerance or vision; and in the interval between these two, Julius Weinbaum had it, Hebrew of most rigid orthodox type imaginable—so they all have left their—"

"Even so," I repeated, yet interested to hear the rest, "what of it?"

"Simply this," said Frances with conviction, "that each in turn has left his layer of concentrated thinking and belief behind him; because each believed intensely, absolutely, beyond the least weakening of any doubt—the kind of strong belief and thinking that is rare anywhere today, the kind that wills, impregnates objects, saturates the atmosphere, haunts, in a word. And each, believing he was utterly and finally right, damned with equally positive conviction the rest of the world. One and all preached that implicitly if not explicitly. It's the root of every creed. Last of the bigoted, grim series came Samuel Franklyn."

I listened in amazement that increased as she went on. Up to this point her explanation was so admirable. It was, indeed, a pretty study in psychology if it were true.

"Then why does nothing ever happen?" I enquired mildly. "A place so thickly haunted ought to produce a crop of no ordinary results!"

"There lies the proof," she went on in a lowered voice, "the proof of the horror and the ugly reality. The thought and belief of each occupant in turn kept all the others under. They gave no sign of life at the time. But the results of thinking never die. They crop out again the moment there's an opening. And, with the return of Mabel in her negative state, believing nothing positive herself the place for the first time found itself free to reproduce its buried stores.

"Damnation, hellfire, and the rest—the most permanent and vital thought of all those creeds, since it was applied to the majority of the world—broke loose again, for there was no restraint to hold it back. Each sought to obtain its former supremacy. None conquered. There results a pandemonium of hate and fear, of striving to escape, of agonized, bitter warring to find safety, peace—salvation. The place is saturated by that appalling stream of thinking—the terror of the damned. It concentrated upon Mabel; whose negative attitude furnished the channel of deliverance. You and I, according to our sympathy with her, were similarly involved. Nothing happened because no one layer could ever gain the supremacy."

I was so interested—I dare not say amused—that I stared in silence while she paused a moment, afraid that she would draw rein and end the fairy tale too soon.

"The beliefs of this man, of his Society rather, vigorously thought and therefore vigorously given out here, will put the whole place straight. It will act as a solvent. These vitriolic layers actively denied, will fuse and disappear in the stream of gentle, tolerant sympathy which is love. For each member, worthy of the name, loves the world, and all creeds go into the melting-pot; Mabel, too, if she joins them out of real conviction, will find salvation—"

"Thinking, I know, is of the first importance," I objected, "but don't you, perhaps, exaggerate the power of feeling and emotion which in religion are au fond always hysterical?"

"What is the world," she told me, "but thinking and feeling? An individual's world is entirely what that individual thinks and believes—interpretation. There is no other. And unless he really thinks and really believes, he has no permanent world at all. I grant that few people think, and still fewer believe, and that most take ready-made suits and make them do. Only the strong make their own things; the lesser fry, Mabel among them, are merely swept up into what has been manufactured for them. They get along somehow. You and I have made for ourselves, Mabel has not. She is a nonentity, and when her belief is taken from her, she goes with it."

It was not in me just then to criticize the evasion, or pick out the sophistry from the truth. I merely waited for her to continue.

"None of us have Truth, my dear Frances," I ventured presently, seeing that she kept silent.

"Precisely," she answered, "but most of us have beliefs. And what one believes and thinks affects the world at large. Consider the legacy of hatred and cruelty involved in the doctrines men have built into their creeds where the sine qua non of salvation is absolute acceptance of one particular set of views or else perishing everlastingly—for only by repudiating history can they disavow it..."

"You're not quite accurate," I put in. "Not all the creeds teach damnation, do they? Franklyn did, of course, but the others are a bit modernized now surely?"

"Trying to get out of it," she admitted, "perhaps they are, but damnation of unbelievers—of most of the world, that is—is their rather favorite idea if you talk with them."

"I never have."

She smiled. "But I have," she said significantly, "so, if you consider what the various occupants of this house have so strongly held and thought and believed, you need not be surprised that the influence they have left behind them should be a dark and dreadful legacy. For thought, you know, does leave—"

The opening of the door, to my great relief, interrupted her, as the Grenadier led in the visitor to see the room. He bowed to both of us with a brief word of apology, looked round him, and withdrew, and with his departure the conversation between us came naturally to an end. I followed him out. Neither of us in any case, I think, cared to argue further.

And, so far as I am aware, the curious history of The Towers ends here too. There was no climax in the story sense. Nothing ever really happened. We left next morning for London. I only know that the Society in question took the house and have since occupied it to their entire satisfaction, and that Mabel, who became a member shortly afterwards, now stays there frequently when in need of repose from the arduous and unselfish labors she took upon herself under its aegis. She dined with us only the other night, here in our tiny Chelsea flat, and a jollier, saner, more interesting and happy guest I could hardly wish for. She was vital—in the best sense; the lay figure had come to life. I found it difficult to believe she was the same woman whose fearful effigy had floated down those dreary corridors and almost disappeared in the depths of that atrocious Shadow.

What her beliefs were now I was wise enough to leave unquestioned, and Frances, to my great relief, kept the conversation well away from such inappropriate topics. It was clear, however, that the woman had in herself some secret source of joy, that she was now an aggressive, positive force, sure of herself, and apparently afraid of nothing in heaven or hell. She radiated something very like hope and courage about her, and talked as though the world were a glorious place and everybody in it kind and beautiful. Her optimism was certainly infectious.

The Towers were mentioned only in passing. The name of Marsh came up— not the Marsh, it so happened, but a name in some book that was being discussed—and I was unable to restrain myself. Curiosity was too strong. I threw out a casual enquiry

Mabel could leave unanswered if she wished. But there was no desire to avoid it. Her reply was frank and smiling.

"Would you believe it? She married," Mabel told me, though obviously surprised that I remembered the housekeeper at all; "and is happy as the day is long. She's found her right niche in life. A sergeant—"

"The army!" I ejaculated.

"Salvation Army," she explained merrily.

Frances exchanged a glance with me. I laughed too, for the information took me by surprise. I cannot say why exactly, but I expected at least to hear that the woman had met some dreadful end, not impossibly by burning.

"And The Towers, now called the Rest House," Mabel chattered on, "seems to me the most peaceful and delightful spot in England—"

"Really," I said politely.

"When I lived there in the old days—while you were there, perhaps, though I won't be sure."

Mabel went on, "the story got abroad that it was haunted. Wasn't it odd? A less likely place for a ghost I've never seen. Why, it had no atmosphere at all." She said this to Frances, glancing up at me with a smile that apparently had no hidden meaning. "Did you notice anything queer about it when you were there?"

This was plainly addressed to me.

"I found it—er—difficult to settle down to anything," I said, after an instant's hesitation. "I couldn't work there—"

"But I thought you wrote that wonderful book on the Deaf and Blind while you stayed with me," she asked innocently.

I stammered a little. "Oh no, not then. I only made a few notes—er—at The Towers. My mind, oddly enough, refused to produce at all down there.

But—why do you ask? Did anything—was anything supposed to happen there?"

She looked searchingly into my eyes a moment before she answered:

"Not that I know of," she said simply.

THE END

The Willows

I

AFTER LEAVING VIENNA, and long before you come to Budapest, the Danube enters a region of singular loneliness and desolation, where its waters spread away on all sides regardless of a main channel, and the country becomes a swamp for miles upon miles, covered by a vast sea of low willow-bushes. On the big maps this deserted area is painted in a fluffy blue, growing fainter in color as it leaves the banks, and across it may be seen in large straggling letters the word Sumpfe, meaning marshes.

In high flood this great acreage of sand, shingle-beds, and willow-grown islands is almost topped by the water, but in normal seasons the bushes bend and rustle in the free winds, showing their silver leaves to the sunshine in an ever-moving plain of bewildering beauty. These willows never attain to the dignity of trees; they have no rigid trunks; they remain humble bushes, with rounded tops and soft outline, swaying on slender stems that answer to the least pressure of the wind; supple as grasses, and so continually shifting that they somehow give the impression that the entire plain is moving and alive. For the wind sends waves rising and falling over the whole surface, waves of leaves instead of waves of water, green swells like the sea, too, until the branches turn and lift, and then silvery white as their underside turns to the sun.

Happy to slip beyond the control of the stern banks, the Danube here wanders about at will among the intricate network of channels intersecting the islands everywhere with broad avenues down which the waters pour with a shouting sound; making whirlpools, eddies, and foaming rapids; tearing at the sandy banks; carrying away masses of shore and willow-clumps; and forming new islands innumerably which shift daily in size and shape and possess at best an impermanent life, since the flood-time obliterates their very existence.

Properly speaking, this fascinating part of the river's life begins soon after leaving Pressburg, and we, in our Canadian canoe,[15] with gipsy tent and frying pan on board, reached it on the crest of a rising flood about mid-July. That very same morning, when the sky was reddening before sunrise, we had slipped swiftly through still-sleeping Vienna, leaving it a couple of hours later a mere patch of smoke against the blue hills of the Wienerwald[16] on the horizon; we had breakfasted below Fischeramend under a grove of birch trees roaring in the wind; and had then swept on the tearing current past Orth, Hainburg, Petronell (the old Roman Carnuntum of Marcus Aurelius),[17] and so under the frowning heights of Thelsen on a spur of the Carpathians, where the March steals in quietly from the left and the frontier is crossed between Austria and Hungary.

Racing along at twelve kilometers an hour soon took us well into Hungary, and the muddy waters—sure sign of flood—sent us aground on many a shingle-bed, and twisted us like a cork in many a sudden belching whirlpool before the towers of Pressburg (Hungarian, Poszony) showed against the sky; and then the canoe, leaping like a spirited horse, flew at top speed under the grey walls, negotiated safely the sunken chain of the Fliegende Brucke ferry, turned the corner sharply to the left, and plunged on yellow foam into the wilderness of islands, sandbanks, and swampland beyond—the land of the willows.

The change came suddenly, as when a series of bioscope pictures snaps down on the streets of a town and shifts without warning into the scenery of lake and forest. We entered the land of desolation on wings, and in less than half an hour there was neither boat nor fishing-hut nor red roof, nor any single sign of human habitation and civilization within sight. The sense of remoteness from the world of humankind, the utter isolation, the fascination of this singular world of willows, winds, and waters, instantly laid its spell upon us both, so that we allowed laughingly to one another that we ought by rights to have held some special kind of passport to admit us, and that we had, somewhat audaciously, come without asking leave into a separate little kingdom of wonder and magic—a kingdom that was reserved for the use of

---

[15] A Canadian canoe is lighter and roomier than, say, a kayak, with space for camping supplies, etc.

[16] The Wienerwald forest is in the district of Mödling, Lower Austria.

[17] Carnuntum was a Roman fort where Emperor Marcus Aurelius composed part of Meditations.

others who had a right to it, with everywhere unwritten warnings to trespassers for those who had the imagination to discover them.

Though still early in the afternoon, the ceaseless buffetings of a most tempestuous wind made us feel weary, and we at once began casting about for a suitable camping ground for the night. But the bewildering character of the islands made landing difficult; the swirling flood carried us in shore and then swept us out again; the willow branches tore our hands as we seized them to stop the canoe, and we pulled many a yard of sandy bank into the water before at length we shot with a great sideways blow from the wind into a backwater and managed to beach the bows in a cloud of spray. Then we lay panting and laughing after our exertions on the hot yellow sand, sheltered from the wind, and in the full blaze of a scorching sun, a cloudless blue sky above, and an immense army of dancing, shouting willow bushes, closing in from all sides, shining with spray and clapping their thousand little hands as though to applaud the success of our efforts.

"What a river!" I said to my companion, thinking of all the way we had traveled from the source in the Black Forest, and how he had often been obliged to wade and push in the upper shallows at the beginning of June.

"Won't stand much nonsense now, will it?" he said, pulling the canoe a little farther into safety up the sand, and then composing himself for a nap.

I lay by his side, happy and peaceful in the bath of the elements—water, wind, sand, and the great fire of the sun—thinking of the long journey that lay behind us, and of the great stretch before us to the Black Sea, and how lucky I was to have such a delightful and charming traveling companion as my friend, the Swede.

We had made many similar journeys together, but the Danube, more than any other river I knew, impressed us from the very beginning with its aliveness. From its tiny bubbling entry into the world among the pinewood gardens of Donaueschingen, until this moment when it began to play the great river-game of losing itself among the deserted swamps, unobserved, unrestrained, it had seemed to us like following the grown of some living creature. Sleepy at first, but later developing violent desires as it became conscious of its deep soul, it rolled, like some huge fluid being, through all the countries we had passed, holding our little craft on its mighty shoulders, playing roughly with us sometimes, yet always friendly and well-meaning, till at length we had come inevitably to regard it as a Great Personage.

How, indeed, could it be otherwise, since it told us so much of its secret life? At night we heard it singing to the moon as we lay in our tent, uttering that odd sibilant note peculiar to itself and said to be caused by the rapid tearing of the pebbles along its bed, so great is its hurrying speed. We knew, too, the voice of its gurgling whirlpools, suddenly bubbling up on a surface previously quite calm; the roar of its shallows and swift rapids; its constant steady thundering below all mere surface sounds; and that ceaseless tearing of its icy waters at the banks. How it stood up and shouted when the rains fell flat upon its face! And how its laughter roared out when the wind blew upstream and tried to stop its growing speed! We knew all its sounds and voices, its tumblings and foamings, its unnecessary splashing against the bridges; that self-conscious chatter when there were hills to look on; the affected dignity of its speech when it passed through the little towns, far too important to laugh; and all these faint, sweet whisperings when the sun caught it fairly in some slow curve and poured down upon it till the steam rose.

It was full of tricks, too, in its early life before the great world knew it. There were places in the upper reaches among the Swabian forests, when yet the first whispers of its destiny had not reached it, where it elected to disappear through holes in the ground, to appear again on the other side of the porous limestone hills and start a new river with another name; leaving, too, so little water in its own bed that we had to climb out and wade and push the canoe through miles of shallows.

And a chief pleasure, in those early days of its irresponsible youth, was to lie low, like Brer Fox, just before the little turbulent tributaries came to join it from the Alps, and to refuse to acknowledge them when in, but to run for miles side by side, the dividing line well marked, the very levels different, the Danube utterly declining to recognize the newcomer. Below Passau, however, it gave up this particular trick, for there the Inn comes in with a thundering power impossible to ignore, and so pushes and incommodes the parent river that there is hardly room for them in the long twisting gorge that follows, and the Danube is shoved this way and that against the cliffs, and forced to hurry itself with great waves and much dashing to and fro in order to get through in time. And during the fight our canoe slipped down from its shoulder to its breast, and had the time of its life among the struggling waves.

But the Inn taught the old river a lesson, and after Passau it no longer pretended to ignore new arrivals.

This was many days back, of course, and since then we had come to know other aspects of the great creature, and across the Bavarian wheat plain of Straubing she wandered so slowly under the blazing June sun that we could well imagine only the surface inches were water, while below there moved, concealed as by a silken mantle, a whole army of Undines,[18] passing silently and unseen down to the sea, and very leisurely too, lest they be discovered.

Much, too, we forgave her because of her friendliness to the birds and animals that haunted the shores. Cormorants lined the banks in lonely places in rows like short black palings; grey crows crowded the shingle-beds; storks stood fishing in the vistas of shallower water that opened up between the islands, and hawks, swans, and marsh birds of all sorts filled the air with glinting wings and singing, petulant cries. It was impossible to feel annoyed with the river's vagaries after seeing a deer leap with a splash into the water at sunrise and swim past the bows of the canoe; and often we saw fawns peering at us from the underbrush, or looked straight into the brown eyes of a stag as we charged full tilt round a corner and entered another reach of the river. Foxes, too, everywhere haunted the banks, tripping daintily among the driftwood and disappearing so suddenly that it was impossible to see how they managed it.

But now, after leaving Pressburg, everything changed a little, and the Danube became more serious. It ceased trifling. It was halfway to the Black Sea, within seeming distance almost of other, stranger countries where no tricks would be permitted or understood. It became suddenly grown-up, and claimed our respect and even our awe. It broke out into three arms, for one thing, that only met again a hundred kilometers farther down, and for a canoe there were no indications which one was intended to be followed.

"If you take a side channel," said the Hungarian officer we met in the Pressburg shop while buying provisions, "you may find yourselves, when the flood subsides, forty miles from anywhere, high and dry, and you may easily starve. There are no people, no farms, no fishermen. I warn you not to continue. The river, too, is still rising, and this wind will increase."

---

[18] Undine is the name of a type of water nymph in the writings of Paracelsus.

The rising river did not alarm us in the least, but the matter of being left high and dry by a sudden subsidence of the waters might be serious, and we had consequently laid in an extra stock of provisions. For the rest, the officer's prophecy held true, and the wind, blowing down a perfectly clear sky, increased steadily till it reached the dignity of a westerly gale.

Undine by John William Waterhouse[19]

It was earlier than usual when we camped, for the sun was a good hour or two from the horizon, and leaving my friend still asleep on the hot sand, I wandered about in desultory examination of our hotel. The island, I found, was less than an acre in extent, a mere sandy bank standing some two or three feet above the level of the river. The far end, pointing into the sunset, was covered with

---

[19] 1872 painting by John William Waterhouse (1849–1917).

flying spray which the tremendous wind drove off the crests of the broken waves. It was triangular in shape, with the apex up stream.

I stood there for several minutes, watching the impetuous crimson flood bearing down with a shouting roar, dashing in waves against the bank as though to sweep it bodily away, and then swirling by in two foaming streams on either side. The ground seemed to shake with the shock and rush, while the furious movement of the willow bushes as the wind poured over them increased the curious illusion that the island itself actually moved. Above, for a mile or two, I could see the great river descending upon me; it was like looking up the slope of a sliding hill, white with foam, and leaping up everywhere to show itself to the sun.

The rest of the island was too thickly grown with willows to make walking pleasant, but I made the tour, nevertheless. From the lower end the light, of course, changed, and the river looked dark and angry. Only the backs of the flying waves were visible, streaked with foam, and pushed forcibly by the great puffs of wind that fell upon them from behind. For a short mile it was visible, pouring in and out among the islands, and then disappearing with a huge sweep into the willows, which closed about it like a herd of monstrous antediluvian creatures crowding down to drink. They made me think of gigantic sponge-like growths that sucked the river up into themselves. They caused it to vanish from sight. They herded there together in such overpowering numbers.

Altogether it was an impressive scene, with its utter loneliness, its bizarre suggestion; and as I gazed, long and curiously, a singular emotion began to stir somewhere in the depths of me. Midway in my delight of the wild beauty, there crept, unbidden and unexplained, a curious feeling of disquietude, almost of alarm.

A rising river, perhaps, always suggests something of the ominous; many of the little islands I saw before me would probably have been swept away by the morning; this resistless, thundering flood of water touched the sense of awe. Yet I was aware that my uneasiness lay deeper far than the emotions of awe and wonder. It was not that I felt. Nor had it directly to do with the power of the driving wind—this shouting hurricane that might almost carry up a few acres of willows into the air and scatter them like so much chaff over the landscape. The wind was simply enjoying itself, for nothing rose out of the flat landscape to stop it, and I was conscious of sharing its great game with a kind of pleasurable excitement. Yet this novel emotion had nothing to do with the wind. Indeed, so vague was the sense of distress I experienced, that it was impossible to trace it to its source and deal with it accordingly, though I was aware somehow that it had to do with my realization of our utter insignificance before this unrestrained power of the elements about me. The huge-grown river had something to do with it too—a vague, unpleasant idea that we had somehow trifled with these great elemental forces in whose power we lay helpless every hour of the day and night. For here, indeed, they were gigantically at play together, and the sight appealed to the imagination.

But my emotion, so far as I could understand it, seemed to attach itself more particularly to the willow bushes, to these acres and acres of willows, crowding, so thickly growing there, swarming everywhere the eye could reach, pressing upon the river as though to suffocate it, standing in dense array mile after mile beneath the sky, watching, waiting, listening. And, apart quite from the elements, the willows connected themselves subtly with my malaise, attacking the mind insidiously somehow by reason of their vast numbers, and contriving in some way or other to represent to the imagination a new and mighty power, a power, moreover, not altogether friendly to us.

Great revelations of nature, of course, never fail to impress in one way or another, and I was no stranger to moods of the kind. Mountains overawe and oceans terrify, while the mystery of great forests exercises a spell peculiarly its own. But all these, at one point or another, somewhere link on intimately with human life and human experience. They stir comprehensible, even if alarming, emotions. They tend on the whole to exalt.

With this multitude of willows, however, it was something far different, I felt. Some essence emanated from them that besieged the heart. A sense of awe awakened, true, but of awe touched somewhere by a vague terror. Their serried ranks, growing everywhere darker about me as the shadows deepened, moving furiously yet softly in the wind, woke in me the curious and unwelcome suggestion that we had trespassed here upon the borders of an alien world, a world where we were intruders, a world where we were not wanted or invited to remain—where we ran grave risks perhaps!

The feeling, however, though it refused to yield its meaning entirely to analysis, did not at the time trouble me by passing into menace. Yet it never left me quite, even during the very practical business of putting up the tent in a hurricane of wind and building a fire for the stewpot. It remained, just enough to bother and perplex, and to rob a most delightful camping-ground of a good portion of its charm. To my companion, however, I said nothing, for he was a man I considered devoid of imagination. In the first place, I could never have explained to him what I meant, and in the second, he would have laughed stupidly at me if I had.

There was a slight depression in the center of the island, and here we pitched the tent. The surrounding willows broke the wind a bit.

"A poor camp," observed the imperturbable Swede when at last the tent stood upright, "no stones and precious little firewood. I'm for moving on early tomorrow—eh? This sand won't hold anything."

But the experience of a collapsing tent at midnight had taught us many devices, and we made the cozy gipsy house as safe as possible, and then set about collecting a store of wood to last till bedtime. Willow bushes drop no branches, and driftwood was our only source of supply. We hunted the shores pretty thoroughly. Everywhere the banks were crumbling as the rising flood tore at them and carried away great portions with a splash and a gurgle.

"The island's much smaller than when we landed," said the accurate Swede. "It won't last long at this rate. We'd better drag the canoe close to the tent, and be ready to start at a moment's notice. I shall sleep in my clothes."

He was a little distance off, climbing along the bank, and I heard his rather jolly laugh as he spoke.

"By Jove!" I heard him call, a moment later, and turned to see what had caused his exclamation. But for the moment he was hidden by the willows, and I could not find him.

"What in the world's this?" I heard him cry again, and this time his voice had become serious.

I ran up quickly and joined him on the bank. He was looking over the river, pointing at something in the water.

"Good heavens, it's a man's body!" he cried excitedly. "Look!"

A black thing, turning over and over in the foaming waves, swept rapidly past. It kept disappearing and coming up to the surface again. It was about twenty feet from the shore, and just as it was opposite to where we stood it lurched round and looked straight at us. We saw its eyes reflecting the sunset, and gleaming an odd yellow as the body turned over. Then it gave a swift, gulping plunge, and dived out of sight in a flash.

"An otter, by gad!" we exclaimed in the same breath, laughing.

It was an otter, alive, and out on the hunt; yet it had looked exactly like the body of a drowned man turning helplessly in the current. Far below it came to the surface once again, and we saw its black skin, wet and shining in the sunlight.

Then, too, just as we turned back, our arms full of driftwood, another thing happened to recall us to the riverbank. This time it really was a man, and what was more, a man in a boat. Now a small boat on the Danube was an unusual sight at any time, but here in this deserted region, and at flood time, it was so unexpected as to constitute a real event. We stood and stared.

Whether it was due to the slanting sunlight, or the refraction from the wonderfully illumined water, I cannot say, but, whatever the cause, I found it difficult to focus my sight properly upon the flying apparition. It seemed, however, to be a man standing upright in a sort of flat-bottomed boat, steering with a long oar, and being carried down the opposite shore at a tremendous pace. He apparently was looking across in our direction, but the distance was too great and the light too uncertain for us to make out very plainly what he was about. It seemed to me that he was gesticulating and making signs at us. His voice came across the water to us shouting something furiously, but the wind drowned it so that no single word was audible. There was something curious about the whole appearance—man, boat, signs, voice—that made an impression on me out of all proportion to its cause.

"He's crossing himself!" I cried. "Look, he's making the sign of the Cross!"

"I believe you're right," the Swede said, shading his eyes with his hand and watching the man out of sight. He seemed to be gone in a moment, melting away down there into the sea of willows where the sun caught them in the bend of the river and turned them into a great crimson wall of beauty. Mist, too, had begun to ruse, so that the air was hazy.

"But what in the world is he doing at nightfall on this flooded river?" I said, half to myself. "Where is he going at such a time, and what did he mean by his signs and shouting? D'you think he wished to warn us about something?"

"He saw our smoke, and thought we were spirits probably," laughed my companion. "These Hungarians believe in all sorts of rubbish; you remember the shop-woman at Pressburg warning us that no one ever landed here because it belonged to some sort of beings outside man's world! I suppose they believe in fairies and elementals, possibly demons, too. That peasant in the boat saw people on the islands for the first time in his life," he added, after a slight pause, "and it scared him, that's all."

The Swede's tone of voice was not convincing, and his manner lacked something that was usually there. I noted the change instantly while he talked, though without being able to label it precisely.

"If they had enough imagination," I laughed loudly—I remember trying to make as much noise as I could—"they might well people a place like this with the old gods of antiquity. The Romans must have haunted all this region more or less with their shrines and sacred groves and elemental deities."

The subject dropped and we returned to our stewpot, for my friend was not given to imaginative conversation as a rule. Moreover, just then I remember feeling distinctly glad that he was not imaginative; his stolid, practical nature suddenly seemed to me welcome and comforting. It was an admirable temperament, I felt; he could steer down rapids like a red Indian, shoot dangerous bridges and whirlpools better than any white man I ever saw in a canoe. He was a grand fellow for an adventurous trip, a tower of strength when untoward things happened. I looked at his strong face and light curly hair as he staggered along under his pile of driftwood (twice the size of mine!), and I experienced a feeling of relief. Yes, I was distinctly glad just then that the Swede was— what he was, and that he never made remarks that suggested more than they said.

"The river's still rising, though," he added, as if following out some thoughts of his own, and dropping his load with a gasp. "This island will be underwater in two days if it goes on."

"I wish the wind would go down," I said. "I don't care a fig for the river."

The flood, indeed, had no terrors for us; we could get off at ten minutes' notice, and the more water the better we liked it. It meant an increasing current and the obliteration of the treacherous shingle-beds that so often threatened to tear the bottom out of our canoe.

Contrary to our expectations, the wind did not go down with the sun. It seemed to increase with the darkness, howling overhead and shaking the willows round us like straws. Curious sounds accompanied it sometimes, like the explosion of heavy guns, and it fell upon the water and the island in great flat blows of immense power. It made me think of the sounds a planet must make, could we only hear it, driving along through space.

But the sky kept wholly clear of clouds, and soon after supper the full moon rose up in the east and covered the river and the plain of shouting willows with a light like the day.

We lay on the sandy patch beside the fire, smoking, listening to the noises of the night round us, and talking happily of the journey we had already made, and of our plans ahead. The map lay spread in the door of the tent, but the high wind made it hard to study, and presently we lowered the curtain and extinguished the lantern. The firelight was enough to smoke and see each other's faces by, and the sparks flew about overhead like fireworks. A few yards beyond, the river gurgled and hissed, and from time to time a heavy splash announced the falling away of further portions of the bank.

Our talk, I noticed, had to do with the faraway scenes and incidents of our first camps in the Black Forest, or of other subjects altogether remote from the present setting, for neither of us spoke of the actual moment more than was necessary—almost as though we had agreed tacitly to avoid discussion of the camp and its incidents. Neither the otter nor the boatman, for instance, received the honor of a single mention, though ordinarily these would have furnished discussion for the greater part of the evening. They were, of course, distinct events in such a place.

The scarcity of wood made it a business to keep the fire going, for the wind, that drove the smoke in our faces wherever we sat, helped at the same time to make a forced draught. We took it in turn to make some foraging expeditions into the darkness, and the quantity the Swede brought back always made me feel that he took an absurdly long time finding it; for the fact was I did not care much about being left alone, and yet it always seemed to be my turn to grub about among the bushes or scramble along the slippery banks in the moonlight. The long day's battle with wind and water—such wind and such water!—had tired us both, and an early bed was the obvious program. Yet neither of us made the move for the tent. We lay there, tending the fire, talking in desultory fashion, peering about us into the dense willow bushes, and listening to the thunder of wind and river. The loneliness of the place had entered our very bones, and silence seemed natural, for after a bit the sound of our voices became a trifle unreal and forced; whispering would have been the fitting mode of communication, I felt, and the human voice, always rather absurd amid the roar of the elements, now carried with it something almost illegitimate. It was like talking out loud in church, or in some place where it was not lawful, perhaps not quite safe, to be overheard.

The eeriness of this lonely island, set among a million willows, swept by a hurricane, and surrounded by hurrying deep waters, touched us both, I fancy. Untrodden by man, almost unknown to man, it lay there beneath the moon, remote from human influence, on the frontier of another world, an alien world, a world tenanted by willows only and the souls of willows. And we, in our rashness, had dared to invade it, even to make use of it! Something more than the power of its mystery stirred in me as I lay on the sand, feet to fire, and peered up through the leaves at the stars. For the last time I rose to get firewood.

"When this has burnt up," I said firmly, "I shall turn in," and my companion watched me lazily as I moved off into the surrounding shadows.

For an unimaginative man I thought he seemed unusually receptive that night, unusually open to suggestion of things other than sensory. He too was touched by the beauty and loneliness of the place. I was not altogether pleased, I remember, to recognize this slight change in him, and instead of immediately collecting sticks, I made my way to the far point of the island where the moonlight on plain and river could be seen to better advantage. The desire to be alone had come suddenly upon me; my former dread returned in force; there was a vague feeling in me I wished to face and probe to the bottom.

When I reached the point of sand jutting out among the waves, the spell of the place descended upon me with a positive shock. No mere "scenery" could have produced such an effect. There was something more here, something to alarm.

I gazed across the waste of wild waters; I watched the whispering willows; I heard the ceaseless beating of the tireless wind; and, one and all, each in its own way, stirred in me this sensation of a strange distress. But the willows especially; forever they went on chattering and talking among themselves, laughing a little, shrilly crying out, sometimes sighing—but what it was they made so much to-do about belonged to the secret life of the great plain they inhabited. And it was utterly alien to the world I knew, or to that of the wild yet kindly elements. They made me think of a host of beings from another plane of life, another evolution altogether, perhaps, all discussing a mystery known only to themselves. I watched them moving busily together, oddly shaking their big bushy heads, twirling their myriad leaves even when there was no wind. They moved of their own will as though alive, and they touched, by some incalculable method, my own keen sense of the horrible.

There they stood in the moonlight, like a vast army surrounding our camp, shaking their innumerable silver spears defiantly, formed all ready for an attack.

The psychology of places, for some imaginations at least, is very vivid; for the wanderer, especially, camps have their "note" either of welcome or rejection. At first it may not always be apparent, because the busy preparations of tent and cooking prevent, but with the first pause—after supper usually—it comes and announces itself. And the note of this willow-camp now became unmistakably plain to me; we were interlopers, trespassers; we were not welcomed. The sense of unfamiliarity grew upon me as I stood there watching. We touched the frontier of a region where our presence was resented. For a night's lodging we might perhaps be tolerated; but for a prolonged and inquisitive stay—No! by all the gods of the trees and wilderness, no! We were the first human influences upon this island, and we were not wanted. The willows were against us.

Strange thoughts like these, bizarre fancies, borne I know not whence, found lodgment in my mind as I stood listening. What, I thought, if, after all, these crouching willows proved to be alive; if suddenly they should rise up, like a swarm of living creatures, marshaled by the gods whose territory we had invaded, sweep towards us off the vast swamps, booming overhead in the night— and then settle down! As I looked it was so easy to imagine they actually moved, crept nearer, retreated a little, huddled together in masses, hostile, waiting for the great wind that should finally start them a-running. I could have sworn their aspect changed a little, and their ranks deepened and pressed more closely together.

The melancholy shrill cry of a night-bird sounded overhead, and suddenly I nearly lost my balance as the piece of bank I stood upon fell with a great splash into the river, undermined by the flood. I stepped back just in time, and went on hunting for firewood again, half laughing at the odd fancies that crowded so thickly into my mind and cast their spell upon me. I recalled the Swede's remark about moving on next day, and I was just thinking that I fully agreed with him, when I turned with a start and saw the subject of my thoughts standing immediately in front of me. He was quite close. The roar of the elements had covered his approach.

"YOU'VE BEEN GONE SO LONG," he shouted above the wind, "I thought something must have happened to you."

But there was that in his tone, and a certain look in his face as well, that conveyed to me more than his usual words, and in a flash I understood the real reason for his coming. It was because the spell of the place had entered his soul too, and he did not like being alone.

"River still rising," he cried, pointing to the flood in the moonlight, "and the wind's simply awful."

He always said the same things, but it was the cry for companionship that gave the real importance to his words.

"Lucky," I cried back, "our tent's in the hollow. I think it'll hold all right." I added something about the difficulty of finding wood, in order to explain my absence, but the wind caught my words and flung them across the river, so that he did not hear, but just looked at me through the branches, nodding his head.

"Lucky if we get away without disaster!" he shouted, or words to that effect; and I remember feeling half angry with him for putting the thought into words, for it was exactly what I felt myself. There was disaster impending somewhere, and the sense of presentiment lay unpleasantly upon me.

We went back to the fire and made a final blaze, poking it up with our feet. We took a last look round. But for the wind the heat would have been unpleasant. I put this thought into words, and I remember my friend's reply struck me oddly: that he would rather have the heat, the ordinary July weather, than this "diabolical wind."

Everything was snug for the night; the canoe lying turned over beside the tent, with both yellow paddles beneath her; the provision sack hanging from a willow-stem, and the washed-up dishes removed to a safe distance from the fire, all ready for the morning meal.

We smothered the embers of the fire with sand, and then turned in. The flap of the tent door was up, and I saw the branches and the stars and the white moonlight. The shaking willows and the heavy buffetings of the wind against our taut little house were the last things I remembered as sleep came down and covered all with its soft and delicious forgetfulness.

Suddenly, I found myself lying awake, peering from my sandy mattress through the door of the tent. I looked at my watch pinned against the canvas, and saw by the bright moonlight that it was past twelve o'clock—the threshold of a new day—and I had therefore slept a couple of hours. The Swede was asleep still beside me; the wind howled as before; something plucked at my heart and made me feel afraid. There was a sense of disturbance in my immediate neighborhood.

I sat up quickly and looked out. The trees were swaying violently to and fro as the gusts smote them, but our little bit of green canvas lay snugly safe in the hollow, for the wind passed over it without meeting enough resistance to make it vicious. The feeling of disquietude did not pass, however, and I crawled quietly out of the tent to see if our belongings were safe. I moved carefully so as not to waken my companion. A curious excitement was on me.

I was halfway out, kneeling on all fours, when my eye first took in that the tops of the bushes opposite, with their moving tracery of leaves, made shapes against the sky. I sat back on my haunches and stared. It was incredible, surely, but there, opposite and slightly above me, were shapes of some indeterminate sort among the willows, and as the branches swayed in the wind they seemed to group themselves about these shapes, forming a series of monstrous outlines that shifted rapidly beneath the moon. Close, about fifty feet in front of me, I saw these things.

My first instinct was to waken my companion, that he too might see them, but something made me hesitate—the sudden realization, probably, that I should not welcome corroboration; and meanwhile I crouched there staring in amazement with smarting eyes. I was wide awake. I remember saying to myself that I was not dreaming.

They first became properly visible, these huge figures, just within the tops of the bushes—immense, bronze-colored, moving, and wholly independent of the swaying of the branches. I saw them plainly and noted, now I came to examine them more calmly, that they were very much larger than human, and indeed that something in their appearance proclaimed them to be not human at all. Certainly they were not merely the moving tracery of the branches against the moonlight. They shifted independently. They rose upwards in a continuous stream from earth to sky, vanishing utterly as soon as they reached the dark of the sky. They were interlaced one with another, making a great column, and I saw their limbs and huge bodies melting in and out of each other, forming this serpentine line that bent and swayed and twisted spirally with the contortions of the wind-tossed trees. They were nude, fluid shapes, passing up the bushes, within the leaves almost; rising up in a living column into the heavens. Their faces I never could see. Unceasingly they poured upwards, swaying in great bending curves, with a hue of dull bronze upon their skins.

I stared, trying to force every atom of vision from my eyes. For a long time I thought they must every moment disappear and resolve themselves into the movements of the branches and prove to be an optical illusion. I searched everywhere for a proof of reality, when all the while I understood quite well that the standard of reality had changed. For the longer I looked the more certain I became that these figures were real and living, though perhaps not according to the standards that the camera and the biologist would insist upon.

Far from feeling fear, I was possessed with a sense of awe and wonder such as I have never known. I seemed to be gazing at the personified elemental forces of this haunted and primeval region. Our intrusion had stirred the powers of the place into activity. It was we who were the cause of the disturbance, and my brain filled to bursting with stories and legends of the spirits and deities of places that have been acknowledged and worshipped by men in all ages of the world's history. But, before I could arrive at any possible explanation, something impelled me to go farther out, and I crept forward on the sand and stood upright. I felt the ground still warm under my bare feet; the wind tore at my hair and face; and the sound of the river burst upon my ears with a sudden roar. These things, I knew, were real, and proved that my senses were acting normally. Yet the figures still rose from earth to heaven, silent, majestically, in a great spiral of grace and strength that overwhelmed me at length with a genuine deep emotion of worship. I felt that I must fall down and worship—absolutely worship.

Perhaps in another minute I might have done so, when a gust of wind swept against me with such force that it blew me sideways, and I nearly stumbled and fell. It seemed to shake the dream violently out of me. At least it gave me another point of view somehow. The figures still remained, still ascended into heaven from the heart of the night, but my reason at last began to assert itself. It must be a subjective experience, I argued—none the less real for that, but still subjective. The moonlight and the branches combined to work out these pictures upon the mirror of my imagination, and for some reason I projected them outwards and made them appear objective. I knew this must be the case, of course. I took courage, and began to move forward across the open patches of sand. By Jove, though, was it all hallucination? Was it merely subjective? Did not my reason argue in the old futile way from the little standard of the known?

I only know that great column of figures ascended darkly into the sky for what seemed a very long period of time, and with a very complete measure of reality as most men are accustomed to gauge reality. Then suddenly they were gone!

And, once they were gone and the immediate wonder of their great presence had passed, fear came down upon me with a cold rush. The esoteric meaning of this lonely and haunted region suddenly flamed up within me, and I began to tremble dreadfully. I took a quick look round—a look of horror that came near to panic—calculating vainly ways of escape; and then, realizing how helpless I was to achieve anything really effective, I crept back silently into the tent and lay down again upon my sandy mattress, first lowering the door-curtain to shut out the sight of the willows in the moonlight, and then burying my head as deeply as possible beneath the blankets to deaden the sound of the terrifying wind.

As though further to convince me that I had not been dreaming, I remember that it was a long time before I fell again into a troubled and restless sleep; and even then only the upper crust of me slept, and underneath there was something that never quite lost consciousness, but lay alert and on the watch.

But this second time I jumped up with a genuine start of terror. It was neither the wind nor the river that woke me, but the slow approach of something that caused the sleeping portion of me to grow smaller and smaller till at last it vanished altogether, and I found myself sitting bolt upright listening.

Outside there was a sound of multitudinous little patterings. They had been coming, I was aware, for a long time, and in my sleep they had first become audible. I sat there nervously wide awake as though I had not slept at all. It seemed to me that my breathing came with difficulty, and that there was a great weight upon the surface of my body. In spite of the hot night, I felt clammy with cold and shivered. Something surely was pressing steadily against the sides of the tent and weighing down upon it from above. Was it the body of the wind? Was this the pattering rain, the dripping of the leaves? The spray blown from the river by the wind and gathering in big drops? I thought quickly of a dozen things.

Then suddenly the explanation leaped into my mind: a bough from the poplar, the only large tree on the island, had fallen with the wind. Still half caught by the other branches, it would fall with the next gust and crush us, and meanwhile its leaves brushed and tapped upon the tight canvas surface of the tent. I raised a loose flap and rushed out, calling to the Swede to follow.

But when I got out and stood upright I saw that the tent was free. There was no hanging bough; there was no rain or spray; nothing approached.

A cold, grey light filtered down through the bushes and lay on the faintly gleaming sand. Stars still crowded the sky directly overhead, and the wind howled magnificently, but the fire no longer gave out any glow, and I saw the east reddening in streaks through the trees. Several hours must have passed since I stood there before watching the ascending figures, and the memory of it now came back to me horribly, like an evil dream. Oh, how tired it made me feel, that ceaseless raging wind! Yet, though the deep lassitude of a sleepless night was on me, my nerves were tingling with the activity of an equally tireless apprehension, and all idea of repose was out of the question. The river I saw had risen further. Its thunder filled the air, and a fine spray made itself felt through my thin sleeping shirt.

Yet nowhere did I discover the slightest evidence of anything to cause alarm. This deep, prolonged disturbance in my heart remained wholly unaccounted for.

My companion had not stirred when I called him, and there was no need to waken him now. I looked about me carefully, noting everything; the turned-over canoe; the yellow paddles—two of them, I'm certain; the provision sack and the extra lantern hanging together from the tree; and, crowding everywhere about me, enveloping all, the willows, those endless, shaking willows. A bird uttered its morning cry, and a string of duck passed with whirring flight overhead in the twilight. The sand whirled, dry and stinging, about my bare feet in the wind.

I walked round the tent and then went out a little way into the bush, so that I could see across the river to the farther landscape, and the same profound yet indefinable emotion of distress seized upon me again as I saw the interminable sea of bushes stretching to the horizon, looking ghostly and unreal in the wan light of dawn. I walked softly here and there, still puzzling over that odd sound of infinite pattering, and of that pressure upon the tent that had wakened me. It must have been the wind, I reflected—the wind bearing upon the loose, hot sand, driving the dry particles smartly against the taut canvas—the wind dropping heavily upon our fragile roof.

Yet all the time my nervousness and malaise increased appreciably.

I crossed over to the farther shore and noted how the coastline had altered in the night, and what masses of sand the river had torn away. I dipped my hands and feet into the cool current, and bathed my forehead. Already there was a glow of sunrise in the sky and the exquisite freshness of coming day. On my way back I passed purposely beneath the very bushes where I had seen the column of figures rising into the air, and midway among the clumps I suddenly found myself overtaken by a sense of vast terror. From the shadows a large figure went swiftly by. Someone passed me, as sure as ever man did....

It was a great staggering blow from the wind that helped me forward again, and once out in the more open space, the sense of terror diminished strangely. The winds were about and walking, I remember saying to myself, for the winds often move like great presences under the trees. And altogether the fear that hovered about me was such an unknown and immense kind of fear, so unlike anything I had ever felt before, that it woke a sense of awe and wonder in me that did much to counteract its worst effects; and when I reached a high point in the middle of the island from which I could see the wide stretch of river, crimson in the sunrise, the whole magical beauty of it all was so overpowering that a sort of wild yearning woke in me and almost brought a cry up into the throat.

But this cry found no expression, for as my eyes wandered from the plain beyond to the island round me and noted our little tent half hidden among the willows, a dreadful discovery leaped out at me, compared to which my terror of the walking winds seemed as nothing at all.

For a change, I thought, had somehow come about in the arrangement of the landscape. It was not that my point of vantage gave me a different view, but that an alteration had apparently been effected in the relation of the tent to the willows, and of the willows to the tent. Surely the bushes now crowded much closer—unnecessarily, unpleasantly close. They had moved nearer.

Creeping with silent feet over the shifting sands, drawing imperceptibly nearer by soft, unhurried movements, the willows had come closer during the night. But had the wind moved them, or had they moved of themselves? I recalled the sound of infinite small patterings and the pressure upon the tent and upon my own heart that caused me to wake in terror. I swayed for a moment in the wind like a tree, finding it hard to keep my upright position on the sandy hillock. There was a suggestion here of personal agency, of deliberate intention, of aggressive hostility, and it terrified me into a sort of rigidity.

Then the reaction followed quickly. The idea was so bizarre, so absurd, that I felt inclined to laugh. But the laughter came no more readily than the cry, for the knowledge that my mind was so receptive to such dangerous imaginings brought the additional terror that it was through our minds and not through our physical bodies that the attack would come, and was coming.

The wind buffeted me about, and, very quickly it seemed, the sun came up over the horizon, for it was after four o'clock, and I must have stood on that little pinnacle of sand longer than I knew, afraid to come down to close quarters with the willows. I returned quietly, creepily, to the tent, first taking another exhaustive look round and—yes, I confess it—making a few measurements. I paced out on the warm sand the distances between the willows and the tent, making a note of the shortest distance particularly.

I crawled stealthily into my blankets. My companion, to all appearances, still slept soundly, and I was glad that this was so. Provided my experiences were not corroborated, I could find strength somehow to deny them, perhaps. With the daylight I could persuade myself that it was all a subjective hallucination, a fantasy of the night, a projection of the excited imagination.

Nothing further came in to disturb me, and I fell asleep almost at once, utterly exhausted, yet still in dread of hearing again that weird sound of multitudinous pattering, or of feeling the pressure upon my heart that had made it difficult to breathe.

The sun was high in the heavens when my companion woke me from a heavy sleep and announced that the porridge was cooked and there was just time to bathe. The grateful smell of frizzling bacon entered the tent door.

"River still rising," he said, "and several islands out in midstream have disappeared altogether. Our own island's much smaller."

"Any wood left?" I asked sleepily.

"The wood and the island will finish tomorrow in a dead heat," he laughed, "but there's enough to last us till then."

I plunged in from the point of the island, which had indeed altered a lot in size and shape during the night, and was swept down in a moment to the landing-place opposite the tent. The water was icy, and the banks flew by like the country from an express train. Bathing under such conditions was an exhilarating operation, and the terror of the night seemed cleansed out of me by a process of evaporation in the brain. The sun was blazing hot; not a cloud showed itself anywhere; the wind, however, had not abated one little jot.

Quite suddenly then the implied meaning of the Swede's words flashed across me, showing that he no longer wished to leave post-haste, and had changed his mind. "Enough to last till tomorrow"—he assumed we should stay on the island another night. It struck me as odd. The night before he was so positive the other way. How had the change come about?

Great crumblings of the banks occurred at breakfast, with heavy splashings and clouds of spray which the wind brought into our frying pan, and my fellow traveler talked incessantly about the difficulty the Vienna-Pesth steamers[20] must have to find the channel in flood. But the state of his mind interested and impressed me far more than the state of the river or the difficulties of the steamers. He had changed somehow since the evening before. His manner was different—a trifle excited, a trifle shy, with a sort of suspicion about his voice and gestures. I hardly know how to describe it now in cold blood, but at the time I remember being quite certain of one thing—that he had become frightened?

He ate very little breakfast, and for once omitted to smoke his pipe. He had the map spread open beside him, and kept studying its markings.

"We'd better get off sharp in an hour," I said presently, feeling for an opening that must bring him indirectly to a partial confession at any rate. And his answer puzzled me uncomfortably: "Rather! If they'll let us."

"Who'll let us? The elements?" I asked quickly, with affected indifference.

"The powers of this awful place, whoever they are," he replied, keeping his eyes on the map. "The gods are here, if they are anywhere at all in the world."

"The elements are always the true immortals," I replied, laughing as naturally as I could manage, yet knowing quite well that my face reflected my true feelings when he looked up gravely at me and spoke across the smoke:

"We shall be fortunate if we get away without further disaster."

---

[20] Danube steamers operated by the Dusseldorf Company.

This was exactly what I had dreaded, and I screwed myself up to the point of the direct question. It was like agreeing to allow the dentist to extract the tooth; it had to come anyhow in the long run, and the rest was all pretense.

"Further disaster! Why, what's happened?"

"For one thing—the steering paddle's gone," he said quietly.

"The steering paddle gone!" I repeated, greatly excited, for this was our rudder, and the Danube in flood without a rudder was suicide. "But what—"

"And there's a tear in the bottom of the canoe," he added, with a genuine little tremor in his voice.

I continued staring at him, able only to repeat the words in his face somewhat foolishly. There, in the heat of the sun, and on this burning sand, I was aware of a freezing atmosphere descending round us. I got up to follow him, for he merely nodded his head gravely and led the way towards the tent a few yards on the other side of the fireplace. The canoe still lay there as I had last seen her in the night, ribs uppermost, the paddles, or rather, the paddle, on the sand beside her.

"There's only one," he said, stooping to pick it up. "And here's the rent in the baseboard."

It was on the tip of my tongue to tell him that I had clearly noticed two paddles a few hours before, but a second impulse made me think better of it, and I said nothing. I approached to see.

There was a long, finely made tear in the bottom of the canoe where a little slither of wood had been neatly taken clean out; it looked as if the tooth of a sharp rock or snag had eaten down her length, and investigation showed that the hole went through. Had we launched out in her without observing it we must inevitably have foundered. At first the water would have made the wood swell so as to close the hole, but once out in midstream the water must have poured in, and the canoe, never more than two inches above the surface, would have filled and sunk very rapidly.

"There, you see an attempt to prepare a victim for the sacrifice," I heard him saying, more to himself than to me, "two victims rather," he added as he bent over and ran his fingers along the slit.

I began to whistle—a thing I always do unconsciously when utterly nonplussed—and purposely paid no attention to his words. I was determined to consider them foolish.

"It wasn't there last night," he said presently, straightening up from his examination and looking anywhere but at me.

"We must have scratched her in landing, of course," I stopped whistling to say. "The stones are very sharp."

I stopped abruptly, for at that moment he turned round and met my eye squarely. I knew just as well as he did how impossible my explanation was. There were no stones, to begin with.

"And then there's this to explain too," he added quietly, handing me the paddle and pointing to the blade.

A new and curious emotion spread freezingly over me as I took and examined it. The blade was scraped down all over, beautifully scraped, as though someone had sandpapered it with care, making it so thin that the first vigorous stroke must have snapped it off at the elbow.

"One of us walked in his sleep and did this thing," I said feebly, "or—or it has been filed by the constant stream of sand particles blown against it by the wind, perhaps."

"Ah," said the Swede, turning away, laughing a little, "you can explain everything."

"The same wind that caught the steering paddle and flung it so near the bank that it fell in with the next lump that crumbled," I called out after him, absolutely determined to find an explanation for everything he showed me.

"I see," he shouted back, turning his head to look at me before disappearing among the willow bushes.

Once alone with these perplexing evidences of personal agency, I think my first thoughts took the form of "One of us must have done this thing, and it certainly was not I." But my second thought decided how impossible it was to suppose, under all the circumstances, that either of us had done it. That my companion, the trusted friend of a dozen similar expeditions, could have knowingly had a hand in it, was a suggestion not to be entertained for a moment. Equally absurd seemed the explanation that this imperturbable and densely practical nature had suddenly become insane and was busied with insane purposes.

Yet the fact remained that what disturbed me most, and kept my fear actively alive even in this blaze of sunshine and wild beauty, was the clear certainty that some curious alteration had come about in his mind—that he was nervous, timid, suspicious, aware of goings on he did not speak about, watching a series of secret and hitherto unmentionable events—waiting, in a word, for a climax that he expected, and, I thought, expected very soon. This grew up in my mind intuitively—I hardly knew how.

I made a hurried examination of the tent and its surroundings, but the measurements of the night remained the same. There were deep hollows formed in the sand I now noticed for the first time, basin-shaped and of various depths and sizes, varying from that of a teacup to a large bowl. The wind, no doubt, was responsible for these miniature craters, just as it was for lifting the paddle and tossing it towards the water. The rent in the canoe was the only thing that seemed quite inexplicable; and, after all, it was conceivable that a sharp point had caught it when we landed. The examination I made of the shore did not assist this theory, but all the same I clung to it with that diminishing portion of my intelligence which I called my "reason." An explanation of some kind was an absolute necessity, just as some working explanation of the universe is necessary—however absurd—to the happiness of every individual who seeks to do his duty in the world and face the problems of life. The simile seemed to me at the time an exact parallel.

I at once set the pitch melting, and presently the Swede joined me at the work, though under the best conditions in the world the canoe could not be safe for traveling till the following day. I drew his attention casually to the hollows in the sand.

"Yes," he said, "I know. They're all over the island. But you can explain them, no doubt!"

"Wind, of course," I answered without hesitation. "Have you never watched those little whirlwinds in the street that twist and twirl everything into a circle? This sand's loose enough to yield, that's all."

He made no reply, and we worked on in silence for a bit. I watched him surreptitiously all the time, and I had an idea he was watching me. He seemed, too, to be always listening attentively to something I could not hear, or perhaps for something that he expected to hear, for he kept turning about and staring into the bushes, and up into the sky, and out across the water where it was visible through the openings among the willows. Sometimes he even put his hand to his ear and held it there for several minutes. He said nothing to me, however, about it, and I asked no questions. And meanwhile, as he mended that torn canoe with the skill and address of a red Indian, I was glad to notice his absorption in the work, for there was a vague dread in my heart that he would speak of the changed aspect of the willows. And, if he had noticed that, my imagination could no longer be held a sufficient explanation of it.

III

AT LENGTH, AFTER A LONG PAUSE, he began to talk.

"Queer thing," he added in a hurried sort of voice, as though he wanted to say something and get it over. "Queer thing. I mean, about that otter last night."

I had expected something so totally different that he caught me with surprise, and I looked up sharply.

"Shows how lonely this place is. Otters are awfully shy things—"

"I don't mean that, of course," he interrupted. "I mean—do you think—did you think it really was an otter?"

"What else, in the name of Heaven, what else?"

"You know, I saw it before you did, and at first it seemed—so much bigger than an otter."

"The sunset as you looked upstream magnified it, or something," I replied.

He looked at me absently a moment, as though his mind were busy with other thoughts.

"It had such extraordinary yellow eyes," he went on half to himself.

"That was the sun too," I laughed, a trifle boisterously. "I suppose you'll wonder next if that fellow in the boat—"

I suddenly decided not to finish the sentence. He was in the act again of listening, turning his head to the wind, and something in the expression of his face made me halt. The subject dropped, and we went on with our caulking. Apparently he had not noticed my unfinished sentence. Five minutes later, however, he looked at me across the canoe, the smoking pitch in his hand, his face exceedingly grave.

"I did rather wonder, if you want to know," he said slowly, "what that thing in the boat was. I remember thinking at the time it was not a man. The whole business seemed to rise quite suddenly out of the water."

I laughed again boisterously in his face, but this time there was impatience, and a strain of anger too, in my feeling.

"Look here now," I cried, "this place is quite queer enough without going out of our way to imagine things! That boat was an ordinary boat, and the man in it was an ordinary man, and they were both going downstream as fast as they could lick. And that otter was an otter, so don't let's play the fool about it!"

He looked steadily at me with the same grave expression. He was not in the least annoyed. I took courage from his silence.

"And, for Heaven's sake," I went on, "don't keep pretending you hear things, because it only gives me the jumps, and there's nothing to hear but the river and this cursed old thundering wind."

"You fool!" he answered in a low, shocked voice, "you utter fool. That's just the way all victims talk. As if you didn't understand just as well as I do!" he sneered with scorn in his voice, and a sort of resignation. "The best thing you can do is to keep quiet and try to hold your mind as firm as possible. This feeble attempt at self-deception only makes the truth harder when you're forced to meet it."

My little effort was over, and I found nothing more to say, for I knew quite well his words were true, and that I was the fool, not he. Up to a certain stage in the adventure he kept ahead of me easily, and I think I felt annoyed to be out of it, to be thus proved less psychic, less sensitive than himself to these extraordinary happenings, and half ignorant all the time of what was going on under my very nose. He knew from the very beginning, apparently. But at the moment I wholly missed the point of his words about the necessity of there being a victim, and that we ourselves were destined to satisfy the want. I dropped all pretense thenceforward, but thenceforward likewise my fear increased steadily to the climax.

"But you're quite right about one thing," he added, before the subject passed, "and that is that we're wiser not to talk about it, or even to think about it, because what one thinks finds expression in words, and what one says, happens."

That afternoon, while the canoe dried and hardened, we spent trying to fish, testing the leak, collecting wood, and watching the enormous flood of rising water. Masses of driftwood swept near our shores sometimes, and we fished for them with long willow branches. The island grew perceptibly smaller as the banks were torn away with great gulps and splashes. The weather kept brilliantly fine till about four o'clock, and then for the first time for three days the wind showed signs of abating. Clouds began to gather in the southwest, spreading thence slowly over the sky.

This lessening of the wind came as a great relief, for the incessant roaring, banging, and thundering had irritated our nerves. Yet the silence that came about five o'clock with its sudden cessation was in a manner quite as oppressive. The booming of the river had everything in its own way then; it filled the air with deep murmurs, more musical than the wind noises, but infinitely more monotonous. The wind held many notes, rising, falling always beating out some sort of great elemental tune; whereas the river's song lay between three notes at most—dull pedal notes, that held a lugubrious quality foreign to the wind, and somehow seemed to me, in my then nervous state, to sound wonderfully well the music of doom.

It was extraordinary, too, how the withdrawal suddenly of bright sunlight took everything out of the landscape that made for cheerfulness; and since this particular landscape had already managed to convey the suggestion of something sinister, the change of course was all the more unwelcome and noticeable. For me, I know, the darkening outlook became distinctly more alarming, and I found myself more than once calculating how soon after sunset the full moon would get up in the east, and whether the gathering clouds would greatly interfere with her lighting of the little island.

With this general hush of the wind—though it still indulged in occasional brief gusts—the river seemed to me to grow blacker, the willows to stand more densely together. The latter, too, kept up a sort of independent movement of their own, rustling among themselves when no wind stirred, and shaking oddly from the roots upwards. When common objects in this way become charged with the suggestion of horror, they stimulate the imagination far more than things of unusual appearance; and these bushes, crowding huddled about us, assumed for me in the darkness a bizarre grotesquerie of appearance that lent to them somehow the aspect of purposeful and living creatures. Their very ordinariness, I felt, masked what was malignant and hostile to us. The forces of the region drew nearer with the coming of night. They were focusing upon our island, and more particularly upon ourselves. For thus, somehow, in the terms of the imagination, did my really indescribable sensations in this extraordinary place present themselves.

I had slept a good deal in the early afternoon, and had thus recovered somewhat from the exhaustion of a disturbed night, but this only served apparently to render me more susceptible than before to the obsessing spell of the haunting. I fought against it, laughing at my feelings as absurd and childish, with very obvious physiological explanations, yet, in spite of every effort, they gained in strength upon me so that I dreaded the night as a child lost in a forest must dread the approach of darkness.

The canoe we had carefully covered with a waterproof sheet during the day, and the one remaining paddle had been securely tied by the Swede to the base of a tree, lest the wind should rob us of that too. From five o'clock onwards I busied myself with the stewpot and preparations for dinner, it being my turn to cook that night. We had potatoes, onions, bits of bacon fat to add flavor, and a general thick residue from former stews at the bottom of the pot; with black bread broken up into it the result was most excellent, and it was followed by a stew of plums with sugar and a brew of strong tea with dried milk. A good pile of wood lay close at hand, and the absence of wind made my duties easy. My companion sat lazily watching me, dividing his attentions between cleaning his pipe and giving useless advice—an admitted privilege of the off-duty man. He had been very quiet all the afternoon, engaged in re-caulking the canoe, strengthening the tent ropes, and fishing for driftwood while I slept. No more talk about undesirable things had passed between us, and I think his only remarks had to do with the gradual destruction of the island, which he declared was not fully a third smaller than when we first landed.

The pot had just begun to bubble when I heard his voice calling to me from the bank, where he had wandered away without my noticing. I ran up.

"Come and listen," he said, "and see what you make of it." He held his hand cup-wise to his ear, as so often before.

"Now do you hear anything?" he asked, watching me curiously.

We stood there, listening attentively together. At first I heard only the deep note of the water and the hissings rising from its turbulent surface. The willows, for once, were motionless and silent. Then a sound began to reach my ears faintly, a peculiar sound—something like the humming of a distant gong. It seemed to come across to us in the darkness from the waste of swamps and willows opposite. It was repeated at regular intervals, but it was certainly neither the sound of a bell nor the hooting of a distant steamer. I can liken it to nothing so much as to the sound of an immense gong, suspended far up in the sky, repeating incessantly its muffled metallic note, soft and musical, as it was repeatedly struck. My heart quickened as I listened.

"I've heard it all day," said my companion. "While you slept this afternoon it came all round the island. I hunted it down, but could never get near enough to see—to localize it correctly. Sometimes it was overhead, and sometimes it seemed under the water. Once or twice, too, I could have sworn it was not outside at all, but within myself—you know—the way a sound in the fourth dimension is supposed to come."

I was too much puzzled to pay much attention to his words. I listened carefully, striving to associate it with any known familiar sound I could think of, but without success. It changed in the direction, too, coming nearer, and then sinking utterly away into remote distance. I cannot say that it was ominous in quality, because to me it seemed distinctly musical, yet I must admit it set going a distressing feeling that made me wish I had never heard it.

"The wind blowing in those sand-funnels," I said determined to find an explanation, "or the bushes rubbing together after the storm perhaps."

"It comes off the whole swamp," my friend answered. "It comes from everywhere at once." He ignored my explanations. "It comes from the willow bushes somehow—"

"But now the wind has dropped," I objected. "The willows can hardly make a noise by themselves, can they?"

His answer frightened me, first because I had dreaded it, and secondly, because I knew intuitively it was true.

"It is because the wind has dropped we now hear it. It was drowned before. It is the cry, I believe, of the—"

I dashed back to my fire, warned by the sound of bubbling that the stew was in danger, but determined at the same time to escape further conversation. I was resolute, if possible, to avoid the exchanging of views. I dreaded, too, that he would begin about the gods, or the elemental forces, or something else disquieting, and I wanted to keep myself well in hand for what might happen later. There was another night to be faced before we escaped from this distressing place, and there was no knowing yet what it might bring forth.

"Come and cut up bread for the pot," I called to him, vigorously stirring the appetizing mixture. That stewpot held sanity for us both, and the thought made me laugh.

He came over slowly and took the provision sack from the tree, fumbling in its mysterious depths, and then emptying the entire contents upon the groundsheet at his feet.

"Hurry up!" I cried; "it's boiling."

The Swede burst out into a roar of laughter that startled me. It was forced laughter, not artificial exactly, but mirthless.

"There's nothing here!" he shouted, holding his sides.

"Bread, I mean."

"It's gone. There is no bread. They've taken it!"

I dropped the long spoon and ran up. Everything the sack had contained lay upon the groundsheet, but there was no loaf.

The whole dead weight of my growing fear fell upon me and shook me. Then I burst out laughing too. It was the only thing to do, and the sound of my laughter also made me understand his. The stain of psychical pressure caused it—this explosion of unnatural laughter in both of us; it was an effort of repressed forces to seek relief; it was a temporary safety-valve. And with both of us it ceased quite suddenly.

"How criminally stupid of me!" I cried, still determined to be consistent and find an explanation. "I clean forgot to buy a loaf at Pressburg. That chattering woman put everything out of my head, and I must have left it lying on the counter or—"

"The oatmeal, too, is much less than it was this morning," the Swede interrupted.

Why in the world need he draw attention to it? I thought angrily.

"There's enough for tomorrow," I said, stirring vigorously, "and we can get lots more at Komorn or Gran. In twenty-four hours we shall be miles from here."

"I hope so—to God," he muttered, putting the things back into the sack, "unless we're claimed first as victims for the sacrifice," he added with a foolish laugh. He dragged the sack into the tent, for safety's sake, I suppose, and I heard him mumbling to himself, but so indistinctly that it seemed quite natural for me to ignore his words.

Our meal was beyond question a gloomy one, and we ate it almost in silence, avoiding one another's eyes, and keeping the fire bright. Then we washed up and prepared for the night, and, once smoking, our minds unoccupied with any definite duties, the apprehension I had felt all day long became more and more acute. It was not then active fear, I think, but the very vagueness of its origin distressed me far more that if I had been able to ticket and face it squarely. The curious sound I have likened to the note of a gong became now almost incessant, and filled the stillness of the night with a faint, continuous ringing rather than a series of distinct notes. At one time it was behind and at another time in front of us. Sometimes I fancied it came from the bushes on our left, and then again from the clumps on our right. More often it hovered directly overhead like the whirring of wings. It was really everywhere at once, behind, in front, at our sides and over our heads, completely surrounding us. The sound really defies description.

But nothing within my knowledge is like that ceaseless muffled humming rising off the deserted world of swamps and willows.

We sat smoking in comparative silence, the strain growing every minute greater. The worst feature of the situation seemed to me that we did not know what to expect, and could therefore make no sort of preparation by way of defense. We could anticipate nothing. My explanations made in the sunshine, moreover, now came to haunt me with their foolish and wholly unsatisfactory nature, and it was more and more clear to us that some kind of plain talk with my companion was inevitable, whether I liked it or not. After all, we had to spend the night together, and to sleep in the same tent side by side. I saw that I could not get along much longer without the support of his mind, and for that, of course, plain talk was imperative. As long as possible, however, I postponed this little climax, and tried to ignore or laugh at the occasional sentences he flung into the emptiness.

Some of these sentences, moreover, were confoundedly disquieting to me, coming as they did to corroborate much that I felt myself; corroboration, too—which made it so much more convincing—from a totally different point of view. He composed such curious sentences, and hurled them at me in such an inconsequential sort of way, as though his main line of thought was secret to himself, and these fragments were mere bits he found it impossible to digest. He got rid of them by uttering them. Speech relieved him. It was like being sick.

"There are things about us, I'm sure, that make for disorder, disintegration, destruction, our destruction," he said once, while the fire blazed between us. "We've strayed out of a safe line somewhere."

And, another time, when the gong sounds had come nearer, ringing much louder than before, and directly over our heads, he said as though talking to himself:

"I don't think a gramophone would show any record of that. The sound doesn't come to me by the ears at all. The vibrations reach me in another manner altogether, and seem to be within me, which is precisely how a fourth dimensional sound might be supposed to make itself heard."

I purposely made no reply to this, but I sat up a little closer to the fire and peered about me into the darkness. The clouds were massed all over the sky, and no trace of moonlight came through. Very still, too, everything was, so that the river and the frogs had things all their own way.

"It has that about it," he went on, "which is utterly out of common experience. It is unknown. Only one thing describes it really; it is a non-human sound; I mean a sound outside humanity."

Having rid himself of this indigestible morsel, he lay quiet for a time, but he had so admirably expressed my own feeling that it was a relief to have the thought out, and to have confined it by the limitation of words from dangerous wandering to and fro in the mind.

The solitude of that Danube camping-place, can I ever forget it? The feeling of being utterly alone on an empty planet! My thoughts ran incessantly upon cities and the haunts of men. I would have given my soul, as the saying is, for the "feel" of those Bavarian villages we had passed through by the score; for the normal, human commonplaces; peasants drinking beer, tables beneath the trees, hot sunshine, and a ruined castle on the rocks behind the red-roofed church. Even the tourists would have been welcome.

Yet what I felt of dread was no ordinary ghostly fear. It was infinitely greater, stranger, and seemed to arise from some dim ancestral sense of terror more profoundly disturbing than anything I had known or dreamed of. We had "strayed," as the Swede put it, into some region or some set of conditions where the risks were great, yet unintelligible to us; where the frontiers of some unknown world lay close about us. It was a spot held by the dwellers in some outer space, a sort of peephole whence they could spy upon the earth, themselves unseen, a point where the veil between had worn a little thin. As the final result of too long a sojourn here, we should be carried over the border and deprived of what we called "our lives," yet by mental, not physical, processes. In that sense, as he said, we should be the victims of our adventure—a sacrifice.

It took us in different fashion, each according to the measure of his sensitiveness and powers of resistance. I translated it vaguely into a personification of the mightily disturbed elements, investing them with the horror of a deliberate and malefic purpose, resentful of our audacious intrusion into their breeding-place; whereas my friend threw it into the unoriginal form at first of a trespass on some ancient shrine, some place where the old gods still held sway, where the emotional forces of former worshippers still clung, and the ancestral portion of him yielded to the old pagan spell.

At any rate, here was a place unpolluted by men, kept clean by the winds from coarsening human influences, a place where spiritual agencies were within reach and aggressive. Never, before or since, have I been so attacked by indescribable suggestions of a "beyond region," of another scheme of life, another revolution not parallel to the human. And in the end our minds would succumb under the weight of the awful spell, and we should be drawn across the frontier into their world.

Small things testified to the amazing influence of the place, and now in the silence round the fire they allowed themselves to be noted by the mind. The very atmosphere had proved itself a magnifying medium to distort every indication: the otter rolling in the current, the hurrying boatman making signs, the shifting willows, one and all had been robbed of its natural character, and revealed in something of its other aspect—as it existed across the border to that other region. And this changed aspect I felt was now not merely to me, but to the race. The whole experience whose verge we touched was unknown to humanity at all. It was a new order of experience, and in the true sense of the word unearthly.

"It's the deliberate, calculating purpose that reduces one's courage to zero," the Swede said suddenly, as if he had been actually following my thoughts. "Otherwise imagination might count for much. But the paddle, the canoe, the lessening food—"

"Haven't I explained all that once?" I interrupted viciously.

"You have," he answered dryly; "you have indeed."

He made other remarks too, as usual, about what he called the "plain determination to provide a victim"; but, having now arranged my thoughts better, I recognized that this was simply the cry of his frightened soul against the knowledge that he was being attacked in a vital part, and that he would be somehow taken or destroyed. The situation called for a courage and calmness of reasoning that neither of us could compass, and I have never before been so clearly conscious of two persons in me—the one that explained everything, and the other that laughed at such foolish explanations, yet was horribly afraid.

Meanwhile, in the pitchy night the fire died down and the wood pile grew small. Neither of us moved to replenish the stock, and the darkness consequently came up very close to our faces. A few feet beyond the circle of firelight it was inky black. Occasionally a stray puff of wind set the willows shivering about us, but apart from this not very welcome sound a deep and depressing silence reigned, broken only by the gurgling of the river and the humming in the air overhead.

We both missed, I think, the shouting company of the winds.

At length, at a moment when a stray puff prolonged itself as though the wind were about to rise again, I reached the point for me of saturation, the point where it was absolutely necessary to find relief in plain speech, or else to betray myself by some hysterical extravagance that must have been far worse in its effect upon both of us. I kicked the fire into a blaze, and turned to my companion abruptly. He looked up with a start.

"I can't disguise it any longer," I said; "I don't like this place, and the darkness, and the noises, and the awful feelings I get. There's something here that beats me utterly. I'm in a blue funk, and that's the plain truth. If the other shore was—different, I swear I'd be inclined to swim for it!"

The Swede's face turned very white beneath the deep tan of sun and wind. He stared straight at me and answered quietly, but his voice betrayed his huge excitement by its unnatural calmness. For the moment, at any rate, he was the strong man of the two. He was more phlegmatic, for one thing.

"It's not a physical condition we can escape from by running away," he replied, in the tone of a doctor diagnosing some grave disease; "we must sit tight and wait. There are forces close here that could kill a herd of elephants in a second as easily as you or I could squash a fly. Our only chance is to keep perfectly still. Our insignificance perhaps may save us."

I put a dozen questions into my expression of face, but found no words. It was precisely like listening to an accurate description of a disease whose symptoms had puzzled me.

"I mean that so far, although aware of our disturbing presence, they have not found us—not 'located' us, as the Americans say," he went on. "They're blundering about like men hunting for a leak of gas. The paddle and canoe and provisions prove that. I think they feel us, but cannot actually see us. We must keep our minds quiet—it's our minds they feel. We must control our thoughts, or it's all up with us."

"Death, you mean?" I stammered, icy with the horror of his suggestion.

"Worse—by far," he said. "Death, according to one's belief, means either annihilation or release from the limitations of the senses, but it involves no change of character. You don't suddenly alter just because the body's gone. But this means a radical alteration, a complete change, a horrible loss of oneself by substitution—far worse than death, and not even annihilation. We happen to have camped in a spot where their region touches ours, where the veil between has worn thin"—horrors! he was using my very own phrase, my actual words—"so that they are aware of our being in their neighborhood."

"But who are aware?" I asked.

I forgot the shaking of the willows in the windless calm, the humming overhead, everything except that I was waiting for an answer that I dreaded more than I can possibly explain.

He lowered his voice at once to reply, leaning forward a little over the fire, an indefinable change in his face that made me avoid his eyes and look down upon the ground.

"All my life," he said, "I have been strangely, vividly conscious of another region—not far removed from our own world in one sense, yet wholly different in kind—where great things go on unceasingly, where immense and terrible personalities hurry by, intent on vast purposes compared to which earthly affairs, the rise and fall of nations, the destinies of empires, the fate of armies and continents, are all as dust in the balance; vast purposes, I mean, that deal directly with the soul, and not indirectly with more expressions of the soul—"

"I suggest just now—" I began, seeking to stop him, feeling as though I was face to face with a madman. But he instantly overbore me with his torrent that had to come.

"You think," he said, "it is the spirit of the elements, and I thought perhaps it was the old gods. But I tell you now it is—neither. These would be comprehensible entities, for they have relations with men, depending upon them for worship or sacrifice, whereas these beings who are now about us have absolutely nothing to do with mankind, and it is mere chance that their space happens just at this spot to touch our own."

The mere conception, which his words somehow made so convincing, as I listened to them there in the dark stillness of that lonely island, set me shaking a little all over. I found it impossible to control my movements.

"And what do you propose?" I began again.

"A sacrifice, a victim, might save us by distracting them until we could get away," he went on, "just as the wolves stop to devour the dogs and give the sleigh another start. But—I see no chance of any other victim now."

I stared blankly at him. The gleam in his eye was dreadful. Presently he continued.

IV

"IT'S THE WILLOWS, OF COURSE. The willows mask the others, but the others are feeling about for us. If we let our minds betray our fear, we're lost, lost utterly." He looked at me with an expression so calm, so determined, so sincere, that I no longer had any doubts as to his sanity. He was as sane as any man ever was. "If we can hold out through the night," he added, "we may get off in the daylight unnoticed, or rather, undiscovered."

"But you really think a sacrifice would—"

That gong-like humming came down very close over our heads as I spoke, but it was my friend's scared face that really stopped my mouth.

"Hush!" he whispered, holding up his hand. "Do not mention them more than you can help. Do not refer to them by name. To name is to reveal; it is the inevitable clue, and our only hope lies in ignoring them, in order that they may ignore us."

"Even in thought?" He was extraordinarily agitated.

"Especially in thought. Our thoughts make spirals in their world. We must keep them out of our minds at all costs if possible."

I raked the fire together to prevent the darkness having everything its own way. I never longed for the sun as I longed for it then in the awful blackness of that summer night.

"Were you awake all last night?" he went on suddenly.

"I slept badly a little after dawn," I replied evasively, trying to follow his instructions, which I knew instinctively were true, "but the wind, of course—"

"I know. But the wind won't account for all the noises."

"Then you heard it too?"

"The multiplying countless little footsteps I heard," he said, adding, after a moment's hesitation, "and that other sound—"

"You mean above the tent, and the pressing down upon us of something tremendous, gigantic?"

He nodded significantly.

"It was like the beginning of a sort of inner suffocation?" I said.

"Partly, yes. It seemed to me that the weight of the atmosphere had been altered—had increased enormously, so that we should have been crushed."

"And that," I went on, determined to have it all out, pointing upwards where the gong-like note hummed ceaselessly, rising and falling like wind. "What do you make of that?"

"It's their sound," he whispered gravely. "It's the sound of their world, the humming in their region. The division here is so thin that it leaks through somehow. But, if you listen carefully, you'll find it's not above so much as around us. It's in the willows. It's the willows themselves humming, because here the willows have been made symbols of the forces that are against us."

I could not follow exactly what he meant by this, yet the thought and idea in my mind were beyond question the thought and idea in his. I realized what he realized, only with less power of analysis than his. It was on the tip of my tongue to tell him at last about my hallucination of the ascending figures and the moving bushes, when he suddenly thrust his face again close into mine across the firelight and began to speak in a very earnest whisper. He amazed me by his calmness and pluck, his apparent control of the situation. This man I had for years deemed unimaginative, stolid!

"Now listen," he said. "The only thing for us to do is to go on as though nothing had happened, follow our usual habits, go to bed, and so forth; pretend we feel nothing and notice nothing. It is a question wholly of the mind, and the less we think about them the better our chance of escape. Above all, don't think, for what you think happens!"

"All right," I managed to reply, simply breathless with his words and the strangeness of it all; "all right, I'll try, but tell me one more thing first. Tell me what you make of those hollows in the ground all about us, those sand-funnels?"

"No!" he cried, forgetting to whisper in his excitement. "I dare not, simply dare not, put the thought into words. If you have not guessed I am glad. Don't try to. They have put it into my mind; try your hardest to prevent their putting it into yours."

He sank his voice again to a whisper before he finished, and I did not press him to explain. There was already just about as much horror in me as I could hold. The conversation came to an end, and we smoked our pipes busily in silence.

Then something happened, something unimportant apparently, as the way is when the nerves are in a very great state of tension, and this small thing for a brief space gave me an entirely different point of view. I chanced to look down at my sandshoe— the sort we used for the canoe—and something to do with the hole at the toe suddenly recalled to me the London shop where I had bought them, the difficulty the man had in fitting me, and other details of the uninteresting but practical operation.

At once, in its train, followed a wholesome view of the modern skeptical world I was accustomed to move in at home. I thought of roast beef, and ale, motorcars, policemen, brass bands, and a dozen other things that proclaimed the soul of ordinariness or utility. The effect was immediate and astonishing even to myself. Psychologically, I suppose, it was simply a sudden and violent reaction after the strain of living in an atmosphere of things that to the normal consciousness must seem impossible and incredible. But, whatever the cause, it momentarily lifted the spell from my heart, and left me for the short space of a minute feeling free and utterly unafraid. I looked up at my friend opposite.

"You damned old pagan!" I cried, laughing aloud in his face. "You imaginative idiot! You superstitious idolater! You—"

I stopped in the middle, seized anew by the old horror. I tried to smother the sound of my voice as something sacrilegious. The Swede, of course, heard it too—the strange cry overhead in the darkness—and that sudden drop in the air as though something had come nearer.

He had turned ashen white under the tan. He stood bolt upright in front of the fire, stiff as a rod, staring at me.

"After that," he said in a sort of helpless, frantic way, "we must go! We can't stay now; we must strike camp this very instant and go on—down the river."

He was talking, I saw, quite wildly, his words dictated by abject terror—the terror he had resisted so long, but which had caught him at last.

"In the dark?" I exclaimed, shaking with fear after my hysterical outburst, but still realizing our position better than he did. "Sheer madness! The river's in flood, and we've only got a single paddle. Besides, we only go deeper into their country! There's nothing ahead for fifty miles but willows, willows, willows!"

He sat down again in a state of semi-collapse. The positions, by one of those kaleidoscopic changes nature loves, were suddenly reversed, and the control of our forces passed over into my hands. His mind at last had reached the point where it was beginning to weaken.

"What on earth possessed you to do such a thing?" he whispered with the awe of genuine terror in his voice and face.

I crossed round to his side of the fire. I took both his hands in mine, kneeling down beside him and looking straight into his frightened eyes.

"We'll make one more blaze," I said firmly, "and then turn in for the night. At sunrise we'll be off full speed for Komorn. Now, pull yourself together a bit, and remember your own advice about not thinking fear!"

He said no more, and I saw that he would agree and obey. In some measure, too, it was a sort of relief to get up and make an excursion into the darkness for more wood. We kept close together, almost touching, groping among the bushes and along the bank. The humming overhead never ceased, but seemed to me to grow louder as we increased our distance from the fire. It was shivery work!

We were grubbing away in the middle of a thickish clump of willows where some driftwood from a former flood had caught high among the branches, when my body was seized in a grip that made me half drop upon the sand. It was the Swede. He had fallen against me, and was clutching me for support. I heard his breath coming and going in short gasps.

"Look! By my soul!" he whispered, and for the first time in my experience I knew what it was to hear tears of terror in a human voice. He was pointing to the fire, some fifty feet away. I followed the direction of his finger, and I swear my heart missed a beat.

There, in front of the dim glow, something was moving.

I saw it through a veil that hung before my eyes like the gauze drop-curtain used at the back of a theater—hazily a little. It was neither a human figure nor an animal. To me it gave the strange impression of being as large as several animals grouped together, like horses, two or three, moving slowly. The Swede, too, got a similar result, though expressing it differently, for he thought it was shaped and sized like a clump of willow bushes, rounded at the top, and moving all over upon its surface—"coiling upon itself like smoke," he said afterwards.

"I watched it settle downwards through the bushes," he sobbed at me. "Look, by God! It's coming this way! Oh, oh!"—he gave a kind of whistling cry. "They've found us."

I gave one terrified glance, which just enabled me to see that the shadowy form was swinging towards us through the bushes, and then I collapsed backwards with a crash into the branches. These failed, of course, to support my weight, so that with the Swede on top of me we fell in a struggling heap upon the sand. I really hardly knew what was happening. I was conscious only of a sort of enveloping sensation of icy fear that plucked the nerves out of their fleshly covering, twisted them this way and that, and replaced them quivering. My eyes were tightly shut; something in my throat choked me; a feeling that my consciousness was expanding, extending out into space, swiftly gave way to another feeling that I was losing it altogether, and about to die.

An acute spasm of pain passed through me, and I was aware that the Swede had hold of me in such a way that he hurt me abominably. It was the way he caught at me in falling.

But it was the pain, he declared afterwards, that saved me; it caused me to forget them and think of something else at the very instant when they were about to find me. It concealed my mind from them at the moment of discovery, yet just in time to evade their terrible seizing of me. He himself, he says, actually swooned at the same moment, and that was what saved him.

I only know that at a later date, how long or short is impossible to say, I found myself scrambling up out of the slippery network of willow branches, and saw my companion standing in front of me holding out a hand to assist me. I stared at him in a dazed way, rubbing the arm he had twisted for me. Nothing came to me to say, somehow.

"I lost consciousness for a moment or two," I heard him say. "That's what saved me. It made me stop thinking about them."

"You nearly broke my arm in two," I said, uttering my only connected thought at the moment. A numbness came over me.

"That's what saved you!" he replied. "Between us, we've managed to set them off on a false tack somewhere. The humming has ceased. It's gone—for the moment at any rate!"

A wave of hysterical laughter seized me again, and this time spread to my friend too—great healing gusts of shaking laughter that brought a tremendous sense of relief in their train. We made our way back to the fire and put the wood on so that it blazed at once. Then we saw that the tent had fallen over and lay in a tangled heap upon the ground.

We picked it up, and during the process tripped more than once and caught our feet in sand.

"It's those sand-funnels," exclaimed the Swede, when the tent was up again, and the firelight lit up the ground for several yards about us. "And look at the size of them!"

All round the tent and about the fireplace where we had seen the moving shadows there were deep funnel-shaped hollows in the sand, exactly similar to the ones we had already found over the island, only far bigger and deeper, beautifully formed, and wide enough in some instances to admit the whole of my foot and leg.

Neither of us said a word. We both knew that sleep was the safest thing we could do, and to bed we went accordingly without further delay, having first thrown sand on the fire and taken the provision sack and the paddle inside the tent with us. The canoe, too, we propped in such a way at the end of the tent that our feet touched it, and the least motion would disturb and wake us.

In case of emergency, too, we again went to bed in our clothes, ready for a sudden start.

It was my firm intention to lie awake all night and watch, but the exhaustion of nerves and body decreed otherwise, and sleep after a while came over me with a welcome blanket of oblivion. The fact that my companion also slept quickened its approach. At first he fidgeted and constantly sat up, asking me if I "heard this" or "heard that." He tossed about on his cork mattress, and said the tent was moving and the river had risen over the point of the island, but each time I went out to look I returned with the report that all was well, and finally he grew calmer and lay still. Then at length his breathing became regular and I heard unmistakable sounds of snoring—the first and only time in my life when snoring has been a welcome and calming influence.

This, I remember, was the last thought in my mind before dozing off.

A difficulty in breathing woke me, and I found the blanket over my face. But something else besides the blanket was pressing upon me, and my first thought was that my companion had rolled off his mattress on to my own in his sleep. I called to him and sat up, and at the same moment it came to me that the tent was surrounded. That sound of multitudinous soft pattering was again audible outside, filling the night with horror.

I called again to him, louder than before. He did not answer, but I missed the sound of his snoring, and also noticed that the flap of the tent was down. This was the unpardonable sin. I crawled out in the darkness to hook it back securely, and it was then for the first time I realized positively that the Swede was not here. He had gone.

I dashed out in a mad run, seized by a dreadful agitation, and the moment I was out I plunged into a sort of torrent of humming that surrounded me completely and came out of every quarter of the heavens at once. It was that same familiar humming—gone mad! A swarm of great invisible bees might have been about me in the air. The sound seemed to thicken the very atmosphere, and I felt that my lungs worked with difficulty.

But my friend was in danger, and I could not hesitate.

The dawn was just about to break, and a faint whitish light spread upwards over the clouds from a thin strip of clear horizon. No wind stirred. I could just make out the bushes and river beyond, and the pale sandy patches. In my excitement I ran frantically to and fro about the island, calling him by name, shouting at the top of my voice the first words that came into my head. But the willows smothered my voice, and the humming muffled it, so that the sound only traveled a few feet round me. I plunged among the bushes, tripping headlong, tumbling over roots, and scraping my face as I tore this way and that among the preventing branches.

Then, quite unexpectedly, I came out upon the island's point and saw a dark figure outlined between the water and the sky. It was the Swede. And already he had one foot in the river! A moment more and he would have taken the plunge.

I threw myself upon him, flinging my arms about his waist and dragging him shoreward with all my strength. Of course he struggled furiously, making a noise all the time just like that cursed humming, and using the most outlandish phrases in his anger about "going inside to Them," and "taking the way of the water and the wind," and God only knows what more besides, that I tried in vain to recall afterwards, but which turned me sick with horror and amazement as I listened. But in the end I managed to get him into the comparative safety of the tent, and flung him breathless and cursing upon the mattress where I held him until the fit had passed.

I think the suddenness with which it all went, and he grew calm, coinciding as it did with the equally abrupt cessation of the humming and pattering outside—I think this was almost the strangest part of the whole business perhaps. For he had just opened his eyes and turned his tired face up to me so that the dawn threw a pale light upon it through the doorway, and said, for all the world just like a frightened child:

"My life, old man—it's my life I owe you. But it's all over now anyhow. They've found a victim in our place!"

Then he dropped back upon his blankets and went to sleep literally under my eyes. He simply collapsed, and began to snore again as healthily as though nothing had happened and he had never tried to offer his own life as a sacrifice by drowning. And when the sunlight woke him three hours later—hours of ceaseless vigil for me—it became so clear to me that he remembered absolutely nothing of what he had attempted to do, that I deemed it wise to hold my peace and ask no dangerous questions.

He woke naturally and easily, as I have said, when the sun was already high in a windless hot sky, and he at once got up and set about the preparation of the fire for breakfast. I followed him anxiously at bathing, but he did not attempt to plunge in, merely dipping his head and making some remark about the extra coldness of the water.

"River's falling at last," he said, "and I'm glad of it."

"The humming has stopped too," I said.

He looked up at me quietly with his normal expression. Evidently he remembered everything except his own attempt at suicide.

"Everything has stopped," he said, "because—"

He hesitated. But I knew some reference to that remark he had made just before he fainted was in his mind, and I was determined to know it.

"Because 'They've found another victim'?" I said, forcing a little laugh.

"Exactly," he answered, "exactly! I feel as positive of it as though—as though—I feel quite safe again, I mean," he finished.

He began to look curiously about him. The sunlight lay in hot patches on the sand. There was no wind. The willows were motionless. He slowly rose to feet.

"Come," he said; "I think if we look, we shall find it."

He started off on a run, and I followed him. He kept to the banks, poking with a stick among the sandy bays and caves and little backwaters, myself always close on his heels.

"Ah!" he exclaimed presently, "ah!"

The tone of his voice somehow brought back to me a vivid sense of the horror of the last twenty-four hours, and I hurried up to join him. He was pointing with his stick at a large black object that lay half in the water and half on the sand. It appeared to be caught by some twisted willow roots so that the river could not sweep it away. A few hours before the spot must have been under water.

"See," he said quietly, "the victim that made our escape possible!"

And when I peered across his shoulder I saw that his stick rested on the body of a man. He turned it over. It was the corpse of a peasant, and the face was hidden in the sand. Clearly the man had been drowned, but a few hours before, and his body must have been swept down upon our island somewhere about the hour of the dawn—at the very time the fit had passed.

"We must give it a decent burial, you know."

"I suppose so," I replied. I shuddered a little in spite of myself, for there was something about the appearance of that poor drowned man that turned me cold.

The Swede glanced up sharply at me, an undecipherable expression on his face, and began clambering down the bank. I followed him more leisurely. The current, I noticed, had torn away much of the clothing from the body, so that the neck and part of the chest lay bare.

Halfway down the bank my companion suddenly stopped and held up his hand in warning; but either my foot slipped, or I had gained too much momentum to bring myself quickly to a halt, for I bumped into him and sent him forward with a sort of leap to save himself. We tumbled together on to the hard sand so that our feet splashed into the water. And, before anything could be done, we had collided a little heavily against the corpse.

The Swede uttered a sharp cry. And I sprang back as if I had been shot.

At the moment we touched the body there rose from its surface the loud sound of humming—the sound of several hummings— which passed with a vast commotion as of winged things in the air about us and disappeared upwards into the sky, growing fainter and fainter till they finally ceased in the distance. It was exactly as though we had disturbed some living yet invisible creatures at work.

My companion clutched me, and I think I clutched him, but before either of us had time properly to recover from the unexpected shock, we saw that a movement of the current was turning the corpse round so that it became released from the grip of the willow roots. A moment later it had turned completely over, the dead face uppermost, staring at the sky. It lay on the edge of the mainstream. In another moment it would be swept away.

The Swede started to save it, shouting again something I did not catch about a "proper burial"—and then abruptly dropped upon his knees on the sand and covered his eyes with his hands. I was beside him in an instant.

I saw what he had seen.

For just as the body swung round to the current the face and the exposed chest turned full towards us, and showed plainly how the skin and flesh were indented with small hollows, beautifully formed, and exactly similar in shape and kind to the sand-funnels that we had found all over the island.

"Their mark!" I heard my companion mutter under his breath. "Their awful mark!"

And when I turned my eyes again from his ghastly face to the river, the current had done its work, and the body had been swept away into midstream and was already beyond our reach and almost out of sight, turning over and over on the waves like an otter.

THE END

The Wendigo

I

A CONSIDERABLE NUMBER OF hunting parties were out that year without finding so much as a fresh trail; for the moose were uncommonly shy, and the various Nimrods returned to the bosoms of their respective families with the best excuses the facts of their imaginations could suggest. Dr. Cathcart, among others, came back without a trophy; but he brought instead the memory of an experience which he declares was worth all the bull moose that had ever been shot. But then Cathcart, of Aberdeen, was interested in other things besides moose—amongst them the vagaries of the human mind. This particular story, however, found no mention in his book on Collective Hallucination for the simple reason (so he confided once to a fellow colleague) that he himself played too intimate a part in it to form a competent judgment of the affair as a whole....

Besides himself and his guide, Hank Davis, there was young Simpson, his nephew, a divinity student destined for the "Wee Kirk" (then on his first visit to Canadian backwoods), and the latter's guide, Défago. Joseph Défago was a French "Canuck," who had strayed from his native Province of Quebec years before, and had got caught in Rat Portage[21] when the Canadian Pacific Railway was a-building; a man who, in addition to his unparalleled knowledge of woodcraft and bush-lore, could also sing the old voyageur songs and tell a capital hunting yarn into the bargain. He was deeply susceptible, moreover, to that singular spell which the wilderness lays upon certain lonely natures, and he loved the wild solitudes with a kind of romantic passion that amounted almost to an obsession. The life of the backwoods fascinated him—whence, doubtless, his surpassing efficiency in dealing with their mysteries.

On this particular expedition he was Hank's choice. Hank knew him and swore by him. He also swore at him, "*jest* as a pal might," and since he had a vocabulary of picturesque, if utterly

---

[21] The city of Rat Portage (French: Portage-aux-Rats) is the old name for Kenora.

meaningless, oaths, the conversation between the two stalwart and hardy woodsmen was often of a rather lively description. This river of expletives, however, Hank agreed to dam a little out of respect for his old "hunting boss," Dr. Cathcart, whom of course he addressed after the fashion of the country as "Doc," and also because he understood that young Simpson was already a "bit of a parson." He had, however, one objection to Défago, and one only—which was, that the French Canadian sometimes exhibited what Hank described as "the output of a cursed and dismal mind," meaning apparently that he sometimes was true to type, Latin type, and suffered fits of a kind of silent moroseness when nothing could induce him to utter speech. Défago, that is to say, was imaginative and melancholy. And, as a rule, it was too long a spell of "civilization" that induced the attacks, for a few days of the wilderness invariably cured them.

This, then, was the party of four that found themselves in camp the last week in October of that "shy moose year" 'way up in the wilderness north of Rat Portage—a forsaken and desolate country. There was also Punk, an Indian, who had accompanied Dr. Cathcart and Hank on their hunting trips in previous years, and who acted as cook. His duty was merely to stay in camp, catch fish, and prepare venison steaks and coffee at a few minutes' notice. He dressed in the worn-out clothes bequeathed to him by former patrons, and, except for his coarse black hair and dark skin, he looked in these city garments no more like a real redskin than a stage Negro looks like a real African. For all that, however, Punk had in him still the instincts of his dying race; his taciturn silence and his endurance survived; also his superstition.

The party round the blazing fire that night were despondent, for a week had passed without a single sign of recent moose discovering itself. Défago had sung his song and plunged into a story, but Hank, in bad humor, reminded him so often that "he kep' mussing-up the fac's so, that it was 'most all nothin' but a petered-out lie," that the Frenchman had finally subsided into a sulky silence which nothing seemed likely to break. Dr. Cathcart and his nephew were fairly done after an exhausting day. Punk was washing up the dishes, grunting to himself under the lean-to of branches, where he later also slept. No one troubled to stir the slowly dying fire. Overhead the stars were brilliant in a sky quite wintry, and there was so little wind that ice was already forming stealthily along the shores of the still lake behind them. The silence of the vast listening forest stole forward and enveloped them.

Hank broke in suddenly with his nasal voice.

"I'm in favor of breaking new ground tomorrow, Doc," he observed with energy, looking across at his employer. "We don't stand a dead Dago's chance around here."

"Agreed," said Cathcart, always a man of few words. "Think the idea's good."

"Sure pop, it's good," Hank resumed with confidence. "S'pose, now, you and I strike west, up Garden Lake way for a change! None of us ain't touched that quiet bit o' land yet—"

"I'm with you."

"And you, Défago, take Mr. Simpson along in the small canoe, skip across the lake, portage over into Fifty Island Water, and take a good squint down that thar southern shore. The moose 'yarded' there like hell last year, and for all we know they may be doin' it agin this year jest to spite us."

Défago, keeping his eyes on the fire, said nothing by way of reply. He was still offended, possibly, about his interrupted story.

"No one's been up that way this year, an' I'll lay my bottom dollar on that!" Hank added with emphasis, as though he had a reason for knowing. He looked over at his partner sharply. "Better take the little silk tent and stay away a couple o' nights," he concluded, as though the matter were definitely settled. For Hank was recognized as general organizer of the hunt, and in charge of the party.

It was obvious to anyone that Défago did not jump at the plan, but his silence seemed to convey something more than ordinary disapproval, and across his sensitive dark face there passed a curious expression like a flash of firelight—not so quickly, however, that the three men had not time to catch it.

"He funked for some reason, I thought," Simpson said afterwards in the tent he shared with his uncle. Dr. Cathcart made no immediate reply, although the look had interested him enough at the time for him to make a mental note of it. The expression had caused him a passing uneasiness he could not quite account for at the moment.

But Hank, of course, had been the first to notice it, and the odd thing was that instead of becoming explosive or angry over the other's reluctance, he at once began to humor him a bit.

"But there ain't no speshul reason why no one's been up there this year," he said with a perceptible hush in his tone; "not the reason you mean, anyway! Las' year it was the fires that kep' folks out, and this year I guess—I guess it jest happened so, that's all!" His manner was clearly meant to be encouraging.

Joseph Défago raised his eyes a moment, then dropped them again. A breath of wind stole out of the forest and stirred the embers into a passing blaze. Dr. Cathcart again noticed the expression in the guide's face, and again he did not like it. But this time the nature of the look betrayed itself. In those eyes, for an instant, he caught the gleam of a man scared in his very soul. It disquieted him more than he cared to admit.

"Bad Indians up that way?" he asked, with a laugh to ease matters a little, while Simpson, too sleepy to notice this subtle by-play, moved off to bed with a prodigious yawn; "or—or anything wrong with the country?" he added, when his nephew was out of hearing.

Hank met his eye with something less than his usual frankness.

"He's jest skeered," he replied good-humoredly. "Skeered stiff about some ole feery tale! That's all, ain't it, ole pard?" And he gave Défago a friendly kick on the moccasined foot that lay nearest the fire.

Défago looked up quickly, as from an interrupted reverie, a reverie, however, that had not prevented his seeing all that went on about him.

"Skeered—nuthin'!" he answered, with a flush of defiance. "There's nuthin' in the Bush that can skeer Joseph Défago, and don't you forget it!" And the natural energy with which he spoke made it impossible to know whether he told the whole truth or only a part of it.

Hank turned towards the doctor. He was just going to add something when he stopped abruptly and looked round. A sound close behind them in the darkness made all three start. It was old Punk, who had moved up from his lean-to while they talked and now stood there just beyond the circle of firelight—listening.

"'Nother time, Doc!" Hank whispered, with a wink, "when the gallery ain't stepped down into the stalls!" And, springing to his feet, he slapped the Indian on the back and cried noisily, "Come up t' the fire an' warm yer dirty red skin a bit." He dragged him towards the blaze and threw more wood on. "That was a mighty good feed you give us an hour or two back," he continued heartily, as though to set the man's thoughts on another scent, "and it ain't

Christian[22] to let you stand out there freezin' yer ole soul to hell while we're gettin' all good an' toasted!" Punk moved in and warmed his feet, smiling darkly at the other's volubility which he only half understood, but saying nothing. And presently Dr. Cathcart, seeing that further conversation was impossible, followed his nephew's example and moved off to the tent, leaving the three men smoking over the now blazing fire.

It is not easy to undress in a small tent without waking one's companion, and Cathcart, hardened and warm-blooded as he was in spite of his fifty odd years, did what Hank would have described as "considerable of his twilight" in the open. He noticed, during the process, that Punk had meanwhile gone back to his lean-to, and that Hank and Défago were at it hammer and tongs, or, rather, hammer and anvil, the little French Canadian being the anvil. It was all very like the conventional stage picture of Western melodrama: the fire lighting up their faces with patches of alternate red and black; Défago, in slouch hat and moccasins in the part of the "badlands" villain; Hank, open-faced and hatless, with that reckless fling of his shoulders, the honest and deceived hero; and old Punk, eavesdropping in the background, supplying the atmosphere of mystery. The doctor smiled as he noticed the details; but at the same time something deep within him—he hardly knew what—shrank a little, as though an almost imperceptible breath of warning had touched the surface of his soul and was gone again before he could seize it. Probably it was traceable to that "scared expression" he had seen in the eyes of Défago; "probably"—for this hint of fugitive emotion otherwise escaped his usually so keen analysis. Défago, he was vaguely aware, might cause trouble somehow ...He was not as steady a guide as Hank, for instance ... Further than that he could not get ...

He watched the men a moment longer before diving into the stuffy tent where Simpson already slept soundly. Hank, he saw, was swearing like a mad African in a New York nigger saloon; but it was the swearing of "affection." The ridiculous oaths flew freely now that the cause of their obstruction was asleep. Presently he put his arm almost tenderly upon his comrade's shoulder, and they moved off together into the shadows where their tent stood

---

22 Blackwood would know; he was raised in a Christian family, and educated at a strict Protestant school in Germany. However, he is said to have developed an interest in Buddhism by reading a book of his father's, which suggests an intellectual environment broad minded enough to account for Blackwood's later fascination with other religions, and the occult.

faintly glimmering. Punk, too, a moment later followed their example and disappeared between his odorous blankets in the opposite direction.

Dr. Cathcart then likewise turned in, weariness and sleep still fighting in his mind with an obscure curiosity to know what it was that had scared Défago about the country up Fifty Island Water way,—wondering, too, why Punk's presence had prevented the completion of what Hank had to say. Then sleep overtook him. He would know tomorrow. Hank would tell him the story while they trudged after the elusive moose.

Deep silence fell about the little camp, planted there so audaciously in the jaws of the wilderness. The lake gleamed like a sheet of black glass beneath the stars. The cold air pricked. In the draughts of night that poured their silent tide from the depths of the forest, with messages from distant ridges and from lakes just beginning to freeze, there lay already the faint, bleak odors of coming winter. White men, with their dull scent, might never have divined them; the fragrance of the wood fire would have concealed from them these almost electrical hints of moss and bark and hardening swamp a hundred miles away. Even Hank and Défago, subtly in league with the soul of the woods as they were, would probably have spread their delicate nostrils in vain....

But an hour later, when all slept like the dead, old Punk crept from his blankets and went down to the shore of the lake like a shadow—silently, as only Indian blood can move. He raised his head and looked about him. The thick darkness rendered sight of small avail, but, like the animals, he possessed other senses that darkness could not mute. He listened—then sniffed the air. Motionless as a hemlock stem he stood there. After five minutes again he lifted his head and sniffed, and yet once again. A tingling of the wonderful nerves that betrayed itself by no outer sign, ran through him as he tasted the keen air. Then, merging his figure into the surrounding blackness in a way that only wild men and animals understand, he turned, still moving like a shadow, and went stealthily back to his lean-to and his bed.

And soon after he slept, the change of wind he had divined stirred gently the reflection of the stars within the lake. Rising among the far ridges of the country beyond Fifty Island Water, it came from the direction in which he had stared, and it passed over the sleeping camp with a faint and sighing murmur through the tops of the big trees that was almost too delicate to be audible. With it, down the desert paths of night, though too faint, too high even for the Indian's hair-like nerves, there passed a curious, thin odor, strangely disquieting, an odor of something that seemed unfamiliar—utterly unknown.

The French Canadian and the man of Indian blood each stirred uneasily in his sleep just about this time, though neither of them woke. Then the ghost of that unforgettably strange odor passed away and was lost among the leagues of tenantless forest beyond.

II

IN THE MORNING THE CAMP WAS astir before the sun. There had been a light fall of snow during the night and the air was sharp. Punk had done his duty betimes, for the odors of coffee and fried bacon reached every tent. All were in good spirits.

"Wind's shifted!" cried Hank vigorously, watching Simpson and his guide already loading the small canoe. "It's across the lake—dead right for you fellers. And the snow'll make bully trails! If there's any moose mussing around up thar, they'll not get so much as a tail-end scent of you with the wind as it is. Good luck, Monsieur Défago!" he added, facetiously giving the name its French pronunciation for once, "bonne chance!"

Défago returned the good wishes, apparently in the best of spirits, the silent mood gone. Before eight o'clock old Punk had the camp to himself, Cathcart and Hank were far along the trail that led westwards, while the canoe that carried Défago and Simpson, with silk tent and grub for two days, was already a dark speck bobbing on the bosom of the lake, going due east.

The wintry sharpness of the air was tempered now by a sun that topped the wooded ridges and blazed with a luxurious warmth upon the world of lake and forest below; loons flew skimming through the sparkling spray that the wind lifted; divers shook their dripping heads to the sun and popped smartly out of sight again; and as far as eye could reach rose the leagues of endless, crowding Bush, desolate in its lonely sweep and grandeur, untrodden by foot of man, and stretching its mighty and unbroken carpet right up to the frozen shores of Hudson Bay.

Simpson, who saw it all for the first time as he paddled hard in the bows of the dancing canoe, was enchanted by its austere beauty. His heart drank in the sense of freedom and great spaces just as his lungs drank in the cool and perfumed wind. Behind him in the stern seat, singing fragments of his native chanties, Défago steered the craft of birch bark like a thing of life, answering cheerfully all his companion's questions. Both were gay and lighthearted. On such occasions men lose the superficial, worldly distinctions; they become human beings working together for a common end. Simpson, the employer, and Défago the employed, among these primitive forces, were simply—two men, the "guider" and the "guided." Superior knowledge, of course, assumed control, and the younger man fell without a second thought into the quasi-subordinate position. He never dreamed of objecting when Défago dropped the "Mr.," and addressed him as "Say, Simpson," or "Simpson, boss," which was invariably the case before they reached the farther shore after a stiff paddle of twelve miles against a head wind. He only laughed, and liked it; then ceased to notice it at all.

For this "divinity student" was a young man of parts and character, though as yet, of course, untraveled; and on this trip—the first time he had seen any country but his own and little Switzerland—the huge scale of things somewhat bewildered him. It was one thing, he realized, to hear about primeval forests, but quite another to see them. While to dwell in them and seek acquaintance with their wildlife was, again, an initiation that no intelligent man could undergo without a certain shifting of personal values hitherto held for permanent and sacred.

Simpson knew the first faint indication of this emotion when he held the new .303 rifle in his hands and looked along its pair of faultless, gleaming barrels. The three days' journey to their headquarters, by lake and portage, had carried the process a stage farther. And now that he was about to plunge beyond even the fringe of wilderness where they were camped into the virgin heart of uninhabited regions as vast as Europe itself, the true nature of the situation stole upon him with an effect of delight and awe that his imagination was fully capable of appreciating. It was himself and Défago against a multitude—at least, against a Titan!

The bleak splendors of these remote and lonely forests rather overwhelmed him with the sense of his own littleness. That stern quality of the tangled backwoods which can only be described as merciless and terrible, rose out of these far blue woods swimming upon the horizon, and revealed itself. He understood the silent warning. He realized his own utter helplessness. Only Défago, as a symbol of a distant civilization where man was master, stood between him and a pitiless death by exhaustion and starvation.

It was thrilling to him, therefore, to watch Défago turn over the canoe upon the shore, pack the paddles carefully underneath, and then proceed to "blaze" the spruce stems for some distance on either side of an almost invisible trail, with the careless remark thrown in, "Say, Simpson, if anything happens to me, you'll find the canoe all correc' by these marks;—then strike doo west into the sun to hit the home camp agin, see?"

It was the most natural thing in the world to say, and he said it without any noticeable inflexion of the voice, only it happened to express the youth's emotions at the moment with an utterance that was symbolic of the situation and of his own helplessness as a factor in it. He was alone with Défago in a primitive world: that was all. The canoe, another symbol of man's ascendancy, was now to be left behind. Those small yellow patches, made on the trees by the axe, were the only indications of its hiding place.

Meanwhile, shouldering the packs between them, each man carrying his own rifle, they followed the slender trail over rocks and fallen trunks and across half-frozen swamps; skirting numerous lakes that fairly gemmed the forest, their borders fringed with mist; and towards five o'clock found themselves suddenly on the edge of the woods, looking out across a large sheet of water in front of them, dotted with pine-clad islands of all describable shapes and sizes.

"Fifty Island Water," announced Défago wearily, "and the sun jest goin' to dip his bald old head into it!" he added, with unconscious poetry; and immediately they set about pitching camp for the night.

In a very few minutes, under those skillful hands that never made a movement too much or a movement too little, the silk tent stood taut and cozy, the beds of balsam boughs ready laid, and a brisk cooking fire burned with the minimum of smoke. While the young Scotchman cleaned the fish they had caught trolling behind the canoe, Défago "guessed" he would "jest as soon" take a turn through the Bush for indications of moose. "May come across a trunk where they bin and rubbed horns," he said, as he moved off, "or feedin' on the last of the maple leaves"—and he was gone.

His small figure melted away like a shadow in the dusk, while Simpson noted with a kind of admiration how easily the forest absorbed him into herself. A few steps, it seemed, and he was no longer visible.

Yet there was little underbrush hereabouts; the trees stood somewhat apart, well-spaced; and in the clearings grew silver birch and maple, spear like and slender, against the immense stems of spruce and hemlock. But for occasional prostrate monsters, and the boulders of grey rock that thrust uncouth shoulders here and there out of the ground, it might well have been a bit of park in the Old Country. Almost, one might have seen in it the hand of man. A little to the right, however, began the great burnt section, miles in extent, proclaiming its real character—brulé, as it is called, where the fires of the previous year had raged for weeks, and the blackened stumps now rose gaunt and ugly, bereft of branches, like gigantic match heads stuck into the ground, savage and desolate beyond words. The perfume of charcoal and rain-soaked ashes still hung faintly about it.

The dusk rapidly deepened; the glades grew dark; the crackling of the fire and the wash of little waves along the rocky lake shore were the only sounds audible. The wind had dropped with the sun, and in all that vast world of branches nothing stirred. Any moment, it seemed, the woodland gods, who are to be worshipped in silence and loneliness, might stretch their mighty and terrific outlines among the trees. In front, through doorways pillared by huge straight stems, lay the stretch of Fifty Island Water, a crescent-shaped lake some fifteen miles from tip to tip, and perhaps five miles across where they were camped. A sky of rose and saffron, more clear than any atmosphere Simpson had ever known, still dropped its pale streaming fires across the waves, where the islands—a hundred, surely, rather than fifty—floated like the fairy barques of some enchanted fleet. Fringed with pines, whose crests fingered most delicately the sky, they almost seemed to move upwards as the light faded—about to weigh anchor and navigate the pathways of the heavens instead of the currents of their native and desolate lake.

And strips of colored cloud, like flaunting pennons, signaled their departure to the stars....

The beauty of the scene was strangely uplifting. Simpson smoked the fish and burnt his fingers into the bargain in his efforts to enjoy it and at the same time tend the frying pan and the fire. Yet, ever at the back of his thoughts, lay that other aspect of the wilderness: the indifference to human life, the merciless spirit of desolation which took no note of man. The sense of his utter loneliness, now that even Défago had gone, came close as he looked about him and listened for the sound of his companion's returning footsteps.

There was pleasure in the sensation, yet with it a perfectly comprehensible alarm. And instinctively the thought stirred in him: "What should I—could I, do—if anything happened and he did not come back—?"

They enjoyed their well-earned supper, eating untold quantities of fish, and drinking unmilked tea strong enough to kill men who had not covered thirty miles of hard "going," eating little on the way. And when it was over, they smoked and told stories round the blazing fire, laughing, stretching weary limbs, and discussing plans for the morrow. Défago was in excellent spirits, though disappointed at having no signs of moose to report. But it was dark, and he had not gone far. The brulé, too, was bad. His clothes and hands were smeared with charcoal. Simpson, watching him, realized with renewed vividness their position—alone together in the wilderness.

"Défago," he said presently, "these woods, you know, are a bit too big to feel quite at home in—to feel comfortable in, I mean!... Eh?" He merely gave expression to the mood of the moment; he was hardly prepared for the earnestness, the solemnity even, with which the guide took him up.

"You've hit it right, Simpson, boss," he replied, fixing his searching brown eyes on his face, "and that's the truth, sure. There's no end to 'em—no end at all." Then he added in a lowered tone as if to himself, "There's lots found out that, and gone plumb to pieces!"

But the man's gravity of manner was not quite to the other's liking; it was a little too suggestive for this scenery and setting; he was sorry he had broached the subject. He remembered suddenly how his uncle had told him that men were sometimes stricken with a strange fever of the wilderness, when the seduction of the uninhabited wastes caught them so fiercely that they went forth, half fascinated, half deluded, to their death. And he had a shrewd idea that his companion held something in sympathy with that queer type. He led the conversation on to other topics, on to Hank and the doctor, for instance, and the natural rivalry as to who should get the first sight of moose.

"If they went doo west," observed Défago carelessly, "there's sixty miles between us now—with ole Punk at halfway house eatin' himself full to bustin' with fish and coffee." They laughed together over the picture. But the casual mention of those sixty miles again made Simpson realize the prodigious scale of this land where they hunted; sixty miles was a mere step; two hundred little more than a step. Stories of lost hunters rose persistently before his memory. The passion and mystery of homeless and wandering men, seduced by the beauty of great forests, swept his soul in a way too vivid to be quite pleasant. He wondered vaguely whether it was the mood of his companion that invited the unwelcome suggestion with such persistence.

"Sing us a song, Défago, if you're not too tired," he asked; "one of those old voyageur songs you sang the other night." He handed his tobacco pouch to the guide and then filled his own pipe, while the Canadian, nothing loth, sent his light voice across the lake in one of those plaintive, almost melancholy chanties with which lumbermen and trappers lessen the burden of their labor. There was an appealing and romantic flavor about it, something that recalled the atmosphere of the old pioneer days when Indians and wilderness were leagued together, battles frequent, and the Old Country farther off than it is today. The sound traveled pleasantly over the water, but the forest at their backs seemed to swallow it down with a single gulp that permitted neither echo nor resonance.

It was in the middle of the third verse that Simpson noticed something unusual—something that brought his thoughts back with a rush from faraway scenes. A curious change had come into the man's voice. Even before he knew what it was, uneasiness caught him, and looking up quickly, he saw that Défago, though still singing, was peering about him into the Bush, as though he heard or saw something. His voice grew fainter—dropped to a hush—then ceased altogether. The same instant, with a movement amazingly alert, he started to his feet and stood upright—sniffing the air. Like a dog scenting game, he drew the air into his nostrils in short, sharp breaths, turning quickly as he did so in all directions, and finally "pointing" down the lake shore, eastwards. It was a performance unpleasantly suggestive and at the same time singularly dramatic. Simpson's heart fluttered disagreeably as he watched it.

"Lord, man! How you made me jump!" he exclaimed, on his feet beside him the same instant, and peering over his shoulder into the sea of darkness. "What's up? Are you frightened—?"

Even before the question was out of his mouth he knew it was foolish, for any man with a pair of eyes in his head could see that the Canadian had turned white down to his very gills. Not even sunburn and the glare of the fire could hide that.

The student felt himself trembling a little, weakish in the knees. "What's up?" he repeated quickly. "D'you smell moose? Or anything queer, anything—wrong?" He lowered his voice instinctively.

The forest pressed round them with its encircling wall; the nearer tree stems gleamed like bronze in the firelight; beyond that—blackness, and, so far as he could tell, a silence of death. Just behind them a passing puff of wind lifted a single leaf, looked at it, then laid it softly down again without disturbing the rest of the covey. It seemed as if a million invisible causes had combined just to produce that single visible effect. Other life pulsed about them—and was gone.

Défago turned abruptly; the livid hue of his face had turned to a dirty grey.

"I never said I heered—or smelt—nuthin'," he said slowly and emphatically, in an oddly altered voice that conveyed somehow a touch of defiance. "I was only—takin' a look round—so to speak. It's always a mistake to be too previous with yer questions." Then he added suddenly with obvious effort, in his more natural voice, "Have you got the matches, Boss Simpson?" and proceeded to light the pipe he had half-filled just before he began to sing.

Without speaking another word they sat down again by the fire. Défago changing his side so that he could face the direction the wind came from. For even a tenderfoot could tell that. Défago changed his position in order to hear and smell—all there was to be heard and smelt. And, since he now faced the lake with his back to the trees it was evidently nothing in the forest that had sent so strange and sudden a warning to his marvelously trained nerves.

"Guess now I don't feel like singing any," he explained presently of his own accord. "That song kinder brings back memories that's troublesome to me; I never oughter've begun it. It sets me on t' imagining things, see?"

Clearly the man was still fighting with some profoundly moving emotion. He wished to excuse himself in the eyes of the other. But the explanation, in that it was only a part of the truth, was a lie, and he knew perfectly well that Simpson was not deceived by it. For nothing could explain away the livid terror that had dropped over his face while he stood there sniffing the air. And nothing—no amount of blazing fire, or chatting on ordinary subjects—could make that camp exactly as it had been before. The shadow of an unknown horror, naked if unguessed, that had flashed for an instant in the face and gestures of the guide, had also communicated itself, vaguely and therefore more potently, to his companion. The guide's visible efforts to dissemble the truth only made things worse. Moreover, to add to the younger man's uneasiness, was the difficulty, nay, the impossibility he felt of asking questions, and also his complete ignorance as to the cause ...Indians, wild animals, forest fires—all these, he knew, were wholly out of the question. His imagination searched vigorously, but in vain....

Yet, somehow or other, after another long spell of smoking, talking and roasting themselves before the great fire, the shadow that had so suddenly invaded their peaceful camp began to shift. Perhaps Défago's efforts, or the return of his quiet and normal attitude accomplished this; perhaps Simpson himself had exaggerated the affair out of all proportion to the truth; or possibly the vigorous air of the wilderness brought its own powers of healing. Whatever the cause, the feeling of immediate horror seemed to have passed away as mysteriously as it had come, for nothing occurred to feed it. Simpson began to feel that he had permitted himself the unreasoning terror of a child. He put it down partly to a certain subconscious excitement that this wild and immense scenery generated in his blood, partly to the spell of solitude, and partly to over fatigue. That pallor in the guide's face was, of course, uncommonly hard to explain, yet it might have been due in some way to an effect of firelight, or his own imagination ...He gave it the benefit of the doubt; he was Scotch.

When a somewhat unordinary emotion has disappeared, the mind always finds a dozen ways of explaining away its causes ...Simpson lit a last pipe and tried to laugh to himself. On getting home to Scotland it would make quite a good story. He did not realize that this laughter was a sign that terror still lurked in the recesses of his soul—that, in fact, it was merely one of the conventional signs by which a man, seriously alarmed, tries to persuade himself that he is not so.

Défago, however, heard that low laughter and looked up with surprise on his face. The two men stood, side by side, kicking the embers about before going to bed. It was ten o'clock—a late hour for hunters to be still awake.

"What's ticklin' yer?" he asked in his ordinary tone, yet gravely.

"I—I was thinking of our little toy woods at home, just at that moment," stammered Simpson, coming back to what really dominated his mind, and startled by the question, "and comparing them to—to all this," and he swept his arm round to indicate the Bush.

A pause followed in which neither of them said anything.

"All the same I wouldn't laugh about it, if I was you," Défago added, looking over Simpson's shoulder into the shadows. "There's places in there nobody won't never see into—nobody knows what lives in there either."

"Too big—too far off?" The suggestion in the guide's manner was immense and horrible.

Défago nodded. The expression on his face was dark. He, too, felt uneasy. The younger man understood that in a hinterland of this size there might well be depths of wood that would never in the life of the world be known or trodden. The thought was not exactly the sort he welcomed. In a loud voice, cheerfully, he suggested that it was time for bed. But the guide lingered, tinkering with the fire, arranging the stones needlessly, doing a dozen things that did not really need doing. Evidently there was something he wanted to say, yet found it difficult to "get at."

"Say, you, Boss Simpson," he began suddenly, as the last shower of sparks went up into the air, "you don't—smell nothing, do you—nothing pertickler, I mean?" The commonplace question, Simpson realized, veiled a dreadfully serious thought in his mind. A shiver ran down his back.

"Nothing but burning wood," he replied firmly, kicking again at the embers. The sound of his own foot made him start.

"And all the evenin' you ain't smelt—nothing?" persisted the guide, peering at him through the gloom; "nothing extrordiny, and different to anything else you ever smelt before?"

"No, no, man; nothing at all!" he replied aggressively, half angrily.

Défago's face cleared. "That's good!" he exclaimed with evident relief. "That's good to hear."

"Have you?" asked Simpson sharply, and the same instant regretted the question.

The Canadian came closer in the darkness. He shook his head. "I guess not," he said, though without overwhelming conviction. "It must've been just that song of mine that did it. It's the song they sing in lumber camps and godforsaken places like that, when they're skeered the Wendigo's somewhere around, doin' a bit of swift traveling."

"And what's the Wendigo, pray?" Simpson asked quickly, irritated because again he could not prevent that sudden shiver of the nerves. He knew that he was close upon the man's terror and the cause of it. Yet a rushing passionate curiosity overcame his better judgment, and his fear.

Défago turned swiftly and looked at him as though he were suddenly about to shriek. His eyes shone, but his mouth was wide open. Yet all he said, or whispered rather, for his voice sank very low, was: "It's nuthin'—nuthin' but what those lousy fellers believe when they've bin hittin' the bottle too long—a sort of great animal that lives up yonder," he jerked his head northwards, "quick as lightning in its tracks, an' bigger'n anything else in the Bush, an' ain't supposed to be very good to look at—that's all!"

"A backwoods superstition—" began Simpson, moving hastily toward the tent in order to shake off the hand of the guide that clutched his arm. "Come, come, hurry up for God's sake, and get the lantern going! It's time we were in bed and asleep if we're going to be up with the sun tomorrow...."

The guide was close on his heels. "I'm coming," he answered out of the darkness, "I'm coming." And after a slight delay he appeared with the lantern and hung it from a nail in the front pole of the tent. The shadows of a hundred trees shifted their places quickly as he did so, and when he stumbled over the rope, diving swiftly inside, the whole tent trembled as though a gust of wind struck it.

The two men lay down, without undressing, upon their beds of soft balsam boughs, cunningly arranged. Inside, all was warm and cozy, but outside the world of crowding trees pressed close about them, marshalling their million shadows, and smothering the little tent that stood there like a wee white shell facing the ocean of tremendous forest.

Between the two lonely figures within, however, there pressed another shadow that was not a shadow from the night. It was the Shadow cast by the strange Fear, never wholly exorcised, that had leaped suddenly upon Défago in the middle of his singing. And Simpson, as he lay there, watching the darkness through the open flap of the tent, ready to plunge into the fragrant abyss of sleep, knew first that unique and profound stillness of a primeval forest when no wind stirs ... and when the night has weight and substance that enters into the soul to bind a veil about it.... Then sleep took him....

III

THUS, IT SEEMED TO HIM, at least. Yet it was true that the lap of the water, just beyond the tent door, still beat time with his lessening pulses when he realized that he was lying with his eyes open and that another sound had recently introduced itself with cunning softness between the splash and murmur of the little waves.

And, long before he understood what this sound was, it had stirred in him the centers of pity and alarm. He listened intently, though at first in vain, for the running blood beat all its drums too noisily in his ears. Did it come, he wondered, from the lake, or from the woods?...

Then, suddenly, with a rush and a flutter of the heart, he knew that it was close beside him in the tent; and, when he turned over for a better hearing, it focused itself unmistakably not two feet away. It was a sound of weeping; Défago upon his bed of branches was sobbing in the darkness as though his heart would break, the blankets evidently stuffed against his mouth to stifle it.

And his first feeling, before he could think or reflect, was the rush of a poignant and searching tenderness. This intimate, human sound, heard amid the desolation about them, woke pity. It was so incongruous, so pitifully incongruous—and so vain! Tears—in this vast and cruel wilderness: of what avail? He thought of a little child crying in mid-Atlantic.... Then, of course, with fuller realization, and the memory of what had gone before, came the descent of the terror upon him, and his blood ran cold.

"Défago," he whispered quickly, "what's the matter?" He tried to make his voice very gentle. "Are you in pain—unhappy—?" There was no reply, but the sounds ceased abruptly. He stretched his hand out and touched him. The body did not stir.

"Are you awake?" for it occurred to him that the man was crying in his sleep. "Are you cold?" He noticed that his feet, which were uncovered, projected beyond the mouth of the tent. He spread an extra fold of his own blankets over them. The guide had slipped down in his bed, and the branches seemed to have been dragged with him. He was afraid to pull the body back again, for fear of waking him.

One or two tentative questions he ventured softly, but though he waited for several minutes there came no reply, nor any sign of movement. Presently he heard his regular and quiet breathing, and putting his hand again gently on the breast, felt the steady rise and fall beneath.

"Let me know if anything's wrong," he whispered, "or if I can do anything. Wake me at once if you feel—queer."

He hardly knew what to say. He lay down again, thinking and wondering what it all meant. Défago, of course, had been crying in his sleep. Some dream or other had afflicted him. Yet never in his life would he forget that pitiful sound of sobbing, and the feeling that the whole awful wilderness of woods listened....

His own mind busied itself for a long time with the recent events, of which this took its mysterious place as one, and though his reason successfully argued away all unwelcome suggestions, a sensation of uneasiness remained, resisting ejection, very deep-seated—peculiar beyond ordinary.

IV

BUT SLEEP, IN THE LONG RUN, proves greater than all emotions. His thoughts soon wandered again; he lay there, warm as toast, exceedingly weary; the night soothed and comforted, blunting the edges of memory and alarm. Half an hour later he was oblivious of everything in the outer world about him.

Yet sleep, in this case, was his great enemy, concealing all approaches, smothering the warning of his nerves.

As, sometimes, in a nightmare events crowd upon each other's heels with a conviction of dreadfulest reality, yet some inconsistent detail accuses the whole display of incompleteness and disguise, so the events that now followed, though they actually happened, persuaded the mind somehow that the detail which could explain them had been overlooked in the confusion, and that therefore they were but partly true, the rest delusion. At the back of the sleeper's mind something remains awake, ready to let slip the judgment. "All this is not quite real; when you wake up you'll understand."

And thus, in a way, it was with Simpson. The events, not wholly inexplicable or incredible in themselves, yet remain for the man who saw and heard them a sequence of separate facts of cold horror, because the little piece that might have made the puzzle clear lay concealed or overlooked.

So far as he can recall, it was a violent movement, running downwards through the tent towards the door, that first woke him and made him aware that his companion was sitting bolt upright beside him—quivering. Hours must have passed, for it was the pale gleam of the dawn that revealed his outline against the canvas. This time the man was not crying; he was quaking like a leaf; the trembling he felt plainly through the blankets down the entire length of his own body. Défago had huddled down against him for protection, shrinking away from something that apparently concealed itself near the door flaps of the little tent.

Simpson thereupon called out in a loud voice some question or other—in the first bewilderment of waking he does not remember exactly what—and the man made no reply. The atmosphere and feeling of true nightmare lay horribly about him, making movement and speech both difficult. At first, indeed, he was not sure where he was—whether in one of the earlier camps, or at home in his bed at Aberdeen. The sense of confusion was very troubling.

And next—almost simultaneous with his waking, it seemed—the profound stillness of the dawn outside was shattered by a most uncommon sound. It came without warning, or audible approach; and it was unspeakably dreadful. It was a voice, Simpson declares, possibly a human voice; hoarse yet plaintive—a soft, roaring voice close outside the tent, overhead rather than upon the ground, of immense volume, while in some strange way most penetratingly and seductively sweet. It rang out, too, in three separate and distinct notes, or cries, that bore in some odd fashion a resemblance, farfetched yet recognizable, to the name of the guide: "Dé-fa-go!"

The student admits he is unable to describe it quite intelligently, for it was unlike any sound he had ever heard in his life, and combined a blending of such contrary qualities. "A sort of windy, crying voice," he calls it, "as of something lonely and untamed, wild and of abominable power...."

And, even before it ceased, dropping back into the great gulfs of silence, the guide beside him had sprung to his feet with an answering though unintelligible cry. He blundered against the tent pole with violence, shaking the whole structure, spreading his arms out frantically for more room, and kicking his legs impetuously free of the clinging blankets. For a second, perhaps two, he stood upright by the door, his outline dark against the pallor of the dawn; then, with a furious, rushing speed, before his companion could move a hand to stop him, he shot with a plunge through the flaps of canvas—and was gone. And as he went—so astonishingly fast that the voice could actually be heard dying in the distance—he called aloud in tones of anguished terror that at the same time held something strangely like the frenzied exultation of delight—

"Oh! oh! My feet of fire! My burning feet of fire! Oh! oh! This height and fiery speed!"

And then the distance quickly buried it, and the deep silence of very early morning descended upon the forest as before.

It had all come about with such rapidity that, but for the evidence of the empty bed beside him, Simpson could almost have believed it to have been the memory of a nightmare carried over from sleep. He still felt the warm pressure of that vanished body against his side; there lay the twisted blankets in a heap; the very tent yet trembled with the vehemence of the impetuous departure. The strange words rang in his ears, as though he still heard them in the distance—wild language of a suddenly stricken mind. Moreover, it was not only the senses of sight and hearing that reported uncommon things to his brain, for even while the man cried and ran, he had become aware that a strange perfume, faint yet pungent, pervaded the interior of the tent. And it was at this point, it seems, brought to himself by the consciousness that his nostrils were taking this distressing odor down into his throat, that he found his courage, sprang quickly to his feet—and went out.

The grey light of dawn that dropped, cold and glimmering, between the trees revealed the scene tolerably well. There stood the tent behind him, soaked with dew; the dark ashes of the fire, still warm; the lake, white beneath a coating of mist, the islands rising darkly out of it like objects packed in wool; and patches of snow beyond among the clearer spaces of the Bush—everything cold, still, waiting for the sun. But nowhere a sign of the vanished guide—still, doubtless, flying at frantic speed through the frozen woods. There was not even the sound of disappearing footsteps, nor the echoes of the dying voice. He had gone—utterly.

There was nothing; nothing but the sense of his recent presence, so strongly left behind about the camp; and—this penetrating, all-pervading odor.

And even this was now rapidly disappearing in its turn. In spite of his exceeding mental perturbation, Simpson struggled hard to detect its nature, and define it, but the ascertaining of an elusive scent, not recognized subconsciously and at once, is a very subtle operation of the mind. And he failed. It was gone before he could properly seize or name it. Approximate description, even, seems to have been difficult, for it was unlike any smell he knew. Acrid rather, not unlike the odor of a lion, he thinks, yet softer and not wholly unpleasing, with something almost sweet in it that reminded him of the scent of decaying garden leaves, earth, and the myriad, nameless perfumes that make up the odor of a big forest. Yet the "odor of lions" is the phrase with which he usually sums it all up.

Then—it was wholly gone, and he found himself standing by the ashes of the fire in a state of amazement and stupid terror that left him the helpless prey of anything that chose to happen. Had a muskrat poked its pointed muzzle over a rock, or a squirrel scuttled in that instant down the bark of a tree, he would most likely have collapsed without more ado and fainted. For he felt about the whole affair the touch somewhere of a great Outer Horror ... and his scattered powers had not as yet had time to collect themselves into a definite attitude of fighting self-control.

Nothing did happen, however. A great kiss of wind ran softly through the awakening forest, and a few maple leaves here and there rustled tremblingly to earth. The sky seemed to grow suddenly much lighter. Simpson felt the cool air upon his cheek and uncovered head; realized that he was shivering with the cold; and, making a great effort, realized next that he was alone in the Bush— and that he was called upon to take immediate steps to find and succor his vanished companion.

Make an effort, accordingly, he did, though an ill-calculated and futile one. With that wilderness of trees about him, the sheet of water cutting him off behind, and the horror of that wild cry in his blood, he did what any other inexperienced man would have done in similar bewilderment: he ran about, without any sense of direction, like a frantic child, and called loudly without ceasing the name of the guide:

"Défago! Défago! Défago!" he yelled, and the trees gave him back the name as often as he shouted, only a little softened—"Défago! Défago! Défago!"

He followed the trail that lay a short distance across the patches of snow, and then lost it again where the trees grew too thickly for snow to lie. He shouted till he was hoarse, and till the sound of his own voice in all that unanswering and listening world began to frighten him. His confusion increased in direct ratio to the violence of his efforts. His distress became formidably acute, till at length his exertions defeated their own object, and from sheer exhaustion he headed back to the camp again. It remains a wonder that he ever found his way. It was with great difficulty, and only after numberless false clues, that he at last saw the white tent between the trees, and so reached safety.

Exhaustion then applied its own remedy, and he grew calmer. He made the fire and breakfasted. Hot coffee and bacon put a little sense and judgment into him again, and he realized that he had been behaving like a boy. He now made another, and more successful attempt to face the situation collectedly, and, a nature naturally plucky coming to his assistance, he decided that he must first make as thorough a search as possible, failing success in which, he must find his way into the home camp as best he could and bring help.

And this was what he did. Taking food, matches and rifle with him, and a small axe to blaze the trees against his return journey, he set forth. It was eight o'clock when he started, the sun shining over the tops of the trees in a sky without clouds. Pinned to a stake by the fire he left a note in case Défago returned while he was away.

This time, according to a careful plan, he took a new direction, intending to make a wide sweep that must sooner or later cut into indications of the guide's trail; and, before he had gone a quarter of a mile he came across the tracks of a large animal in the snow, and beside it the light and smaller tracks of what were beyond question human feet—the feet of Défago. The relief he at once experienced was natural, though brief; for at first sight he saw in these tracks a simple explanation of the whole matter: these big marks had surely been left by a bull moose that, wind against it, had blundered upon the camp, and uttered its singular cry of warning and alarm the moment its mistake was apparent. Défago, in whom the hunting instinct was developed to the point of uncanny perfection, had scented the brute coming down the wind hours before. His excitement and disappearance were due, of course, to—to his—

Then the impossible explanation at which he grasped faded, as common sense showed him mercilessly that none of this was true. No guide, much less a guide like Défago, could have acted in so irrational a way, going off even without his rifle ...! The whole affair demanded a far more complicated elucidation, when he remembered the details of it all—the cry of terror, the amazing language, the grey face of horror when his nostrils first caught the new odor; that muffled sobbing in the darkness, and—for this, too, now came back to him dimly—the man's original aversion for this particular bit of country....

Besides, now that he examined them closer, these were not the tracks of a bull moose at all! Hank had explained to him the outline of a bull's hoofs, of a cow's or calf's, too, for that matter; he had drawn them clearly on a strip of birch bark. And these were wholly different. They were big, round, ample, and with no pointed outline as of sharp hoofs. He wondered for a moment whether bear tracks were like that. There was no other animal he could think of, for caribou did not come so far south at this season, and, even if they did, would leave hoof marks.

They were ominous signs—these mysterious writings left in the snow by the unknown creature that had lured a human being away from safety—and when he coupled them in his imagination with that haunting sound that broke the stillness of the dawn, a momentary dizziness shook his mind, distressing him again beyond belief. He felt the threatening aspect of it all. And, stooping down to examine the marks more closely, he caught a faint whiff of that sweet yet pungent odor that made him instantly straighten up again, fighting a sensation almost of nausea.

Then his memory played him another evil trick. He suddenly recalled those uncovered feet projecting beyond the edge of the tent, and the body's appearance of having been dragged towards the opening; the man's shrinking from something by the door when he woke later. The details now beat against his trembling mind with concerted attack. They seemed to gather in those deep spaces of the silent forest about him, where the host of trees stood waiting, listening, watching to see what he would do. The woods were closing round him.

With the persistence of true pluck, however, Simpson went forward, following the tracks as best he could, smothering these ugly emotions that sought to weaken his will. He blazed innumerable trees as he went, ever fearful of being unable to find the way back, and calling aloud at intervals of a few seconds the name of the guide. The dull tapping of the axe upon the massive trunks, and the unnatural accents of his own voice became at length sounds that he even dreaded to make, dreaded to hear. For they drew attention without ceasing to his presence and exact whereabouts, and if it were really the case that something was hunting himself down in the same way that he was hunting down another—

With a strong effort, he crushed the thought out the instant it rose. It was the beginning, he realized, of a bewilderment utterly diabolical in kind that would speedily destroy him.

Although the snow was not continuous, lying merely in shallow flurries over the more open spaces, he found no difficulty in following the tracks for the first few miles. They went straight as a ruled line wherever the trees permitted. The stride soon began to increase in length, till it finally assumed proportions that seemed absolutely impossible for any ordinary animal to have made. Like huge flying leaps they became. One of these he measured, and though he knew that "stretch" of eighteen feet must be somehow wrong, he was at a complete loss to understand why he found no signs on the snow between the extreme points. But what perplexed him even more, making him feel his vision had gone utterly awry, was that Défago's stride increased in the same manner, and finally covered the same incredible distances. It looked as if the great beast had lifted him with it and carried him across these astonishing intervals. Simpson, who was much longer in the limb, found that he could not compass even half the stretch by taking a running jump.

And the sight of these huge tracks, running side by side, silent evidence of a dreadful journey in which terror or madness had urged to impossible results, was profoundly moving. It shocked him in the secret depths of his soul. It was the most horrible thing his eyes had ever looked upon. He began to follow them mechanically, absentmindedly almost, ever peering over his shoulder to see if he, too, were being followed by something with a gigantic tread.... And soon it came about that he no longer quite realized what it was they signified—these impressions left upon the snow by something nameless and untamed, always accompanied by the footmarks of the little French Canadian, his guide, his comrade, the man who had shared his tent a few hours before, chatting, laughing, even singing by his side....

V

FOR A MAN OF HIS YEARS AND INEXPERIENCE, only a canny Scot, perhaps, grounded in common sense and established in logic, could have preserved even that measure of balance that this youth somehow or other did manage to preserve through the whole adventure. Otherwise, two things he presently noticed, while forging pluckily ahead, must have sent him headlong back to the comparative safety of his tent, instead of only making his hands close more tightly upon the rifle stock, while his heart, trained for the Wee Kirk, sent a wordless prayer winging its way to heaven. Both tracks, he saw, had undergone a change, and this change, so far as it concerned the footsteps of the man, was in some undecipherable manner—appalling.

It was in the bigger tracks he first noticed this, and for a long time he could not quite believe his eyes. Was it the blown leaves that produced odd effects of light and shade, or that the dry snow, drifting like finely ground rice about the edges, cast shadows and high lights? Or was it actually the fact that the great marks had become faintly colored? For round about the deep, plunging holes of the animal there now appeared a mysterious, reddish tinge that was more like an effect of light than of anything that dyed the substance of the snow itself. Every mark had it, and had it increasingly—this indistinct fiery tinge that painted a new touch of ghastliness into the picture.

But when, wholly unable to explain or to credit it, he turned his attention to the other tracks to discover if they, too, bore similar witness, he noticed that these had meanwhile undergone a change that was infinitely worse, and charged with far more horrible suggestion. For, in the last hundred yards or so, he saw that they had grown gradually into the semblance of the parent tread. Imperceptibly the change had come about, yet unmistakably. It was hard to see where the change first began. The result, however, was beyond question. Smaller, neater, more cleanly modeled, they formed now an exact and careful duplicate of the larger tracks beside them. The feet that produced them had, therefore, also changed. And something in his mind reared up with loathing and with terror as he saw it.

Simpson, for the first time, hesitated; then, ashamed of his alarm and indecision, took a few hurried steps ahead; the next instant stopped dead in his tracks. Immediately in front of him all signs of the trail ceased; both tracks came to an abrupt end. On all sides, for a hundred yards and more, he searched in vain for the least indication of their continuance. There was—nothing.

The trees were very thick just there, big trees all of them, spruce, cedar, hemlock; there was no underbrush. He stood, looking about him, all distraught; bereft of any power of judgment. Then he set to work to search again, and again, and yet again, but always with the same result: nothing. The feet that printed the surface of the snow thus far had now, apparently, left the ground!

And it was in that moment of distress and confusion that the whip of terror laid its most nicely calculated lash about his heart. It dropped with deadly effect upon the sorest spot of all, completely unnerving him. He had been secretly dreading all the time that it would come—and come it did.

Far overhead, muted by great height and distance, strangely thinned and wailing, he heard the crying voice of Défago, the guide.

The sound dropped upon him out of that still, wintry sky with an effect of dismay and terror unsurpassed. The rifle fell to his feet. He stood motionless an instant, listening as it were with his whole body, then staggered back against the nearest tree for support, disorganized hopelessly in mind and spirit. To him, in that moment, it seemed the most shattering and dislocating experience he had ever known, so that his heart emptied itself of all feeling whatsoever as by a sudden draught.

"Oh! oh! This fiery height! Oh, my feet of fire! My burning feet of fire ...!" ran in far, beseeching accents of indescribable appeal this voice of anguish down the sky. Once it called—then silence through all the listening wilderness of trees.

And Simpson, scarcely knowing what he did, presently found himself running wildly to and fro, searching, calling, tripping over roots and boulders, and flinging himself in a frenzy of undirected pursuit after the Caller. Behind the screen of memory and emotion with which experience veils events, he plunged, distracted and half-deranged, picking up false lights like a ship at sea, terror in his eyes and heart and soul. For the Panic of the Wilderness had called to him in that far voice—the Power of untamed Distance— the Enticement of the Desolation that destroys. He knew in that moment all the pains of someone hopelessly and irretrievably lost, suffering the lust and travail of a soul in the final Loneliness. A vision of Défago, eternally hunted, driven and pursued across the sky-like vastness of those ancient forests fled like a flame across the dark ruin of his thoughts ...

It seemed ages before he could find anything in the chaos of his disorganized sensations to which he could anchor himself steady for a moment, and think ...

The cry was not repeated; his own hoarse calling brought no response; the inscrutable forces of the Wild had summoned their victim beyond recall—and held him fast.

Yet he searched and called, it seems, for hours afterwards, for it was late in the afternoon when at length he decided to abandon a useless pursuit and return to his camp on the shores of Fifty Island Water. Even then he went with reluctance, that crying voice still echoing in his ears. With difficulty he found his rifle and the homeward trail. The concentration necessary to follow the badly blazed trees, and a biting hunger that gnawed, helped to keep his mind steady. Otherwise, he admits, the temporary aberration he had suffered might have been prolonged to the point of positive disaster. Gradually the ballast shifted back again, and he regained something that approached his normal equilibrium.

But for all that the journey through the gathering dusk was miserably haunted. He heard innumerable following footsteps; voices that laughed and whispered; and saw figures crouching behind trees and boulders, making signs to one another for a concerted attack the moment he had passed. The creeping murmur of the wind made him start and listen. He went stealthily, trying to hide where possible, and making as little sound as he could. The shadows of the woods, hitherto protective or covering merely, had now become menacing, challenging; and the pageantry in his frightened mind masked a host of possibilities that were all the more ominous for being obscure. The presentiment of a nameless doom lurked ill-concealed behind every detail of what had happened.

It was really admirable how he emerged victor in the end; men of riper powers and experience might have come through the ordeal with less success. He had himself tolerably well in hand, all things considered, and his plan of action proves it. Sleep being absolutely out of the question and traveling an unknown trail in the darkness equally impracticable, he sat up the whole of that night, rifle in hand, before a fire he never for a single moment allowed to die down. The severity of the haunted vigil marked his soul for life; but it was successfully accomplished; and with the very first signs of dawn he set forth upon the long return journey to the home camp to get help. As before, he left a written note to explain his absence, and to indicate where he had left a plentiful cache of food and matches—though he had no expectation that any human hands would find them!

How Simpson found his way alone by the lake and forest might well make a story in itself, for to hear him tell it is to know the passionate loneliness of soul that a man can feel when the Wilderness holds him in the hollow of its illimitable hand—and laughs. It is also to admire his indomitable pluck.

He claims no skill, declaring that he followed the almost invisible trail mechanically, and without thinking. And this, doubtless, is the truth. He relied upon the guiding of the unconscious mind, which is instinct. Perhaps, too, some sense of orientation, known to animals and primitive men, may have helped as well, for through all that tangled region he succeeded in reaching the exact spot where Défago had hidden the canoe nearly three days before with the remark, "Strike doo west across the lake into the sun to find the camp."

There was not much sun left to guide him, but he used his compass to the best of his ability, embarking in the frail craft for the last twelve miles of his journey with a sensation of immense relief that the forest was at last behind him. And, fortunately, the water was calm; he took his line across the center of the lake instead of coasting round the shores for another twenty miles. Fortunately, too, the other hunters were back. The light of their fires furnished a steering point without which he might have searched all night long for the actual position of the camp.

It was close upon midnight all the same when his canoe grated on the sandy cove, and Hank, Punk and his uncle, disturbed in their sleep by his cries, ran quickly down and helped a very exhausted and broken specimen of Scotch humanity over the rocks toward a dying fire.

VI

THE SUDDEN ENTRANCE OF HIS PROSAIC UNCLE into this world of wizardry and horror that had haunted him without interruption now for two days and two nights, had the immediate effect of giving to the affair an entirely new aspect. The sound of that crisp "Hulloa, my boy! And what's up now?" and the grasp of that dry and vigorous hand introduced another standard of judgment. A revulsion of feeling washed through him. He realized that he had let himself "go" rather badly. He even felt vaguely ashamed of himself. The native hard-headedness of his race reclaimed him.

And this doubtless explains why he found it so hard to tell that group round the fire—everything. He told enough, however, for the immediate decision to be arrived at that a relief party must start at the earliest possible moment, and that Simpson, in order to guide it capably, must first have food and, above all, sleep. Dr. Cathcart observing the lad's condition more shrewdly than his patient knew, gave him a very slight injection of morphine. For six hours he slept like the dead.

From the description carefully written out afterwards by this student of divinity, it appears that the account he gave to the astonished group omitted sundry vital and important details. He declares that, with his uncle's wholesome, matter-of-fact countenance staring him in the face, he simply had not the courage to mention them. Thus, all the search party gathered, it would seem, was that Défago had suffered in the night an acute and inexplicable attack of mania, had imagined himself "called" by someone or something, and had plunged into the bush after it without food or rifle, where he must die a horrible and lingering death by cold and starvation unless he could be found and rescued in time. "In time," moreover, meant at once.

In the course of the following day, however—they were off by seven, leaving Punk in charge with instructions to have food and fire always ready—Simpson found it possible to tell his uncle a good deal more of the story's true inwardness, without divining that it was drawn out of him as a matter of fact by a very subtle form of cross examination. By the time they reached the beginning of the trail, where the canoe was laid up against the return journey, he had mentioned how Défago spoke vaguely of "something he called a 'Wendigo'"; how he cried in his sleep; how he imagined an unusual scent about the camp; and had betrayed other symptoms of mental excitement. He also admitted the bewildering effect of "that extraordinary odor" upon himself, "pungent and acrid like the odor of lions." And by the time they were within an easy hour of Fifty Island Water he had let slip the further fact—a foolish avowal of his own hysterical condition, as he felt afterwards—that he had heard the vanished guide call "for help." He omitted the singular phrases used, for he simply could not bring himself to repeat the preposterous language. Also, while describing how the man's footsteps in the snow had gradually assumed an exact miniature likeness of the animal's plunging tracks, he left out the fact that they measured a wholly incredible distance. It seemed a question, nicely balanced between individual pride and honesty, what he should reveal and what suppress. He mentioned the fiery tinge in the snow, for instance, yet shrank from telling that body and bed had been partly dragged out of the tent....

With the net result that Dr. Cathcart, adroit psychologist that he fancied himself to be, had assured him clearly enough exactly where his mind, influenced by loneliness, bewilderment and terror, had yielded to the strain and invited delusion. While praising his conduct, he managed at the same time to point out where, when, and how his mind had gone astray. He made his nephew think himself finer than he was by judicious praise, yet more foolish than he was by minimizing the value of the evidence. Like many another materialist, that is, he lied cleverly on the basis of insufficient knowledge, because the knowledge supplied seemed to his own particular intelligence inadmissible.

"The spell of these terrible solitudes," he said, "cannot leave any mind untouched, any mind, that is, possessed of the higher imaginative qualities. It has worked upon yours exactly as it worked upon my own when I was your age. The animal that haunted your little camp was undoubtedly a moose, for the 'belling' of a moose may have, sometimes, a very peculiar quality of sound. The colored appearance of the big tracks was obviously a defect of vision in your own eyes produced by excitement. The size and stretch of the tracks we shall prove when we come to them. But the hallucination of an audible voice, of course, is one of the commonest forms of delusion due to mental excitement—an excitement, my dear boy, perfectly excusable, and, let me add, wonderfully controlled by you under the circumstances. For the rest, I am bound to say, you have acted with a splendid courage, for the terror of feeling oneself lost in this wilderness is nothing short of awful, and, had I been in your place, I don't for a moment believe I could have behaved with one quarter of your wisdom and decision. The only thing I find it uncommonly difficult to explain is—that—damned odor."

"It made me feel sick, I assure you," declared his nephew, "positively dizzy!" His uncle's attitude of calm omniscience, merely because he knew more psychological formulae, made him slightly defiant. It was so easy to be wise in the explanation of an experience one has not personally witnessed. "A kind of desolate and terrible odor is the only way I can describe it," he concluded, glancing at the features of the quiet, unemotional man beside him.

"I can only marvel," was the reply, "that under the circumstances it did not seem to you even worse." The dry words, Simpson knew, hovered between the truth, and his uncle's interpretation of "the truth."

And so at last they came to the little camp and found the tent still standing, the remains of the fire, and the piece of paper pinned to a stake beside it—untouched. The cache, poorly contrived by inexperienced hands, however, had been discovered and opened—by musk rats, mink and squirrel. The matches lay scattered about the opening, but the food had been taken to the last crumb.

"Well, fellers, he ain't here," exclaimed Hank loudly after his fashion. "And that's as sartain as the coal supply down below! But whar he's got to by this time is 'bout as unsartain as the trade in crowns in t'other place." The presence of a divinity student was no barrier to his language at such a time, though for the reader's sake it may be severely edited. "I propose," he added, "that we start out at once an' hunt for'm like hell!"

The gloom of Défago's probable fate oppressed the whole party with a sense of dreadful gravity the moment they saw the familiar signs of recent occupancy. Especially the tent, with the bed of balsam branches still smoothed and flattened by the pressure of his body, seemed to bring his presence near to them. Simpson, feeling vaguely as if his world were somehow at stake, went about explaining particulars in a hushed tone. He was much calmer now, though over-wearied with the strain of his many journeys. His uncle's method of explaining—"explaining away," rather—the details still fresh in his haunted memory helped, too, to put ice upon his emotions.

"And that's the direction he ran off in," he said to his two companions, pointing in the direction where the guide had vanished that morning in the grey dawn. "Straight down there he ran like a deer, in between the birch and the hemlock...."[23]

Hank and Dr. Cathcart exchanged glances.

"And it was about two miles down there, in a straight line," continued the other, speaking with something of the former terror in his voice, "that I followed his trail to the place where—it stopped—dead!"

"And where you heered him callin' an' caught the stench, an' all the rest of the wicked entertainment," cried Hank, with a volubility that betrayed his keen distress.

"And where your excitement overcame you to the point of producing illusions," added Dr. Cathcart under his breath, yet not so low that his nephew did not hear it.

It was early in the afternoon, for they had traveled quickly, and there were still a good two hours of daylight left. Dr. Cathcart and Hank lost no time in beginning the search, but Simpson was too exhausted to accompany them. They would follow the blazed marks on the trees, and where possible, his footsteps. Meanwhile the best thing he could do was to keep a good fire going, and rest.

But after something like three hours' search, the darkness already down, the two men returned to camp with nothing to report. Fresh snow had covered all signs, and though they had followed the blazed trees to the spot where Simpson had turned back, they had not discovered the smallest indication of a human being—or for that matter, of an animal. There were no fresh tracks of any kind; the snow lay undisturbed.

It was difficult to know what was best to do, though in reality there was nothing more they could do. They might stay and search for weeks without much chance of success. The fresh snow destroyed their only hope, and they gathered round the fire for supper, a gloomy and despondent party. The facts, indeed, were sad enough, for Défago had a wife at Rat Portage, and his earnings were the family's sole means of support.

Now that the whole truth in all its ugliness was out, it seemed useless to deal in further disguise or pretense. They talked openly of the facts and probabilities. It was not the first time, even in the experience of Dr. Cathcart, that a man had yielded to the singular seduction of the Solitudes and gone out of his mind; Défago, moreover, was predisposed to something of the sort, for he already had

___

23 Blackwood's repeated use of the word hemlock, with its witchcraft and black magic connotations, creates a cadence of creeping suspense.

a touch of melancholia in his blood, and his fiber was weakened by bouts of drinking that often lasted for weeks at a time. Something on this trip—one might never know precisely what—had sufficed to push him over the line, that was all. And he had gone, gone off into the great wilderness of trees and lakes to die by starvation and exhaustion. The chances against his finding camp again were overwhelming; the delirium that was upon him would also doubtless have increased, and it was quite likely he might do violence to himself and so hasten his cruel fate. Even while they talked, indeed, the end had probably come. On the suggestion of Hank, his old pal, however, they proposed to wait a little longer and devote the whole of the following day, from dawn to darkness, to the most systematic search they could devise. They would divide the territory between them. They discussed their plan in great detail. All that men could do they would do. And, meanwhile, they talked about the particular form in which the singular Panic of the Wilderness had made its attack upon the mind of the unfortunate guide. Hank, though familiar with the legend in its general outline, obviously did not welcome the turn the conversation had taken. He contributed little, though that little was illuminating. For he admitted that a story ran over all this section of country to the effect that several Indians had "seen the Wendigo" along the shores of Fifty Island Water in the "fall" of last year, and that this was the true reason of Défago's disinclination to hunt there. Hank doubtless felt that he had in a sense helped his old pal to death by over persuading him. "When an Indian goes crazy," he explained, talking to himself more than to the others, it seemed, "it's always put that he's 'seen the Wendigo.' An' pore old Défaygo was superstitious down to his heels!"

And then Simpson, feeling the atmosphere more sympathetic, told over again the full story of his astonishing tale; he left out no details this time; he mentioned his own sensations and gripping fears. He only omitted the strange language used.

"But Défago surely had already told you all these details of the Wendigo legend, my dear fellow," insisted the doctor. "I mean, he had talked about it, and thus put into your mind the ideas which your own excitement afterwards developed?"

Whereupon Simpson again repeated the facts. Défago, he declared, had barely mentioned the beast. He, Simpson, knew nothing of the story, and, so far as he remembered, had never even read about it. Even the word was unfamiliar.

Of course he was telling the truth, and Dr. Cathcart was reluctantly compelled to admit the singular character of the whole affair. He did not do this in words so much as in manner, however. He kept his back against a good, stout tree; he poked the fire into a blaze the moment it showed signs of dying down; he was quicker than any of them to notice the least sound in the night about them—a fish jumping in the lake, a twig snapping in the bush, the dropping of occasional fragments of frozen snow from the branches overhead where the heat loosened them. His voice, too, changed a little in quality, becoming a shade less confident, lower also in tone.

Fear, to put it plainly, hovered close about that little camp, and though all three would have been glad to speak of other matters, the only thing they seemed able to discuss was this—the source of their fear. They tried other subjects in vain; there was nothing to say about them. Hank was the most honest of the group; he said next to nothing. He never once, however, turned his back to the darkness. His face was always to the forest, and when wood was needed he didn't go farther than was necessary to get it.

VII

A WALL OF SILENCE WRAPPED THEM IN, for the snow, though not thick, was sufficient to deaden any noise, and the frost held things pretty tight besides. No sound but their voices and the soft roar of the flames made itself heard. Only, from time to time, something soft as the flutter of a pine moth's wings went past them through the air. No one seemed anxious to go to bed. The hours slipped towards midnight.

"The legend is picturesque enough," observed the doctor after one of the longer pauses, speaking to break it rather than because he had anything to say, "for the Wendigo is simply the Call of the Wild personified, which some natures hear to their own destruction."

"That's about it," Hank said presently. "An' there's no misunderstandin' when you hear it. It calls you by name right 'nough."

Another pause followed. Then Dr. Cathcart came back to the forbidden subject with a rush that made the others jump.

"The allegory is significant," he remarked, looking about him into the darkness, "for the Voice, they say, resembles all the minor sounds of the Bush—wind, falling water, cries of the animals, and so forth. And, once the victim hears that—he's off for good, of course! His most vulnerable points, moreover, are said to be the feet and the eyes; the feet, you see, for the lust of wandering, and the eyes for the lust of beauty. The poor beggar goes at such a dreadful speed that he bleeds beneath the eyes, and his feet burn."

Dr. Cathcart, as he spoke, continued to peer uneasily into the surrounding gloom. His voice sank to a hushed tone.

"The Wendigo," he added, "is said to burn his feet—owing to the friction, apparently caused by its tremendous velocity—till they drop off, and new ones form exactly like its own."

Simpson listened in horrified amazement; but it was the pallor on Hank's face that fascinated him most. He would willingly have stopped his ears and closed his eyes, had he dared.

"It don't always keep to the ground neither," came in Hank's slow, heavy drawl, "for it goes so high that he thinks the stars have set him all a-fire. An' it'll take great thumpin' jumps sometimes, an' run along the tops of the trees, carrying its partner with it, an' then droppin' him jest as a fish hawk'll drop a pickerel to kill it before eatin'. An' its food, of all the muck in the whole Bush is— moss!" And he laughed a short, unnatural laugh. "It's a moss-eater, is the Wendigo," he added, looking up excitedly into the faces of his companions. "Moss-eater," he repeated, with a string of the most outlandish oaths he could invent.

But Simpson now understood the true purpose of all this talk. What these two men, each strong and "experienced" in his own way, dreaded more than anything else was—silence. They were talking against time. They were also talking against darkness, against the invasion of panic, against the admission reflection might bring that they were in an enemy's country—against anything, in fact, rather than allow their inmost thoughts to assume control. He himself, already initiated by the awful vigil with terror, was beyond both of them in this respect. He had reached the stage where he was immune. But these two, the scoffing, analytical doctor, and the honest, dogged backwoodsman, each sat trembling in the depths of his being. Thus the hours passed; and thus, with lowered voices and a kind of taut inner resistance of spirit, this little group of humanity sat in the jaws of the wilderness and talked foolishly of the terrible and haunting legend. It was an unequal contest, all things considered, for the wilderness had already the advantage of first attack—and of a hostage. The fate of their comrade hung over them with a steadily increasing weight of oppression that finally became insupportable.

It was Hank, after a pause longer than the preceding ones that no one seemed able to break, who first let loose all this pent-up emotion in very unexpected fashion, by springing suddenly to his feet and letting out the most ear-shattering yell imaginable into the night. He could not contain himself any longer, it seemed. To make it carry even beyond an ordinary cry he interrupted its rhythm by shaking the palm of his hand before his mouth.

"That's for Défago," he said, looking down at the other two with a queer, defiant laugh, "for it's my belief"—the sandwiched oaths may be omitted—"that my ole partner's not far from us at this very minute."

There was a vehemence and recklessness about his performance that made Simpson, too, start to his feet in amazement, and betrayed even the doctor into letting the pipe slip from between his lips. Hank's face was ghastly, but Cathcart's showed a sudden weakness—a loosening of all his faculties, as it were. Then a momentary anger blazed into his eyes, and he too, though with deliberation born of habitual self-control, got upon his feet and faced the excited guide. For this was unpermissible, foolish, dangerous, and he meant to stop it in the bud.

What might have happened in the next minute or two one may speculate about, yet never definitely know, for in the instant of profound silence that followed Hank's roaring voice, and as though in answer to it, something went past through the darkness of the sky overhead at terrific speed—something of necessity very large, for it displaced much air, while down between the trees there fell a faint and windy cry of a human voice, calling in tones of indescribable anguish and appeal, "Oh, oh! This fiery height! Oh, oh! My feet of fire! My burning feet of fire!"

White to the very edge of his shirt, Hank looked stupidly about him like a child. Dr. Cathcart uttered some kind of unintelligible cry, turning as he did so with an instinctive movement of blind terror towards the protection of the tent, then halting in the act as though frozen. Simpson, alone of the three, retained his presence of mind a little. His own horror was too deep to allow of any immediate reaction. He had heard that cry before.

Turning to his stricken companions, he said almost calmly—

"That's exactly the cry I heard—the very words he used!"

Then, lifting his face to the sky, he cried aloud, "Défago, Défago! Come down here to us! Come down—!"

And before there was time for anybody to take definite action one way or another, there came the sound of something dropping heavily between the trees, striking the branches on the way down, and landing with a dreadful thud upon the frozen earth below. The crash and thunder of it was really terrific.

"That's him, s'help me the good Gawd!" came from Hank in a whispering cry half choked, his hand going automatically toward the hunting knife in his belt. "And he's coming! He's coming!" he added, with an irrational laugh of horror, as the sounds of heavy footsteps crunching over the snow became distinctly audible, approaching through the blackness towards the circle of light.

And while the steps, with their stumbling motion, moved nearer and nearer upon them, the three men stood round that fire, motionless and dumb. Dr. Cathcart had the appearance of a man suddenly withered; even his eyes did not move. Hank, suffering shockingly, seemed on the verge again of violent action; yet did nothing. He, too, was hewn of stone. Like stricken children they seemed. The picture was hideous. And, meanwhile, their owner still invisible, the footsteps came closer, crunching the frozen snow. It was endless—too prolonged to be quite real—this measured and pitiless approach. It was accursed.

VIII

THEN AT LENGTH THE DARKNESS, having thus laboriously conceived, brought forth—a figure. It drew forward into the zone of uncertain light where fire and shadows mingled, not ten feet away; then halted, staring at them fixedly. The same instant it started forward again with the spasmodic motion as of a thing moved by wires, and coming up closer to them, full into the glare of the fire, they perceived then that—it was a man; and apparently that this man was—Défago.

Something like a skin of horror almost perceptibly drew down in that moment over every face, and three pairs of eyes shone through it as though they saw across the frontiers of normal vision into the Unknown.

Défago advanced, his tread faltering and uncertain; he made his way straight up to them as a group first, then turned sharply and peered close into the face of Simpson. The sound of a voice issued from his lips—

"Here I am, Boss Simpson. I heered someone calling me." It was a faint, dried up voice, made wheezy and breathless as by immense exertion. "I'm havin' a reg'lar hellfire kind of a trip, I am." And he laughed, thrusting his head forward into the other's face.

But that laugh started the machinery of the group of waxwork figures with the wax-white skins. Hank immediately sprang forward with a stream of oaths so farfetched that Simpson did not recognize them as English at all, but thought he had lapsed into Indian or some other lingo. He only realized that Hank's presence, thrust thus between them, was welcome—uncommonly welcome. Dr. Cathcart, though more calmly and leisurely, advanced behind him, heavily stumbling.

Simpson seems hazy as to what was actually said and done in those next few seconds, for the eyes of that detestable and blasted visage peering at such close quarters into his own utterly bewildered his senses at first. He merely stood still. He said nothing. He had not the trained will of the older men that forced them into action in defiance of all emotional stress. He watched them moving as behind a glass that half destroyed their reality; it was dreamlike; perverted. Yet, through the torrent of Hank's meaningless phrases, he remembers hearing his uncle's tone of authority—hard and forced—saying several things about food and warmth, blankets, whisky and the rest ... and, further, that whiffs of that penetrating, unaccustomed odor, vile yet sweetly bewildering, assailed his nostrils during all that followed.

It was no less a person than himself, however—less experienced and adroit than the others though he was—who gave instinctive utterance to the sentence that brought a measure of relief into the ghastly situation by expressing the doubt and thought in each one's heart.

"It is—you, isn't it, Défago?" he asked under his breath, horror breaking his speech.

And at once Cathcart burst out with the loud answer before the other had time to move his lips. "Of course it is! Of course it is! Only—can't you see—he's nearly dead with exhaustion, cold and terror! Isn't that enough to change a man beyond all recognition?" It was said in order to convince himself as much as to convince the others. The overemphasis alone proved that. And continually, while he spoke and acted, he held a handkerchief to his nose. That odor pervaded the whole camp.

For the "Défago" who sat huddled by the big fire, wrapped in blankets, drinking hot whisky and holding food in wasted hands, was no more like the guide they had last seen alive than the picture of a man of sixty is like a daguerreotype of his early youth in the costume of another generation. Nothing really can describe that ghastly caricature, that parody, masquerading there in the firelight as Défago. From the ruins of the dark and awful memories he still retains, Simpson declares that the face was more animal than human, the features drawn about into wrong proportions, the skin loose and hanging, as though he had been subjected to extraordinary pressures and tensions. It made him think vaguely of those bladder faces blown up by the hawkers on Ludgate Hill, that change their expression as they swell, and as they collapse emit a faint and wailing imitation of a voice. Both face and voice suggested some such abominable resemblance. But Cathcart long afterwards, seeking to describe the indescribable, asserts that thus might have looked a face and body that had been in air so rarified that, the weight of atmosphere being removed, the entire structure threatened to fly asunder and become—incoherent....

It was Hank, though all distraught and shaking with a tearing volume of emotion he could neither handle nor understand, who brought things to a head without much ado. He went off to a little distance from the fire, apparently so that the light should not dazzle him too much, and shading his eyes for a moment with both hands, shouted in a loud voice that held anger and affection dreadfully mingled:

"You ain't Défago! You ain't Défago at all! I don't give a—damn, but that ain't you, my ole pal of twenty years!" He glared upon the huddled figure as though he would destroy him with his eyes. "An' if it is I'll swab the floor of hell with a wad of cotton wool on a toothpick, s'help me the good Gawd!" he added, with a violent fling of horror and disgust.

It was impossible to silence him. He stood there shouting like one possessed, horrible to see, horrible to hear—because it was the truth. He repeated himself in fifty different ways, each more outlandish than the last. The woods rang with echoes. At one time it looked as if he meant to fling himself upon "the intruder," for his hand continually jerked towards the long hunting knife in his belt.

But in the end he did nothing, and the whole tempest completed itself very shortly with tears. Hank's voice suddenly broke, he collapsed on the ground, and Cathcart somehow or other persuaded him at last to go into the tent and lie quiet. The remainder of the affair, indeed, was witnessed by him from behind the canvas, his white and terrified face peeping through the crack of the tent door flap.

Then Dr. Cathcart, closely followed by his nephew who so far had kept his courage better than all of them, went up with a determined air and stood opposite to the figure of Défago huddled over the fire. He looked him squarely in the face and spoke. At first his voice was firm.

"Défago, tell us what's happened—just a little, so that we can know how best to help you?" he asked in a tone of authority, almost of command. And at that point, it was command. At once afterwards, however, it changed in quality, for the figure turned up to him a face so piteous, so terrible and so little like humanity, that the doctor shrank back from him as from something spiritually unclean. Simpson, watching close behind him, says he got the impression of a mask that was on the verge of dropping off, and that underneath they would discover something black and diabolical, revealed in utter nakedness. "Out with it, man, out with it!" Cathcart cried, terror running neck and neck with entreaty. "None of us can stand this much longer ...!" It was the cry of instinct over reason.

And then "Défago," smiling whitely, answered in that thin and fading voice that already seemed passing over into a sound of quite another character—

"I seen that great Wendigo thing," he whispered, sniffing the air about him exactly like an animal. "I been with it too—"

Whether the poor devil would have said more, or whether Dr. Cathcart would have continued the impossible cross examination cannot be known, for at that moment the voice of Hank was heard yelling at the top of his voice from behind the canvas that concealed all but his terrified eyes. Such a howling was never heard.

"His feet! Oh, Gawd, his feet! Look at his great changed—feet!"

Défago, shuffling where he sat, had moved in such a way that for the first time his legs were in full light and his feet were visible. Yet Simpson had no time, himself, to see properly what Hank had seen. And Hank has never seen fit to tell. That same instant, with a leap like that of a frightened tiger, Cathcart was upon him, bundling the folds of blanket about his legs with such speed that the young student caught little more than a passing glimpse of something dark and oddly massed where moccasined feet ought to have been, and saw even that but with uncertain vision.

Then, before the doctor had time to do more, or Simpson time to even think a question, much less ask it, Défago was standing upright in front of them, balancing with pain and difficulty, and upon his shapeless and twisted visage an expression so dark and so malicious that it was, in the true sense, monstrous.

"Now you seen it too," he wheezed, "you seen my fiery, burning feet! And now—that is, unless you kin save me an' prevent—it's 'bout time for—"

His piteous and beseeching voice was interrupted by a sound that was like the roar of wind coming across the lake. The trees overhead shook their tangled branches. The blazing fire bent its flames as before a blast. And something swept with a terrific, rushing noise about the little camp and seemed to surround it entirely in a single moment of time. Défago shook the clinging blankets from his body, turned towards the woods behind, and with the same stumbling motion that had brought him—was gone; gone before anyone could move muscle to prevent him, gone with an amazing, blundering swiftness that left no time to act. The darkness positively swallowed him; and less than a dozen seconds later, above the roar of the swaying trees and the shout of the sudden wind, all three men, watching and listening with stricken hearts, heard a cry that seemed to drop down upon them from a great height of sky and distance—

"Oh, oh! This fiery height! Oh, oh! My feet of fire! My burning feet of fire ...!" then died away, into untold space and silence.

Dr. Cathcart—suddenly master of himself, and therefore of the others—was just able to seize Hank violently by the arm as he tried to dash headlong into the Bush.

"But I want ter know,—you!" shrieked the guide. "I want ter see! That ain't him at all, but some—devil that's shunted into his place ...!"

Somehow or other—he admits he never quite knew how he accomplished it—he managed to keep him in the tent and pacify him. The doctor, apparently, had reached the stage where reaction had set in and allowed his own innate force to conquer. Certainly he "managed" Hank admirably. It was his nephew, however, hitherto so wonderfully controlled, who gave him most cause for anxiety, for the cumulative strain had now produced a condition of lachrymose hysteria which made it necessary to isolate him upon a bed of boughs and blankets as far removed from Hank as was possible under the circumstances.

And there he lay, as the watches of that haunted night passed over the lonely camp, crying startled sentences, and fragments of sentences, into the folds of his blanket. A quantity of gibberish about speed and height and fire mingled oddly with biblical memories of the classroom. "People with broken faces all on fire are coming at a most awful, awful, pace towards the camp!" he would moan one minute; and the next would sit up and stare into the woods, intently listening, and whisper, "How terrible in the wilderness are—are the feet of them that—" until his uncle came across to change the direction of his thoughts and comfort him.

The hysteria, fortunately, proved but temporary. Sleep cured him, just as it cured Hank.

Till the first signs of daylight came, soon after five o'clock, Dr. Cathcart kept his vigil. His face was the color of chalk, and there were strange flushes beneath the eyes. An appalling terror of the soul battled with his will all through those silent hours. These were some of the outer signs ...

At dawn he lit the fire himself, made breakfast, and woke the others, and by seven they were well on their way back to the home camp—three perplexed and afflicted men, but each in his own way having reduced his inner turmoil to a condition of more or less systematized order again.

IX

THEY TALKED LITTLE, AND THEN only of the most wholesome and common things, for their minds were charged with painful thoughts that clamored for explanation, though no one dared refer to them. Hank, being nearest to primitive conditions, was the first to find himself, for he was also less complex. In Dr. Cathcart "civilization" championed his forces against an attack singular enough. To this day, perhaps, he is not quite sure of certain things. Anyhow, he took longer to "find himself."

Simpson, the student of divinity, it was who arranged his conclusions probably with the best, though not most scientific, appearance of order. Out there, in the heart of unreclaimed wilderness, they had surely witnessed something crudely and essentially primitive. Something that had survived somehow the advance of humanity had emerged terrifically, betraying a scale of life still monstrous and immature. He envisaged it rather as a glimpse into prehistoric ages, when superstitions, gigantic and uncouth, still oppressed the hearts of men; when the forces of nature were still untamed, the Powers that may have haunted a primeval universe not yet withdrawn. To this day he thinks of what he termed years later in a sermon "savage and formidable Potencies lurking behind the souls of men, not evil perhaps in themselves, yet instinctively hostile to humanity as it exists."

With his uncle he never discussed the matter in detail, for the barrier between the two types of mind made it difficult. Only once, years later, something led them to the frontier of the subject—of a single detail of the subject, rather—

"Can't you even tell me what—they were like?" he asked; and the reply, though conceived in wisdom, was not encouraging, "It is far better you should not try to know, or to find out."

"Well—that odor...?" persisted the nephew. "What do you make of that?"

Dr. Cathcart looked at him and raised his eyebrows.

"Odors," he replied, "are not so easy as sounds and sights of telepathic communication. I make as much, or as little, probably, as you do yourself."

He was not quite so glib as usual with his explanations. That was all.

At the fall of day, cold, exhausted, famished, the party came to the end of the long portage and dragged themselves into a camp that at first glimpse seemed empty. Fire there was none, and no

Punk came forward to welcome them. The emotional capacity of all three was too over-spent to recognize either surprise or annoyance; but the cry of spontaneous affection that burst from the lips of Hank, as he rushed ahead of them towards the fireplace, came probably as a warning that the end of the amazing affair was not quite yet. And both Cathcart and his nephew confessed afterwards that when they saw him kneel down in his excitement and embrace something that reclined, gently moving, beside the extinguished ashes, they felt in their very bones that this "something" would prove to be Défago—the true Défago, returned.

And so, indeed, it was.

It is soon told. Exhausted to the point of emaciation, the French Canadian—what was left of him, that is—fumbled among the ashes, trying to make a fire. His body crouched there, the weak fingers obeying feebly the instinctive habit of a lifetime with twigs and matches. But there was no longer any mind to direct the simple operation. The mind had fled beyond recall. And with it, too, had fled memory. Not only recent events, but all previous life was a blank.

This time it was the real man, though incredibly and horribly shrunken. On his face was no expression of any kind whatever—fear, welcome, or recognition. He did not seem to know who it was that embraced him, or who it was that fed, warmed and spoke to him the words of comfort and relief. Forlorn and broken beyond all reach of human aid, the little man did meekly as he was bidden. The "something" that had constituted him "individual" had vanished forever.

In some ways it was more terribly moving than anything they had yet seen—that idiot smile as he drew wads of coarse moss from his swollen cheeks and told them that he was "a damned moss-eater"; the continued vomiting of even the simplest food; and, worst of all, the piteous and childish voice of complaint in which he told them that his feet pained him—"burn like fire"—which was natural enough when Dr. Cathcart examined them and found that both were dreadfully frozen. Beneath the eyes there were faint indications of recent bleeding.

The details of how he survived the prolonged exposure, of where he had been, or of how he covered the great distance from one camp to the other, including an immense detour of the lake on foot since he had no canoe—all this remains unknown. His memory had vanished completely. And before the end of the winter whose beginning witnessed this strange occurrence, Défago, bereft of mind, memory and soul, had gone with it. He lingered only a few weeks.

And what Punk was able to contribute to the story throws no further light upon it. He was cleaning fish by the lake shore about five o'clock in the evening—an hour, that is, before the search party returned—when he saw this shadow of the guide picking its way weakly into camp. In advance of him, he declares, came the faint whiff of a certain singular odor.

That same instant old Punk started for home. He covered the entire journey of three days as only Indian blood could have covered it. The terror of a whole race drove him. He knew what it all meant. Défago had "seen the Wendigo."

THE END

Printed in Great Britain
by Amazon